D1455701

THE TALES OF N. S. LESKOV

THE MUSK-OX
AND OTHER TALES

The Hyperion Library of World Literature

CLASSICS OF RUSSIAN LITERATURE

THE TALES OF N. S. LESKOV

THE
MUSK-OX
AND OTHER
TALES

HYPERION PRESS, INC.
Westport, Connecticut

Published in 1944 by George Routledge & Sons Ltd., London
Hyperion reprint edition 1977
Library of Congress Catalog Number 76-23887
ISBN 0-88355-499-2 (cloth ed.)
ISBN 0-88355-500-X (paper ed.)
Printed in the United States of America

Library of Congress Cataloging in Publication Data

Leskov, Nikolai Semenovich, 1831-1895.
  The tales of N.S. Leskov.

  *(Classics of Russian literature) (The Hyperion
library of world literature)*
  *Reprint of the 1945 ed. published by Routledge,
London.*
  CONTENTS: [1] The musk-ox and other tales.
PZ3.L5647Tal12   [PG3337.L5]   891.7'3'3   76-23887
ISBN 0-88355-499-2
ISBN 0-88355-500-X pbk.

CONTENTS

INTRODUCTION

Had Leskov become aware of his vocation as a writer at an earlier period of his life, he would doubtless be spoken of now with Turgenev, Goncharov and Aksakov. But it is doubtful if he could have become the great painter of Russian national life in its numerous manifestations, had he not spent the first thirty years of his existence in studying this life with no thoughts of literary fame.

N. S. Leskov was born in 1831 in a village near Orel. His father belonged to the "personal" or courtesy gentry, since he held a post in the Russian Civil Service; his mother was a member of the hereditary landed gentry; one of his grandfathers was a priest, and his grandmother came from the merchant class. Thus in Leskov's veins ran the blood of four distinct classes of Russian society.

Most of his childhood was spent in the country under the care of nurses (a soldier's widow, a former serf girl of Count Kamensky, etc.). This resulted in his early acquaintance with the lot of the common people, and the simple tales of his nurses filled him with deep sympathy for the wretchedness of the peasants.

The spirit of kindliness and toleration which illuminates all his writing was fed and developed in infancy. Very soon he began to observe that, even then, during "The Iron Forties", in that period of general stagnation, lethargy, callousness and indifference to the higher problems of existence—there were many, in different walks of life, who were naturally devoted to good, who went about quietly giving help and service to their neighbours, and often displayed great moral and physical courage when faced with seemingly insurmountable difficulties. Such a character was the poor village priest, Father Alexis (described in "The Beast"), or the serf Hraposhka ("The Beast"), the peasant Selivan ("The Bogey"), Leskov's aunt Polly ("The Dale"), or his grandmother, who was taken in marriage "not for her riches, but for her beauty" ("The Musk-Ox", "The Inexhaustible Rouble", "Golovan the Deathless").

Two most vivid impressions of the practical application of the spirit of Christianity which he witnessed as a child, and which profoundly *influenced his future views, are concerned with foreigners—a ridiculous German tutor, who threw away his post because an injustice had been done to a peasant boy, and an English Quaker girl, who came to the village to succour his father's starving peasants during the famine of 1840. Both these people are described with deep affection in two lovely tales, " The Anguish of the Spirit" and " The Dale".*

When, at the age of 16, he left the state school at Orel, Leskov found himself faced with having to earn his living. His parents were dead; his property at Orel had been destroyed in a fire; his country property was loaded with debt. So he became a government clerk, and, at 18, was appointed to the local Court of Exchequer at Kiev. Here he made a number of friends among the students of the University and some of the professors. He had always read everything, and he now plunged into the whirl of intellectual activity, spending nights discussing Kant and Hegel, Strauss, Feuerbach, etc. But to Leskov books and intellectual debates were merely aids to forming a view of the very rich, colourful life which teemed all round him and which he knew so well from infancy. The feeling for that complex and irrational life was too strong in him to be sacrificed to abstract theories. And this sense of wonder and sympathy for all that was happening about him was chiefly responsible for his peculiar position later on in Russian literature, a position that earned him, with every justice, the title of " The Russian Dickens".

Soon Leskov's uncle by marriage, an Englishman named Scott, an upright, hard-working man, who managed some vast estates near Kiev, suggested to Leskov that he should come and work for him. Leskov agreed with joy. For the next ten years he travelled all over Russia as Scott's agent and enriched still more his knowledge of Russian life in various parts of the country.

In 1860 Russia was on the eve of the greatest series of reforms the world had ever seen, conducted by the ruler of the destinies of over 100,000,000 human beings. Public excitement was feverous. Suggestions, opinions, ideas, poured into the papers and periodicals from all over Russia. Leskov, like so many others, burning to help the movement practically, sent in several articles on various social problems. At the same time, some of his literary friends who had read the reports he sent to his uncle from his travels, urged him to take up writing seriously. As a result, Leskov came to St. Petersburg.

INTRODUCTION

But alas for his dreams! He found the educated youth of the capital divided into a number of camps, groups, movements, which pursued one or another intellectual theory of the correct method of assisting mankind. The government's call to the cultured forces to rally round and concentrate on the practical side of reorganization in the spirit of the new decrees was little answered among the younger people. The reforms were vast and momentous, and their success depended much on active collaboration and goodwill. But the intellectual class was found to be ill-equipped for the task. The new liberties granted to the people by a stroke of the Emperor's pen, the many rights conceded to women, the sudden removal of many of the restrictions on printed matter, and the resulting spate of imported theories and doctrines, swept many of the educated youngsters off their feet. Extreme ideas were eagerly disseminated, and intellectual chaos was widespread.

A definite "direction" was demanded of writers. Two opposing literary groups—Liberal and Conservative—came into being. By far the most influential group—the "Progressive Liberals", were entirely "utilitarian", and the directions were supplied by a number of critics, or rather publicists, who were acknowledged as the leaders of the main literary movements. Writers of the time had but to join one or the other movement or circle and make clear their "direction", and their bread and butter was assured.

On his arrival at St. Petersburg, Leskov naturally joined the Liberal camp, only to find very soon that the Liberals were primarily occupied in intrigue and recrimination. The pillars of contemporary literature—Turgenev, Goncharov, Dostoyevsky, Pisemsky, were working on novels in which they expressed all their bitter disappointment with this degeneracy of the Liberal movement. Hertzen from London was appealing for common sense and discipline and was fast losing his influence in the new Russia.

And so Leskov, bearing in his mind's eye the haunting pictures of the backwardness of provincial and rural Russia, so familiar to him, published an article "Concerning the Unseemly Behaviour of some Authors". Then, in 1861, in the "Severnaya Pchela", appeared his fateful letter on the epidemic of arson which had broken out about that time.

After the liberation of the serfs there were sporadic disorders in some parts of Russia, followed by a wave of mysterious fires which swept the country. The general public was on the verge of panic: political extremists were suspected, and for some reason students and schoolboys were identified with these extremists.

Leskov's balanced and judicious letter was written to pacify the public and to defend the youth of Russia, but appearing as it did at a moment of hysteria, it was seized upon by the Liberal Press and Leskov was accused of inciting the police against the students. He was deeply shaken. But since the fat was in the fire, he went on and wrote his famous novel "The Impasse" (Nekuda). In this he tried to explain and illustrate his view that babblers, doctrinaires and countless hangers-on and adventurers in the progressive movement were heading for an impasse, and hindering progress towards a truly cultured Russia.

The appearance of this book caused a storm among the Liberals. It was denounced as a libel on young Russia, Leskov was branded a traitor to the cause—a turncoat. The critical attitude towards the young extremist intellectuals, which was noted "with profound regret" in the old-established writers, who had greatly helped to bring about the period of reform and liberation, could not be tolerated in a young beginner. Leskov was damned by the Liberals. Pisarev, the impetuous and powerful leader of the influential "Enlightened Realist" movement, doubted whether there would be found in Russia a single periodical that would "dare" to print anything written by Leskov: to print anything of Leskov's would show a "lack of caution" and indifference towards one's reputation, and he followed this by advice to take care and not "risk an obvious danger".

Under this threat, all the Liberal magazines shut Leskov out once and for all. Vengerov, an independent progressive critic, was probably alone when he wrote at the time: "Leskov's sentence is exceedingly harsh and to a considerable degree unjust."

From then on, Leskov could appear only in Conservative magazines, where his stories were printed with those of Turgenev, Goncharov and other former "Liberals". His popularity and renown grew rapidly among the public. Many of his works have become classics. Even his enemies were compelled to concede that in his writings Leskov displayed "a very rare talent" (Skabichevsky).

In 1870 appeared Leskov's other large political novel, "At Dagger

Drawn". This was a more uncompromising condemnation of the "nihilists" and was much despised by the Liberals. But in 1880 he provoked a storm among the Conservatives as well with his "Snippets of Clerical Life". These sketches cost Leskov his posts at the Ministries of Education and State Properties.

Still he continued to write as his conscience moved him—beloved by the public, and ignored by the critics. He died in 1895.

Because of the cloud that hung over Leskov's name, he was not studied much by the Russian intelligentsia during the years immediately following his death. So he is almost unknown in England. Then, in 1917, came the Revolution. In the crash and tumult, in the terrific debacle of the aspirations and dreams of the cultured classes, many of the former idols of Russian thought were hauled off their pedestals and buried for ever under the general wreckage. Gone were the names of many Liberal writers who filled pages in textbooks and who preached a vague Liberty and an amorphous "humanity". They brought no comfort after the great disillusionment. But two Russian authors were read greedily and hopefully by all classes in Russia after the Revolution—Tolstoi and Leskov.

.   .   .   .   .

Leskov undoubtedly belongs to the Russian "immortals", and he has a twofold claim to be included among the great writers of the world.

First, there is his surprising range in portraying characters from every level of Russian society and every walk of life, which enables him to picture so comprehensively late nineteenth-century Russia. He reflects every aspect of the life he saw before him, and it is an attractive reflection, full of sympathy, humour and colour. And since all the characters are so true, so creditable, we gain a picture of that "Holy Russia" which readers of Russian literature seek vainly in the work of lesser writers, and which they are apt to regard as the creation of the "theopneustic" genius of Dostoyevsky, of the intellectual speculations of Tolstoi in the rôle of reformer, or of the intense humanitarianism of Turgenev.

Secondly, Leskov is one of the very few writers who have succeeded in creating characters of genuine virtue who can stand the test of time.

Some of the most brilliant and moving authors become stilted and insincere when faced with showing what, to their mind, constitutes the perfect human being, and their positive types so often lack conviction. Also the manner in which positive types in literature lose their appeal and vividness with the change of outlook upon "absolute" moral values and the change of "fashion" in ethical behaviour, must have struck every thoughtful reader. In Russia, where the Golden Age of Literature passed against a background of systems of thought and philosophical programmes, Russian men of letters were always striving to create characters that would win the admiration and emulation of the public. The influence of these "positive" types in literature was usually brief. They at once became the objects of furious attack and merciless criticism by differing schools of thought, and as some new philosophical movement gathered force, new idols were rapidly created in fiction, to be brought down again just as quickly. Many giants of Russian literature failed to create enduring types of inspiring human beings.

Leskov's ability to present to us men and women of real virtue is explained by the fact that he is completely uninfluenced by any passing or fashionable philosophy. He accepts unreservedly the precepts of the Gospel, without any religious accretions, and then shows us men and women he has come across who interpret these precepts in their daily life. And because they are mostly actual people he has known, and thanks to his vigorous, racy style, these characters are gripping, convincing and lovable. Tales which are specifically concerned with them, are grouped together under the general heading of "Men of Virtues", but such characters also invade most of his other tales and novels. For instance, there is Princess Protozanov, the dour, forceful and level-headed heroine of "A Family Chronicle"; there is Pasha, the simple servant-friend of an author, in "The Lady and the Bumpkin"; Maria Ivanovna in "The Disinherited", and so on.

But Leskov had too much love for humanity to limit the expression of true virtue to the influence of the teaching of Christ. Indeed, he hated "official" Christianity. All faiths that enjoin love for one's neighbour, in other words, all the moral forces, influences and impulses that have gone to the creation and revelation of values and principles which the majority of those living to-day profess to hold inviolable, and which the ancients acknowledged, are absolute virtues to him. Thus, in his story "On the Edge of the World", it is a *primitive native who saves the life of a bishop, while a native proselyte displays contemptible cowardice. In his later tales, in which he developed anecdotes from the "Prologues of the Lives of the Saints", it is often the pagans who are the true heroes, and the official Christians who are weaklings and sinners. In "The Beast of Askelon", the Christian Theodor is an easy-going egotist, and the Christian agent of the Empress Theodora, the villain. In "Panphalon the Buffoon", it is a mountebank, an associate of the hetairas of Alexandria, who confounds a virtuous stylite.*

With the present-day spread of the new morality, when more and more countries have succumbed to dictatorships and blamed Christianity because it has failed to produce for them a state of economic well-being and security, with the officially fostered and strenuously propagated creed of class hatred, race hatred—hatred that is presumed to create the perfect state that Christian love has failed to do—it is a relief to plunge into the world of Leskov. Although it is a Russian world, depicted with the greatest skill and artistry, it is also illuminated by sentiments that have been worshipped the world over for countless generations; and the darker the night, the brighter these sentiments shine in the gloom.

.   .   .   .

All the tales in this volume have been taken from a standard edition of the complete works of Leskov, in 36 volumes, brought out in St. Petersburg in 1902–1903, by A. F. Marx. "The Musk-Ox" and "The Devilchase" come from Volume XIV of this edition; "Kotin and Platonida" and "A Flaming Patriot" from Volume XVI; "The Stinger" from Volume XXII; "The Alexandrite" from Volume XX. "The Spirit of Madame de Genlis" and "The Clothes-Mender" are taken from Volume XVIII, which is devoted to a collection of Leskov's Christmas tales.

R. NORMAN.

THE MUSK-OX

WHEN I FIRST MADE THE ACQUAINTANCE OF
Vasilii Petrovich, he was already known as "The Musk-Ox".
He got this name because his appearance reminded one strangely
of a musk-ox, portrayed in the "Illustrated Guide to Zoology",
by Julian Simashko. He was twenty-eight, but looked much
older. He was neither an athlete nor a giant, but a man of
outstanding strength and good health, small in stature, squarely
built and broad-shouldered. His face was of a sallow complexion and round; but the face alone was round, his skull
presenting a strange deformity. At first glance it looked rather
like the skull of a Kaffir, but on closer study it was quite impossible to classify it according to any known phrenological group.
He dressed his hair in such a manner that he seemed to want to
mislead everyone about the configuration of his "upper storey".
The back of his head was clipped very short, while in front his
dark auburn hair fell in two long, thick locks. Vasilii Petrovich
constantly twirled these locks, and they always lay in curled
rolls upon his temples and curved away from his cheeks, like
the horns of the animal from which he derived his nickname.
It was these two locks which were mainly responsible for his
resemblance to a musk-ox. There was nothing ridiculous in
Vasilii Petrovich's figure. Anyone meeting him for the first
time would merely have remarked that Vasilii Petrovich was
—as the saying goes—"badly cut, but strongly put together",
and looking into his brown, very wide-set eyes, no one could
help reading in them the presence of a clear mind, a strong will
and determination of purpose. There was much that was
uncommon in the character of Vasilii Petrovich. His distinctive
trait was an evangelic heedlessness of the morrow. The son of
a village sexton—brought up in the most dreadful poverty—his
father died when he was quite small—he never lent a thought
to any lasting betterment of his position in life and never in
fact worried about what was in store for him. He had no

precious possessions to give away, but he was capable of presenting his last shirt to anyone in need and believed the same of all the people he made friends with; while all the others he termed, bluntly and briefly, "pigs". When Vasilii Petrovich had no boots, that's to say, when his boots, to use his own expression, were "gasping for air", he would come to you and, without further ceremony, he would take your spare boots, if by any chance they fitted him, and would leave his cast-offs as a souvenir. Whether you were in or not, didn't make the slightest difference to Vasilii Petrovich; he would make himself perfectly at home, take what he needed—but always in as small a quantity as possible—and sometimes on meeting you, would mention that he had helped himself to your tobacco, or tea, or boots; but, more often, he did not think these small matters worth mentioning. He had no patience with modern literature and read only the Gospels and ancient classics; he could not bear conversations about women, considered them all and every one as "fools", and very seriously regretted that his aged mother was a woman, and not some sexless creature. The self-sacrifice of Vasilii Petrovich was boundless. He never showed any of us that he was fond of anyone; but we were all perfectly aware that there was no limit to what he would do for the sake of every one of his friends and acquaintances. His readiness to sacrifice himself in the cause of his chosen ideal no one ever thought of doubting, but it was not easy to discover this ideal beneath the skull of the Musk-Ox. He did not laugh at the many theories in which we then believed fervently, but entertained a profound and sincere contempt for them.

The Musk-Ox was not fond of talk and did everything in silence, and did precisely the thing which, at that moment, one would have least expected of him.

How and why he had become a member of the little circle to which I also belonged during my brief stay in our Provincial centre, I do not know. About three years before my arrival, the Musk-Ox had completed a course of studies at the Kursk Seminary. His mother, who had brought him up on the crumbs she procured by way of alms, was filled with impatience for the time to come when her son would be ordained a priest and have a parish of his own and a young wife. But visions of a young wife never entered his head. Vasilii Petrovich had not the least desire to marry. His course of studies was over, his mother was busy making enquiries about suitable brides, while Vasilii Petrovich just said nothing and one fine morning disappeared no one knew where. Six months later he sent his mother twenty-five roubles and a letter in which he informed the poverty-stricken old woman that he had walked to Kazan and had entered the local Ecclesiastical Academy. How he had managed to get on foot to Kazan—a walk of over six hundred miles—and by what means he had obtained the twenty-five roubles, remained a mystery. The Musk-Ox did not mention a word of it to his mother. But the old woman had scarcely had time to conjure up visions of her Vasya becoming an arch-priest, when she would live with him and have her own bright room with a white tile stove and would drink tea with currants twice a day, when, like a bolt from the blue, Vasya appeared in Kursk again. He was plied with questions: What had happened? How? Why was he back?—but precious little could be got out of him. "Couldn't get on," the Musk-Ox would reply briefly, and nothing further would he vouchsafe. Only to one person did he confide a little more—"Don't want to be a monk"—and that was the most anyone ever learnt from him.

The person to whom the Musk-Ox said more than he did to the rest was Yakov Chelnovsky, a kindly, decent soul, who was incapable of hurting a fly and was prepared to do all he could for his neighbour. Chelnovsky happened to be a very distant relative of mine. And at Chelnovsky's I made the acquaintance of the stocky hero of my story.

It was in the summer of 1854. I was busy over a lawsuit that was being dealt with by the Kursk Government Offices.

I arrived in Kursk about seven in the morning. It was in the merry month of May, and I went straight to Chelnovsky. At the time he was occupied with coaching youngsters for the University, taught Russian and History at a couple of boarding-schools for girls, and didn't do so badly; he had a nice little apartment of three rooms, a considerable library, comfortable furniture, a few pots of exotic plants, and a bulldog called "Box", with bared teeth, a most obscene behind, and a gait which slightly resembled a can-can.

Chelnovsky was exceedingly glad to see me, and made me promise that I would stop with him all the time I was at Kursk. He himself was usually on the run all day, hurrying about his lessons, while I either went to the Civic Hall or strolled aimlessly along the banks of the Tuskar or the Seim. The first of these rivers you may perhaps not find on many Russian maps, while the second is famous for its particularly tasty crayfish, but has achieved still greater notoriety because of the system of locks which had been built on it and which swallowed up an enormous amount of money, without changing the classification of the Seim as a river "unsuitable for navigation".

A fortnight had elapsed since my arrival at Kursk. The Musk-Ox I had not heard mentioned anywhere, and I had not the least suspicion of the existence of so strange a beast within the precincts of our Black Earth Belt, so rich in wheat, beggars, and thieves.

One day, tired and exhausted, I returned home soon after one in the afternoon. In the hall I was met by Box, who guarded our abode more thoroughly than the eleven-year-old boy who served us in the rank of man-servant. . . . On the table, in the main room, lay a terribly dilapidated cloth cap, half of a most filthy pair of braces with a leather strap attached, a greasy black kerchief twisted into a rope, and a thin stick of wild walnut. In the second room, lined with bookcases and furnished with rather smart library furniture, was seated on the sofa an appallingly dusty individual. He wore a pink cotton shirt and light-yellow trousers which were through at the knees. The stranger's boots were covered with a thick mantle of white dust, while on his lap lay a weighty book which he was reading without inclining his head. When I entered the library, the dusty figure cast one cursory glance at me and turned again to the book. In the bedroom everything was in order. The striped linen blouse of Chelnovsky, which he put on as soon as he got home, hung in its place, and bore witness that the master was out. I could not for the life of me decide who the strange guest was

who had made himself so perfectly at home. The ferocious
Box regarded him as an old friend and desisted from fawning
merely because a fondness for being petted, natural to dogs of
French breeds, is not in the nature of dogs of Anglo-Saxon
species. Again I went through into the entrance hall, having
in mind a twofold purpose—first, to ask the boy about the
guest, and secondly, to draw, by my appearance, some observation from the guest himself. I failed in both respects. The
entrance hall was as deserted as before, and the guest did not
even raise his eyes to me, and sat quietly in the position I had
found him in five minutes earlier. There remained but one
course open to me, and that was, to address myself directly to
the guest.

"You are no doubt waiting for Yakov Ivanovich?" I
enquired, placing myself before the stranger.

The guest glanced at me lazily, then raised himself from the
sofa, spat between his teeth in a manner peculiar to Russian
artisans and ecclesiastical seminarists, and emitted in a deep
bass: "No."

"Who is it you want to see, then?" I asked, taken aback by
the surprising answer.

"Oh, I merely dropped in on the way," the guest replied,
pacing up and down and twirling his side locks.

"But may I be permitted to know whom I have the honour
to address?"

Here I gave my name and stated that I was a relative of
Yakov Ivanovich.

"And I'm just no one in particular," answered the guest,
picking up his book again.

Thereon the conversation ended. Abandoning all attempts
to solve the mystery of the individual's presence by myself, I
retired to my bed book in hand. When you come out of
the glare of a scorching sun into a clean, cool room where there
are no pestering flies, and where there is a neat, tidy bed, you
can drop off to sleep with the greatest of ease. On this occasion
I proved it in practice and never noticed how the book slipped
out of my hand. Through a sweet drowsiness, peculiar to
persons who are full of hope and faith, I could just make out

how Chelnovsky was lecturing the boy, to which the boy had
long accustomed himself and paid not the slightest heed. My
full awakening, however, occurred only when my relative
entered the study and cried:

"Hello, Musk-Ox! What brings you here?"

"I have come," was the guest's reply to this unusual greeting.

"I know you have come, but where from? Where have you
been?"

"Too far to see from here."

"Oh, stop fooling! Have you been gracing my abode long?"
Yakov Ivanovich again enquired of his guest, as he entered the
bedroom. "Here!—but you're asleep," he said, turning to me.
"Get up, man, I'll show you a beastie."

"What beastie?" I asked, not fully restored to what is known
as a waking state from the state known as sleep.

Chelnovsky did not answer me, but removed his frock-coat
and slipped on his blouse—which was a matter of a minute—
went into the study, and dragging the stranger out by the hand,
made a mock bow, and with a sweep of the hand towards the
resisting guest announced: "I have the honour of presenting
to you—the Musk-Ox. His staple food is grass, but when no
grass is to be had, he has been known to eat lichen."

I got up and gave my hand to the Musk-Ox, who, throughout
the introduction, had been listlessly studying a thick cluster of
lilac that screened the open window of our bedroom.

"I have already introduced myself," I said to the Musk-Ox.

"I heard you," the Musk-Ox replied. I am a sort of Devil-
dodger—Vasilii Bogoslovsky."

"What do you mean, you've introduced yourself?" asked
Yakov Ivanovich. "Have you met already?"

"Yes, I found Vasilii . . . I haven't the honour of knowing
your patronymic."

"Petrovich, it used to be," replied Bogoslovsky.

"That's what it used to be—now he's just called Musk-Ox."

"I don't mind what you call me."

"E-e-eh, you're wrong there, brother! A musk-ox you are,
and musk-ox you'll remain."

We sat down at table. Vasilii Petrovich poured himself out

6

a tot of vodka, tipped it into his mouth, held it for a while behind his cheek-bone and then, swallowing it, cast a knowing look at the plate of soup that had been placed before him.

"Haven't you any galantine?" he enquired of our host.

"No, brother, I haven't any. We didn't expect so illustrious a guest to-day," replied Chelnovsky. "We haven't provided for him."

"You could have been having some yourselves."

"We are just as happy with soup."

"Namby-pambies!" remarked the Musk-Ox.

"What—no goose either?" he asked with increasing astonishment, when rissoles were served.

"No goose either," our host replied, smiling his gentle smile. "To-morrow you'll have galantine and goose and 'kasha' with goose fat."

"To-morrow isn't to-day."

"Well, it can't be helped! I suppose you haven't had goose for a long time."

The Musk-Ox regarded him fixedly and announced with an air of gratification:

"You'd better ask when I last had anything to eat at all."

"You don't mean it!"

"Four evenings ago I had a bun at Sevsk."

"In Sevsk?"

The Musk-Ox made an affirmative gesture of the hand.

"What were you doing in Sevsk?"

"Just passing through."

"Gracious—where has the Devil been taking you?"

The Musk-Ox interrupted the swing of his fork, with which he had been transporting enormous pieces of the rissoles to his mouth, again stared fixedly at Chelnovsky, and ignoring his question, remarked:

"Been taking snuff, or what, to-day?"

"What do you mean, taking snuff?"

Chelnovsky and I burst out laughing at the extraordinary question.

"Just what I say."

"But do talk sense, my dear beastie!"

7

"Seems your tongue is itching to-day."

"But why shouldn't I ask? It's a whole month since you've gone and lost yourself!"

"Me—lost?" the Musk-Ox echoed. "I'll never get lost, brother, and if I do, it'll be in a good cause."

"The urge to preach has bitten deep into us!" Chelnovsky explained to me. "The passion devours us, but Fate is so unkind! In our enlightened times it is forbidden to preach on street corners and in the market-place; we cannot become a priest, because we dare not touch Woman—the source of all evil—and something prevents us from becoming a monk. What exactly it is that stands in the way, I really don't know."

"It's just as well you don't know."

"Why is it well? The more we know the better it is."

"You go and turn monk yourself—you'll know all right."

"And you don't want to place your experience at the service of Mankind?"

"Other people's experiences are worthless, brother," declared the weird creature, rising from the table and wiping his napkin across his entire face, which had become covered in perspiration as a result of his exertions over dinner. He deposited his napkin, made his way to the entrance hall, and there produced from his overcoat a small clay pipe, with a blackened, deeply indented stem, and a small cotton tobacco-bag. He filled his pipe, placed the tobacco in the pocket of his trousers and again made his way to the entrance hall.

"Smoke here," Chelnovsky told him.

"You'll start sneezing for all I know, or it'll give you a headache."

The Musk-Ox stood in the doorway, smiling. I never met a man who smiled as Bogoslovsky did. His face remained perfectly serene; not a single line of it moved, and in his eyes there lay the same deep and sad expression, and yet you saw that these same eyes were laughing—laughing with the kindliest laughter a Russian sometimes laughs with at himself and his bitter lot.

"The new Diogenes!" Chelnovsky said, as the Musk-Ox went out. "Keeps on looking for Men of the Gospel."

We lit our cigars and, stretching on our beds, talked about

8

various human foibles which came into our minds in connection with the eccentricities of Vasilii Petrovich. A quarter of an hour later, enter Vasilii Petrovich himself. He stood his little pipe on the floor by the stove, sat down at the feet of Chelnovsky, and after scratching his left shoulder with his right hand, said *sotto voce*: "I've been looking for a tutor's job."

"When?" Chelnovsky asked him.

"Why, just now."

"Where did you look for one?"

"I just looked as I went."

Chelnovsky broke into a fit of laughter, but the Musk-Ox took not the slightest notice.

"Well, and what did the Good Lord provide?" enquired Chelnovsky.

"A fig He provided."

"You are an idiot! Whoever heard of anyone looking for a tutor's job on the road?"

"I called at the landowners' houses, enquired there," the Musk-Ox went on in all seriousness.

"And what happened?"

"They wouldn't have me."

"Of course they will never have you."

The Musk-Ox contemplated Chelnovsky with that fixed look of his and asked in the same even voice:

"And why—may I ask—shouldn't they have me?"

"Because tramps who come from nowhere are not taken into a house without testimonials."

"I showed them my Diploma."

"And in it stands: 'Conduct—fairish'."

"Well, what of it? I'll tell you, brother, that isn't the reason —it's because . . ."

"You are the Musk-Ox," Chelnovsky completed for him.

"Yes, the Musk-Ox, maybe."

"Well, what are you thinking of doing now?"

"I'm thinking of smoking another pipe," Vasilii Petrovich replied, getting to his feet and again turning to his pipe.

"But do smoke here."

"Oh, shut up!"

"Go on—the window is open, isn't it?"

"Shut up."

"But, damn it all, man, it won't be the first time you've smoked your shag in my room."

"They wouldn't like it," said the Musk-Ox, pointing at me.

"Please smoke, Vasilii Petrovich. I am quite used to it; no shag can possibly have any effect on me."

"Yes—but my shag is the one that made the Devil take to his heels," retorted the Musk-Ox—he pronounced it "shagg" with plenty of emphasis—and the captivating smile again flickered in his kindly eyes.

"Well, I won't take to mine."

"You're stronger than the Devil, then?"

"In this case."

"He has the highest opinion of the strength of the Devil," said Chelnovsky.

"Only Woman, brother, is more vicious than the Devil."

Vasilii Petrovich stuffed his pipe with shag, emitted a thin ribbon of acrid smoke through his lips, rammed down the burning tobacco with his finger and said:

"I'll start copying exercises."

"What exercises?" said Chelnovsky, cupping his hand to his ear.

"Exercises—Seminary exercises, I can copy, I reckon, for the time being—the boys' copybooks—don't you get me?"

"Oh, I see now. That isn't much of a job, brother."

"Makes no odds."

"A couple of roubles a month, that's all you can hope to earn."

"That won't worry me."

"Well—and after that—what?"

"Get me a tutor's post."

"In the country again?"

"I like it better in the country."

"And I suppose you'll walk out again after a week. Do you know what he did last spring?" said Chelnovsky, turning to me. "I got him a post—a hundred and twenty roubles a year, all found—and he had to coach a boy for the second form of a Gymnasium School. We fitted him out with all he needed—

poshed up the lad. Now—I figured—our Musk-Ox is fixed
up at last! And would you believe it: back he was after a
month—anyone would have said he had sprung from the
earth. And what's more, he'd left all his clothes behind in
payment for the coaching."

"Well, what of it, if it was the only way?" the Musk-Ox
put in with a frown, and rose from his chair.

"You ask him why it was the only way," said Chelnovsky,
again turning to me. "Because they wouldn't let him pull the
wretched little brat's miserable hair."

"Any more lies?" growled the Musk-Ox.

"Well, you tell us how it all happened."

The Musk-Ox stopped in front of me, and after a moment's
deliberation said:

"It's quite a different story."

"Sit down, Vasilii Petrovich," I said, making room for him
on my bed.

"No, don't bother. It was nothing of the kind . . .," he
began again. "The little stinker was getting on for fifteen and
quite a little gentleman at that—in other words, as shameless
a blackguard as ever I saw."

"That's how it is with us!" grinned Chelnovsky.

"Yeh," continued the Musk-Ox. "They had a chef there—
Yegor—a young lad. He got married—found himself a sexton's
daughter from among our ecclesiastical paupers. My young
gent had been instructed in everything, and there he was, making
up to her. The wench was young, of course, and spirited, and
not that kind, and stood no nonsense. She complained to her
husband, and the husband to the lady of the house. She said
something or other to her son, but he was back at his old pranks.
This happened again, and then a third time; again the chef
went to the lady to say his wife had no peace from the young
master—again nothing happened. I was wild. 'See here,' said
I to him: 'If ever I catch you pinching Alenka again, I'll give
you such a crack.' He went as red as a tomato with annoyance
—it made his noble blood boil, you know—and off he dashed
to his mamma, with me behind. There she was, sitting in her
armchair, also as red as a tomato, while her precious darling

11

was detailing a complaint against me in French. No sooner did she catch sight of me than she takes his hand and simpers, the Devil alone knows why. 'There—there,' she says, 'my friend Vasilii Petrovich doubtless thought he saw something—he is jesting—and you will prove to him that he is making a mistake.' And all the time I see her looking at me from the corner of her eye. The little blighter went out, and she—you know—instead of speaking to me about her son, says to me: 'How chivalrous you are, Vasilii Petrovich! You're not sweet on someone too, are you?' Well, I just can't stand that sort of thing," said the Musk-Ox with a determined jerk of his arm. "I just can't listen to that sort of thing," he repeated, his voice rising, and he began to pace the room once more.

"So you left the house there and then?"

"No, six weeks later."

"And continued to live on good terms?"

"Well, I didn't speak to anyone."

"And what about at dinner?"

"I used to have dinner with the clerk."

"How do you mean—with the clerk?"

"Well, to put it plainly—with the underlings. But that didn't make any difference to me; I can't be insulted, you know. . . ."

"In what way?"

"Of course I can't be insulted. . . . But don't let's talk about that. . . . Only, you know, one day I was sitting under the window, after dinner. I was reading my Tacitus, when I became aware that someone was hollering in the servants' quarters. What the hullabaloo was about I couldn't make out, only it was Alenka's voice. The little skunk must be having his bit of fun, I reckoned. Up I got and went to the servants' hall. Then I heard Alenka crying and screaming through her tears: 'You ought to be ashamed of yourself', 'Have you no fear of God', and all that sort of thing. Well, I looked in, and there was Alenka in the loft, over a step-ladder, while my young hopeful was under the step-ladder, so that the good woman couldn't possibly get down. It was too embarrassing—you know how they go about in the country . . . nothing on underneath. And the little swine was egging her: 'Go on, now; come down,' he was saying, 'or

I'll pull the ladder away.' I was so furious, I went into the lobby and gave him such a tap !"

"So that the blood spurted from his ear and nose," Chelnovsky prompted, laughing gaily.

"Well—whatever kind of tap he was fated to have. . . ."

"And what did the mother have to say about it ?"

"Well, I didn't go to look at her after that. I went straight from the servants' hall to Kursk."

"How many miles would that be ?"

"A hundred and thirteen; but it wouldn't have mattered if it had been thirteen hundred."

If you could have seen the Musk-Ox just then, you would have had no doubt whatever that to him it really did not make the slightest difference how many miles he would have had to walk and whom he would have had to "tap", if, in his opinion, "a tap" was required.

CHAPTER THE SECOND

A SWELTERING June set in. Vasilii Petrovich appeared at our abode with the utmost regularity every day about twelve o'clock, removed his calico neckerchief and braces, and, after bidding us both "Good morning", settled down to his classics. So the hours would pass before dinner. After dinner he lit his pipe and, stationing himself by the window, he would usually enquire : "What about that tutor's job ?" A month had gone by and the Musk-Ox repeated his question to Chelnovsky every day, and every day for a month he heard the same hopeless reply. There was not the remotest prospect of a job. Yet apparently Vasilii Petrovich was not in the least put out by this. He took his food with an excellent appetite and was constantly in his wonted good spirits. Only on one or two occasions did I see him at all irritated. But this irritation had nothing to do with the state of the fortunes of Vasilii Petrovich. It arose from two entirely extraneous causes. On one occasion he met a peasant woman who was sobbing and keening, and asked her in his booming voice : "Why are you howling, fool?" The woman was quite frightened at first, and then she told him that her boy had been caught and would be taken to the Recruiting Office the following morning. Vasilii Petrovich recalled that the clerk at the Recruiting Office had been with him at the Seminary, went to see him next morning, and returned extremely upset. His intercession had not worked. On another occasion a party of recruits, made up of little Jewish boys, was being taken through the town. About that time there were frequent recruiting drives. Vasilii Petrovich, biting his upper lip, and arms akimbo, was standing beneath the window and closely studying the train of carts loaded with recruits. The clumsy local conveyances were slowly filing past; the carts, bumping from side to side over the uneven street, jolted the heads of the children dressed in grey topcoats made of heavy military cloth. The outsize grey sheepskin caps tilted forward over their eyes and lent a profoundly sad expression to their pretty little faces and intelligent eyes which gazed with longing and, at the same time, with childish curiosity at the new town and the crowds of street arabs who raced—hopping and skipping—after the carts. Behind them came a couple of cooks.

"Mothers' sons, too," said one of the cooks—a strapping, pock-marked female—as she passed our windows.

"Aye, they've got mothers, I shouldn't wonder," the other one replied, slipping her hands inside her sleeves and scratching her elbows.

"And they'd be missing them too—even if they are Yidds."

"Well, I suppose it can't be helped, dearie."

"'Course; but a mother's feeling, you know."

"That's right—a mother's feeling, of course. . . . One's own flesh and blood. . . . But what must be must be."

"'Course."

"Fools!" Vasilii Petrovich roared after them.

The women stopped, looked at him in astonishment, and both said simultaneously: "What are you yapping at, you sleek tyke?" and went on their way.

I wanted to go and see how these hapless children would be unloaded at the garrison barracks.

"Let's go to the barracks, Vasilii Petrovich," I called to Bogoslovsky.

"Why?"

"To see what'll happen to them there."

Vasilii Petrovich made no reply; but when I picked up my hat he joined me and came too. The garrison barracks, to which the little Jewish recruits were brought, was quite a distance from our house. When we got there, the carts had already been emptied and the children were lined up in two even ranks. The officer in charge of the party and the N.C.O. were calling the roll. Onlookers crowded round. By one of the carts, also, stood several ladies and a priest with a bronze cross on a ribbon of the Order of St. Vladimir. We approached this cart. In it sat a sick boy, aged about nine, who greedily devoured a cheese tart; another boy lay covered with a great-coat, taking no notice of anything around him; judging by his flushed face and by his eyes, which burned with a sickly glow, one would suppose he was suffering from fever—even typhus perhaps.

"Are you ill?" asked one of the ladies of the boy who was swallowing a tart in lumps.

"Eh?"

"Are you sick?"

The boy shook his head vigorously.

"You are not sick?" the lady enquired again.

Again the boy shook his head.

"He not comprenny—doesn't understand," remarked the priest, and immediately asked in turn: "Have you been baptized already?"

The child pondered, as though recalling something familiar in the question that had been put to him, and with another shake of the head said: "Neh, Neh."

"What a darling!" exclaimed the lady, taking the child by the chin and tilting upwards his pretty face with its dark eyes.

"Where is your mother?" suddenly asked the Musk-Ox, giving a tug at the child's greatcoat.

The child started, looked at Vasilii Petrovich, then at the people about him, then at the N.C.O., and again at Vasilii Petrovich.

"Mother, where is mother?" repeated the Musk-Ox.

15

"Mama?"

"Yês, mama, mama."

"Mama . . ."—the child waved his hand towards the horizon.

"At home?"

The recruit thought for a moment and nodded his head in agreement.

"Still remembers her," interjected the priest, and asked: "Any bruders?"

The child made a slight negative sign.

"Now that's a fib, that's a fib, they don't take only sons as recruits. Telling stories, nicht gut, nein," continued the priest, imagining that by making use of nominative cases, he would add clearness to his conversation.

"I—tramp," declared the boy.

"Wha-a-at?"

"Tramp," the boy stated more clearly.

"Ah, a tramp! That's what we call in Russian a vagrant— he's been taken for vagrancy; I've read this law about them, about Jewish infants, yes. . . . Vagrancy is to be rooted out. Well, that, of course, is quite right: a settled person will stay at home—moving from place to place makes no odds to a vagrant, and he will taste of Holy Baptism and will mend his ways and become a man," the priest was saying; and meanwhile the roll-call was over and the N.C.O., taking the horse by the bridle, jerked the cart with the sick boys towards the doorway of the barracks, through which bustled the long line of little recruits, dragging after them their little haversacks and clutching the skirts of their clumsy greatcoats. I began to look for my Musk-Ox, but he was no longer there. He didn't return by nightfall and was not there for dinner on the second and third day. We sent the boy to his lodgings where he lived with some Seminarists—but he was not there either. The little Seminarists with whom the Musk-Ox lived had long ago got used to not seeing Vasilii Petrovich for weeks on end and took no notice of his disappearance. Chelnovsky also was not in the least bit concerned.

"He'll come back," he maintained, "he's roaming some- where, or sleeping in the rye—that's all."

It might here be observed that Vasilii Petrovich, in his own words, was very fond of his "lairs", and of these hide-outs he had a goodly number. The bed with the bare boards which stood in his lodgings never rested his body for long. Only every now and again would he drop in, stretch himself on the bed and initiate an unexpected examination for the boys, with some curious question at the end of each test, after which the bed would again remain unoccupied. He rarely spent the night with us, and then he usually slept either in the porch or, if a heated debate developed in the evening and was not over by nightfall, the Musk-Ox would make his bed on the floor, between our beds, refusing anything in the nature of bedding, except a flimsy little floor-runner. Early in the morning he went either into the fields or to the graveyard. He visited the graveyard every day. He would arrive there, make himself comfortable on a mossy grave, place before him the work of some Latin author and proceed to read it; or else— closing the book—he would place it under his head and gaze into the sky.

"You are a denizen of the graves, Vasilii Petrovich!" Chelnovsky's lady friends would say to him.

"You are talking nonsense," Vasilii Petrovich would reply.

"You are a vampire," he would be told by the pale district school teacher, who enjoyed a reputation as a man of letters since the Provincial newspaper had printed one of his articles on Science.

"You invent nonsense," the Musk-Ox would retort to him as well, and would again retire to his corpses.

The eccentricities of Vasilii Petrovich had taught the little circle of his friends not to be surprised at any of his odd actions. And therefore no one was surprised at his sudden and unexpected disappearance. For he would undoubtedly pop up again. No one entertained the least doubt that he would return: the only question was where he had got to and where he was roaming. What was the cause of his irritation and how was he doctoring himself against it? These were questions which were of great interest to me in my boredom.

CHAPTER THE THIRD

THREE more days went by. A spell of gorgeous weather
had set in. Our rich and fecund part of the country was living
its life to the full. There was a new moon. After a broiling
day, a sparkling luxuriant night had descended. On nights
like these the inhabitants of Kursk love to listen to their
nightingales. Their famous nightingales trill to them from
dusk till dawn, and they listen to them from dusk till dawn in
their spacious and dense public park. They will walk about
softly and in silence, and only the young school-teachers debate
heatedly on "lofty and beauteous subjects" or on "dilettantism
in Science". These loud debates were carried on with great
earnestness. To the remotest corners of the ornamental gardens
in the ancient park would be wafted exclamations such as : "Here
is a dilemma!", "One moment, please : you cannot argue
a priori", "You should proceed by an inductive method", etc.
In those days we still argued about matters of this kind. Nowadays such debates are not heard any longer. "Every age has
its birds, and every bird has its song." Present-day middle-
class Russian society in no way resembles the one I lived in at
Kursk at the time of this tale. Questions which now occupy
our minds still had not been raised then, and in numerous
heads romanticism held its sway, freely and powerfully, un-
conscious of the coming of new ideas which would claim their
rights to the Russian thinking man and which the Russian
thinking man of a certain intellectual level would accept as he
accepts everything, that is to say, not altogether sincerely, but
vehemently, with affectation and with extravagance. In those
days men were still unashamed to speak of feelings for the lofty
and the beautiful, while women loved ideal heroes, listened to
the nightingales that trilled in the flowering lilac bushes, and
hearkened spell-bound to the windbags who trundled them
under the arm up and down the dark paths and settled with
them the esoteric problems of *sacred love*.

Chelnovsky and I remained in the park till midnight, heard
much that was ennobling about lofty ideals and sacred love,

and slipped into our beds with the greatest of pleasure. The light in our room was already out; but we were not yet asleep, and, tucked up under our blankets, were telling each other of our impressions. The night was at the height of its grandeur and a nightingale right under our window sang passionately. We were on the point of bidding each other good-night, when suddenly, from beyond the fence which separated the street from the little garden under our bedroom window, someone called out : "Boys !"

"That's the Musk-Ox," said Chelnovsky, jerking his head from his pillow.

I fancied he was mistaken.

"Oh yes, that's the Musk-Ox right enough," insisted Chelnovsky, and jumping out of bed, leaned out of the window. All was still.

"Boys !" the same voice cried again beneath the fence.

"Musk-Ox !" Chelnovsky called.

"That's me."

"Come along, then."

"The gates are shut."

"Well, give a knock."

"Oh, I don't want to wake anyone. I just wanted to know if you were asleep."

A series of heavy movements sounded behind the fence, following which, Vasilii Petrovich dropped into the little garden like a load of earth.

"There's an Ariel for you !" Chelnovsky said, laughing, and watching Vasilii Petrovich lifting himself from the ground and making his way towards the window through the thick clusters of acacia and lilac.

"Greetings !" the Musk-Ox saluted us gaily, appearing at our window.

Chelnovsky moved the dressing-table with our toilet things from the window, and Vasilii Petrovich first swung over one of his legs, then seated himself astride the window-sill, then swung over the other leg, and finally appeared complete in the room.

"Ooph ! I'm about done in," he announced, took his coat off, and grasped our hands.

"How many miles have you done now?" Chelnovsky asked, getting into bed again.

"I've been to Pogodov."

"At the tavern-keeper's?"

"At the tavern-keeper's."

"Will you eat?"

"If you've got anything."

"Wake the boy."

"Oh, don't bother the little snorer!"

"Why not?"

"Let him sleep."

"Don't be an idiot!" Chelnovsky gave a loud shout: "Moisei!"

"Don't wake him, I tell you; let him sleep."

"Well, I won't find what to give you."

"All the better."

"But you want to eat, don't you?"

"Don't bother, I tell you; now look here, brothers . . ."

"What is it, brother?"

"I've come to say good-bye to you." Vasilii Petrovich sat down on Chelnovsky's bed and placed a friendly hand on his knee.

"What do you mean, 'say good-bye'?"

"Don't you know how people say good-bye?"

"Where are you off to now?"

"I am going far away, brothers."

Chelnovsky got out of bed and lit the candle. Vasilii Petrovich sat very quietly, and on his face was an expression of serenity and even happiness.

"Let me have a good look at you," said Chelnovsky.

"Go on—look as much as you like," the Musk-Ox replied, smiling his awkward smile.

"What's your tavern-keeper doing, then?"

"Selling hay and oats."

"And have you thrashed out with him the subject of human wrongs and injustice?"

"I have."

"It was he, then—was it—who advised you on this pilgrimage?"

THE MUSK-OX

"No, I decided it all on my own."
"What distant lands are you off to, then?"
"To Perm."
"To Perm?"
"Yes. Now isn't it marvellous!"
"Lost anything there?"
Vasilii Petrovich got up, took a turn round the room, gave his side locks a twist and muttered to himself: "That's my concern."
"Now then, Vasilii: don't be an ass," said Chelnovsky. The Musk-Ox was silent, and we were silent too.
It was an oppressive silence. Both Chelnovsky and I divined that there, before us, stood an agitator—a sincere and fearless agitator. And he understood that we had understood him, and suddenly exclaimed:
"What will you have me do? My heart cannot stand this civilization, this nobilization, this scoundrelization!..."—and he crashed his fist on his bosom and collapsed heavily into an armchair.
"But what can you do?"
"Oh, if only I knew what can be done with this! If I could only tell! I'm groping ahead."
There was a general silence.
"May I smoke?" asked Bogoslovsky after a lengthy pause.
"Sure. Go ahead."
"I'll have a lie-down with you, here, on the floor.—This will be my last supper."
"That's a good idea."
"We'll talk—you know . . . I sort of go about saying nothing, and then suddenly I get an urge to talk."
"Something has upset you."
"I am sorry for the kids," said he, and spat between his teeth.
"What kids?"
"Well, my little priests-to-be."
"Why are you sorry for *them*?"
"They'll be ruined without me."
"It's you who are ruining them."
"Go on!"

21

"Of course: they are taught one thing, and you go and tell them something quite different."

"Well, what's wrong in that?"

"Well, no good will come of it."

A pause ensued.

"Now, you listen to me, man," said Chelnovsky: "why don't you marry and take your old mother to live with you, and become a good priest—now, there you would be doing something worth while."

"Don't you talk to me about that! Don't you talk to me about that!"

"Oh, all right—God forgive you," answered Chelnovsky with a wave of his hand.

Vasilii Petrovich began to pace the room again, and halting before the window recited:

> "Stand alone before the storm,
> Take not a wife unto thyself."

"Hark to him: he's learnt some verses too," Chelnovsky said to me, smiling and pointing at Vasilii Petrovich.

"Intelligent ones only," replied the other without leaving the window.

"There's any amount of intelligent verses like these, Vasilii Petrovich," said I.

"All rubbish."

"And women are all trash?"

"All trash."

"And Lidochka?"

"Well, what of Lidochka?" asked Vasilii Petrovich when he was reminded of the name of a very charming and exceptionally unhappy young girl—the only female creature in the town who exhibited the warmest sympathy for Vasilii Petrovich.

"You won't miss her?"

"What's this you are talking about?" queried the Musk-Ox, opening wide his eyes and staring fixedly at me.

"I am only saying she is a good girl!"

"Well, what if she is a good girl?" Vasilii Petrovich lapsed into silence, knocked out his pipe against the window-sill and grew thoughtful.

"The lousy crowd!" he muttered, lighting another pipe. Chelnovsky and I burst out laughing.

"What's biting you?" demanded Vasilii Petrovich.

"Is it the ladies by any chance that are lousy according to you?"

"Ladies! Ladies be damned—it's the Jews."

"What have the Jews got to do with it?"

"Oh, the Devil alone knows—I keep thinking of them: I have a mother, and every one of them has a mother too, and everyone knows—" Vasilii Petrovich observed, and blowing out the candle, pipe in mouth, settled down on the floor-runner.

"Haven't you forgotten that yet?"

"I don't easily forget, brother." Vasilii Petrovich heaved a deep sigh.

"They'll probably all peg out on the way, the homeless brats."

"Perhaps."

"About the best thing they can do."

"Now, if this isn't a most involved sort of compassion," commented Chelnovsky.

"No, it's you who get everything involved. With me, brother, everything is straightforward, peasant-like. I can't follow all your la-di-das. Your heads are full of stuff about the sheep being safe and the wolves being in good fettle too, only it can't be done. It never happens that way?"

"Then how do you think things will be all right?"

"They'll only be all right as God wills."

"God Himself does nothing in what appertains to human affairs."

"Naturally—all that will be done by the people themselves."

"When they become human beings," observed Chelnovsky.

"Ha! Aren't you clever now! To look at you all, anyone might think that you actually know something, yet you know nothing," cried Vasilii Petrovich fiercely. "You can't see anything beyond your aristocratic noses, and you never will. Now if you had stood in my shoes, living with the people,—had tramped about as much as I have done, you would have known that sentimentalism gets you nowhere. Ugh—there's another brute for you! He's also acquired the habits of a regular gent"—the Musk-Ox suddenly flew off at a tangent and rose to his feet.

"Who's got the habits of a gent?"

"That dog of yours—Box—who else do you think?"

"And what sort of habits peculiar to the nobility has he got?" asked Chelnovsky.

"Leaves doors open."

Only then did we become aware that a draught was indeed scurrying across the room.

Vasilii Petrovich got up, closed the door into the passage and hooked the door.

"Thank you," Chelnovsky said to him when he returned and stretched himself on the mat again.

Vasilii Petrovich made no reply, refilled his pipe, lit it, and suddenly asked:

"What sort of lies are they printing in books nowadays?"

"In what books?"

"Well, in your periodicals?"

"Oh, they write about all sorts of things; I can't tell you in so many words."

"All about progress, no doubt."

"Yes, about progress also."

"And about the people?"

"About the people too."

"Oh, woe to these scribes and pharisees!" the Musk-Ox remarked with a sigh. "Blah-blah, without knowing a thing themselves."

"Why do you imagine, Vasilii Petrovich, that there is no one besides you who knows anything about the people? That's pride, you know, speaking within you."

"No, it isn't pride. All I see is that everyone is doing the business in a dirty way. They're all building up a reputation with blah-blah, and when it comes to doing things, there isn't a soul who's willing. No—what I say is: get doing things—don't blather. Their love for the people is all so much talk

24

over a good dinner. Writing novels—books!" he added after a pause, "oh idolaters! cursed pharisees! They never move; they're afraid the dry oatmeal our peasants eat will choke them.—It's just as well they don't move," he added after a pause.

"Why?"

"Well, it's just as I said: if the oatmeal choked them, they would need thumping on the back, to make them get their breath back, and then they'd set up a holler: 'We're being thrashed!' Who would believe people like that! Now, if you want to serve," he continued, seating himself on the bed, "don't be afraid to put on a working smock, and see it fits you; eat bread and dripping and don't mind it; and don't be superior when it comes to driving a pig into the yard: then they'll have confidence in you. Put your heart into it, and do it so that everyone can see what sort of a heart you have; don't go about spinning yarns. Oh, my people, my people! What would I not do for you?... My people, my people! What would I not give unto you?" Vasilii Petrovich pondered a while, then rose to his full height, and extending his arms towards me and Chelnovsky cried: "Boys! Troubled days are coming—days of distress. There is not an hour to lose, for false prophets will otherwise arise, and I hear their voices—their cursed, hateful voices. In the name of the people they will ensnare you and corrupt you. Do not be tempted by these alluring voices, and if you feel not the strength of bullocks in your shoulders, do not set the yoke upon them. It is not a matter of numbers. You cannot catch a flea with your five fingers, you can only do it with one. I expect no more profit from you than from the rest of them. It isn't your fault—you are too flabby for a great cause. But I beg of you to observe a brotherly commandment of mine: Don't ever yap for the sake of yapping! Honestly—it does a lot of harm! It is evil! Don't hinder—that's all you are asked to do; but for us—the Musk-Oxen"—he smote his bosom—"for us, that is not enough. Heaven will smite us if we don't do more. We are of the people and the people shall know us."

Vasilii Petrovich continued to speak in the same strain and went on and on for hours. I had never known him speak so much and express himself so clearly. The first streaks of dawn were in the sky and a noticeable greyness suffused the room, yet Vasilii Petrovich was still speaking. His stocky figure was making vigorous gestures, and through the rents of his ancient cotton shirt his hairy chest could be seen heaving with unrestrained emotion.

We dropped off to sleep at four in the morning and awoke at nine. The Musk-Ox was no longer there, and from that day I saw him no more for exactly three years. The weird creature left that very morning for the land recommended to him by his crony, the tavern-keeper at Pogodov.

CHAPTER THE FOURTH

THERE exist in our Province a considerable number of monasteries, built amid forests and known as "Hermitages". My grandmother was a very pious old soul. An old-world lady, she was possessed by an insuperable passion for making the round of them. She not only knew by heart the history of each and every one of these isolated monasteries, but was familiar with all the monastic legends, the history of every ikon, miracles which were told there, knew all about the monastic funds, the state of the Sacristy, and all the rest. In the monasteries, too, everyone knew the old lady and gave her the warmest welcome, despite the fact that she never made any very costly donations, except palls that she occupied herself with embroidering throughout the autumn and winter, when the weather prevented her from travelling. In the hospices of the P— and L— Hermitages, rooms were always kept reserved for her before the Feast of St. Peter and Assumption Day. They were carefully swept out and were not allotted to anyone else even on the eve of the Feasts.

"Alexandra Vasilievna is coming," the Father-Treasurer would tell everyone, "I cannot let you have the rooms."

And my grandmother would invariably arrive.

On one occasion she happened to be very late, while a very large influx of visitors arrived at the Hermitages for the Feast.

In the evening, before Midnight Mass, some General or other arrived at the L— Hermitage and demanded to be given the best room in the hospice. The Father-Treasurer was on the horns of a dilemma. It was the first time my grandmother was missing the solemn Feast in honour of which the Hermitage church had been named. "The old woman must have died," he figured, but, consulting his ancient bulbous watch, and finding that another two hours remained before the Midnight Mass, he still refused to give up the rooms to the General, and, quite unperturbed, betook himself to his cell to read his orisons. The great bell of the monastery boomed thrice; the darkness of the church was broken by the flame of a little wax taper with which a novice was bustling about by the reredos, lighting the candles before the ikons in the side panels. The worshippers, yawning and crossing their mouths, began to throng into the church, and my dear granny, wearing a neat dress of home-spun linen and a snow-white bonnet of a style that had been the fashion in Moscow in 1812, entered through the North doors, crossing herself devoutly and whispering: "Hear my voice in the morning, O Lord my God." When the Arch-deacon uttered his solemn: "Arise ye all!", granny was already in a dark corner, bowing to the ground for the souls of the dead. Father-Treasurer, as he shepherded the congregation towards the cross, after the early matins, was not in the least surprised to behold the ancient lady, and handing her a wafer, which he produced from under his cassock, said, as though nothing had occurred: "Welcome, Mother Alexandra!" Only the young novices at the Hermitages used to address grand-mama as "Alexandra Vasilievna"; the older men never called her anything but "Mother Alexandra", yet the pious old soul was never a sanctimonious hypocrite and never laid claims to being a nun.

Despite her sixty-odd years, she was always as neat and clean as a new pin. Her trim dress of linen or green cotton, her billowy cap of tulle with unbleached ribbons, and her handbag with an embroidered dog upon it—all were full of freshness and a complete absence of affectation. She used to travel to the Hermitages in an unsprung, covered, country cart drawn by two aged bay mares of a very good breed. One of these (the mother) was called "Beauty", and the other (the daughter), "Surprise". The latter received her name because she arrived in the world unexpectedly. Both these horses were extremely well-behaved, playful and good-tempered, and to travel with them—accompanied by the pious old lady and her very placid and aged coachman, Ilya Vasilievich—was one of the greatest delights of my childhood days.

I was A.D.C. to the aged lady from earliest infancy. I was only six when for the first time I went with her to the L— Hermitage, conveyed by the two bay mares, and from that time onwards, escorted her on every occasion until, at the age of ten, I was sent to the Provincial High School. The visits to the monasteries were full of attraction to me. The old lady had a knack of weaving a lot of poetry and romance into her travels. We would be rattling along at a brisk trot—everything around would be so lovely: the fragrant air, the jackdaws pottering about in the greenery of the trees. We would meet people who bowed to us, and we would bow back to them. We would proceed on foot through the forests: granny would be telling me all about 1812, about the gentry of Mozhaisk, about her flight from Moscow, of the proud way the French approached the city, and how, later, they were mercilessly frozen to death and exterminated. And then we would come across a wayside guest-house, with inn-keepers whom we knew, and countrywomen with fat bellies and aprons laced criss-cross above their breasts, and spacious meadows where one could run about to one's heart's content. All this captivated me and held for me a world of enchantment. Grandmama would be attending to her toilet in her little room, while I would repair to the cool, shady wainshed, where I would join Ilya Vasilievich, stretch myself by his side on a heap of hay, and listen to his story of how Ilya drove the Emperor Alexander when he visited Orel, would learn what a dangerous business that was, what a lot of carriages there were, and the danger to which the Emperor's carriage was exposed when, as it descended the hill towards the river Orlik, one of the coachman's reins snapped, and how he, Ilya Vasilievich, alone, by his presence of mind, saved the life of the Emperor, who was already preparing to jump out of the carriage. The Phaeacians never listened to Ulysses with such breathless absorption as I listened to our coachman Ilya Vasilievich.

At the Hermitages themselves I had my bosom friends. I was a great favourite with two ancient greybeards : the Abbot of P— Hermitage and Father-Treasurer of the L— Hermitage. The former, a gaunt and pale old man, with a kindly, yet austere countenance, I was not, however, attached to: but Father-Treasurer I loved with all the ardour of my little heart. He was the most genial creature in this sublunary world of ours, of which, may it here be mentioned, he knew nothing, and in this ignorance of his—now I come to think of it—lay the secret of the boundless love this old man felt for all humanity.

But apart from these, so to speak, aristocratic acquaintances among the hermits, I also possessed democratic connections with the plebeians of the Hermitages. I was very fond of the novices—the strange class of creatures among whom, as a rule, two passions predominate — indolence and touchiness, but where sometimes is also to be met a rich store of gay light-heartedness and typically Russian indifference to oneself.

"How did you experience the call to monastic life ?" I would sometimes ask a novice.

"No," he would reply, "I felt no call—I just entered the monastery ;—just like that."

"And you will take the vow ?"

"Of course."

A novice seemed to think that it was quite impossible for him to leave the monastery, though he was perfectly well aware that no one would have prevented him from doing so. As a child I was very fond of this crowd—gay, mischievous, daring and blandly hypocritical. So long as a novice remains a novice, or *slimak*, i.e. "slug", no one takes much notice of him, and consequently no one is aware of his true nature ; but the moment a novice dons a cassock and cowl he completely alters, both in character and in his attitude towards his fellow-creatures. Yet so long as he remains a novice he is a most sociable animal. What epic fisticuff fights I recall in the monastery bakeries. What gallant songs were sung *sotto voce* upon the battlements, when five or six tall, handsome novices strolled leisurely along them and shot keen glances across the river, beyond which another song was sung by ringing and alluring female voices—a song in which fluttered a yearning appeal: "Cast yourself—fling yourself—into the green woods hurl yourself." And I remember how the "slugs" would grow fidgety, listening to these songs, and, unable to withstand their seductive call any longer, would dive into the green wood. Oh! I remember it all very well. I have not forgotten a single lesson—neither the singing of cantatas composed upon the most unusual themes; nor the lessons in gymnastics, for the exercise of which, incidentally, the lofty walls of the monastery were not very suitable; nor yet the lessons in keeping silent and laughing while preserving a perfectly straight face. But above all else I loved the fishing expeditions to the monastery lake. My pals, the novices, also regarded an expedition to the lake as a kind of picnic. Fishing, in their monotonous existence, was the only occupation which gave them an opportunity of having some real fun and of testing the strength of their young muscles. Indeed, there was much that was poetic in this type of fishing.

The distance from the monastery to the lake was about five or six miles, which had to be travelled on foot through a very dense and rough forest. We usually set out before Evensong. In a cart, to which was harnessed a fat and very ancient cob belonging to the monastery, lay the drag-net, several buckets, a barrel for the fish and long poles; but no one rode in the cart. The reins were made fast to the front rail, and if the horse strayed off the road, the novice who acted as the driver merely came up and tugged at the reins. Actually, the cob scarcely ever got off the road, and indeed could not very well do so, because from the monastery to the lake a single track went through the wood, and this track was so deeply rutted that the horse never felt like pulling the wheels out of the ruts. As supervisor over us, we invariably had the same deaf and purblind old man, the venerable Father Ignatii, who, many years ago, had received in his little cell the Emperor Alexander I, and who constantly forgot that Alexander I was no longer on the throne. Father Ignatii rode in a tiny little cart and himself managed the other podgy little horse. I, personally, had always the right to ride with Father Ignatii, to whose care my grandmother especially entrusted me, and Father Ignatii would even allow me to drive the roly-poly kind of animal harnessed to the short shafts of his little cart. But as a rule I preferred to walk with the novices, and they never kept to the track. By and by we would scatter all over the forest and would begin by singing: "A young monk was a-journeying on the road and met Jesus Christ Himself", and then someone would launch into a new song and we would sing them one after another. . . . Those carefree, beloved days! Bless you—and a blessing on you too, all you who have provided me with these memories. . . .

It was not until nightfall that we would thus reach the lake. Here, on the shore, stood a little cabin in which lived two aged men, cassocked lay-brothers, Father Sergii and Father Vavila. They were both "unlettered", i.e. illiterate, and did a "watchman's novitiate" on the monastery lake. Father Sergii was extremely clever with his hands. I still possess a lovely spoon and a filigree cross which he made. He also produced nets, peg-tops, chips, baskets and various similar articles. Also he had a very cleverly carved little wooden statue of some saint or other; but he only showed it to me once, and made me promise that I would tell no one. Father Vavila, on the contrary, did nothing. He was a poet. He loved freedom, indolence and peace. He was prepared to stand for hours by the lake in a contemplative pose and observe how the wild ducks flew, how the dignified heron stepped out, every now and again stabbing the water with his long beak, as he picked out the frogs who had persuaded Zeus to make him their king. Immediately before the cabin of the two "unlettered" monks lay a broad stretch of sand, and beyond it was the lake. Inside, the cabin was very clean and well kept. There were two ikons on a little shelf, and two heavy wooden beds painted in green oil paint, a table covered with an unbleached cloth, and two chairs, while along the side walls were two wooden benches just as in a peasant cottage. In the corner was a small cupboard with the tea-things, and under the cupboard, on a special stool, stood a copper samovar, which shone like the boiler of a royal yacht. Everything was very neat and cosy. Besides the "unlettered" Fathers, no one else lived in the cell, with the exception of a black-and-yellow cat, called "Captain", and remarkable only because, bearing a masculine name and having for long been regarded as a real tom, he suddenly scandalized everybody by producing a litter of kittens, and from then on never stopped increasing his progeny, as behoves a proper she-cat.

Of all our company, only Father Ignatii would make his bed inside the cabin with the "unlettered" Fathers. As a rule I would excuse myself this honour and sleep with the novices in the open, near the cabin. Truth to tell, we scarcely slept at all. By the time we had made a fire, boiled a cauldron of water, made a thin gruel, into which we would throw a few dried carp, and by the time we had eaten it all out of a large wooden bowl, it would be midnight. And then, no sooner had we lain down than someone would begin a tale, and always a most terrifying one, full of the most lurid sins. From tales we would switch over to real-life reminiscences, into which each teller would, of course, always introduce countless inventions made up on the spur of the moment. So the night would often pass before anyone expressed any intention of going to sleep. The stories usually were about pilgrims and robbers. A particularly rich store of tales of this kind was possessed by Timofei Nevstruev, a middle-aged novice, who enjoyed among us the reputation of a real Samson and who was always about to join in some Crusade for the liberation of the Christians, with the intention of subjugating the lot. He had, it would appear, tramped all over Russia, had even been to Palestine and Greece, and had espied the fact that they could all be subjugated. We would be sprawling on our sacking, the fire would still be glowing, the tubby horses, tied up near by, would be emitting contented little snorts over their oats, and then someone would start yet another yarn. I have forgotten the vast majority of these stories now, and can

only recall the last night which, thanks to the indulgence of
my grandmother, I spent with the novices on the shore of
lake P—. Timofei Nevstruev was out of spirits—he had, that
day, been made to stand in the middle of the church and make
deep obeisances as a penance for having clambered over the
wall of the Abbot's garden the previous night—and the story-
telling was begun by Emelian Vysotsky, a young man of about
eighteen. He came from Courland, was abandoned as a baby
in our Province and became a novice. His mother had been
a variety actress and he knew nothing more about her, but
had been brought up by some kind-hearted shopkeeper's wife,
who placed him as a novice in the monastery when he was ten.
The conversation began because one of the novices, after someone had told a story, heaved a deep sigh and asked:

"Why is it, brothers, that you don't get good robbers
nowadays?"

No one replied, and I was becoming greatly exercised by
the problem, which for a long time past I had been unable to
resolve to my own satisfaction. In those days I was very fond
of robbers and used to draw them in my copy-book, dressed in
flowing capes, with pretty feathers in their hats.

"You still get robbers now," remarked the novice from
Courland in a high-pitched voice.

"Well, go on, tell us what sort of robbers you get nowadays,"
challenged Nevstruev, and buried himself up to his chin in his
calico robe.

"Well, for instance, when I was still living at Puzaniha,"
began the Courlander, "I happened to be making a pilgrimage
once, with Mother Natalia—the one from Borovsk—and with
Alena, another pilgrim from near Chernigov, to the Shrine of
St. Nicholas at Mzensk."

"Which Natalia is that? The tall blonde one? Would that
be the one?" interrupted Nevstruev.

"That's her," the story-teller replied hastily, and went on:
"Now, on the way there is a village called Otrada—seventeen
miles from Orel. We came to this village at nightfall. We
asked the peasants to put us up for the night—they wouldn't
let us in, so we went to the inn. At the inn they only charge

you a grosh, but it was frightfully crowded. All flax-beaters—about forty of them were there, I reckon. They started drinking and swearing something awful. In the morning, when Mother Natalia woke me, all the beaters had gone, only three of them remained, and they were strapping their satchels to their beaters' tools. We also tied up our satchels, paid the three groshes for our beds and set out too. We were out of the village, when we turned round and saw that the three beaters were following us. Well, there was nothing wrong in that. We didn't mind. Only Mother Natalia kind of said: 'That's queer! Yesterday,' says she, 'these same flax-beaters said, as they were supping, that they were going to Orel, and now, look, they are going with us to Mzensk.' On we went—the beaters some distance behind us. And then we came to a little wood on the road. Now, as we neared this wood, the beaters began to gain on us. We put on speed, and so did they. 'What are you running for?' they said. 'You can't get away,' and with that two of them ran up and grabbed Mother Natalia's hands. She fairly yelled, in a voice that was like nothing on earth, while Mother Alena and I just sprinted. We were haring along, with the robbers hollering after us: 'Hold them, hold them!' they were roaring and Mother Natalia was shrieking. 'They must have knifed her,' we figured, and ran all the faster. Mother Alena, she just streaked out of sight, but I went all kind of limp. . . . I felt I couldn't go on any more, so I just tumbled under a bush. 'Whatever it is,' I reckoned, 'that God has predestined cannot be avoided.' There I was lying under that bush, scarcely daring to breathe. I was expecting them to come across me any moment! But no one appeared. All I could hear was how they were still wrestling with Mother Natalia. She is a hefty big woman, they just couldn't finish her off. It was very still in the wood, and you can hear a lot in the early morning air. Every now and again I could hear Mother Natalia give another shriek. 'The Lord rest her soul,' I thought to myself. As for myself, I didn't know whether I had better get to my feet and run, or wait where I was for some passer-by to come along. Then I fancied someone was approaching. I lay quite still, half dead with fright, and watched from under my bush.

34

And what do you think I saw, brothers?—Why, Mother Natalia going past! Her black kerchief had slipped from her head; her thick plait of golden hair was all in a mess, she was carrying her satchel in her arms and seemed to be tripping over things. 'I'll speak to her,' I decided, and called to her, softly like. She stopped and stared at the bush, and I called to her again. 'Who's that?' says she. I jumped to my feet and ran to her, and she fairly gaped. I looked all about me—there was no one behind or ahead of us. 'Are they after us?' I says to her. 'Let's run!' And she was standing as though turned to stone—only her lips were trembling. I saw that her dress had been torn, her arms were all scratched nearly up to her elbows, and her forehead, too, was all scratched as if by someone's nails. 'Let us go,' I says to her again. 'Were they throttling you?' I asked. 'Yes, they were,' says she. 'Let's hurry,' and off we went! 'How did you get away from them?' I asked. But she said nothing more till we got to the village, where we met Mother Alena."

"And what did she say then?" asked Nevstruev, who, like the rest of us, had listened to the tale in dead silence.

"Well, all she said even then was how they chased her all over the place, and how she kept repeating a prayer and flinging sand into their eyes."

"And they didn't take anything from her?" asked someone.

"Not a thing. She only lost a shoe off her foot and a sacred charm that was hanging round her neck. They were looking for money, she said, which they thought she was carrying in her dress."

"Tcha! Call them robbers! All they were fit for was to search women," ejaculated Nevstruev, and then began telling of better robbers, who had given him a fright in the Oboyan district. "There," he maintained, "were real, Russian robbers."

Things were becoming desperately thrilling, and we were all ears about these real, good robbers.

Nevstruev began: "I was walking," he said, "from the Korennaya one day. I went there to fulfil a vow over a matter of a toothache. I had with me about two roubles in money and a parcel of shirts. On the road I fell in with a couple—

35

artisans they looked like. 'Where,' they asked,' are you going?' I told them. 'That's where we are going,' they said. 'Let's go together.'—'All right, let's.' So we went. We came to a village; night was falling. 'Let's spend the night here,' says I to them, but they said: 'It's no good here; let's do another mile: there is a jolly good inn there. There,' they said, 'they will give us every pleasure.' 'It's as far as I go,' I said. 'I don't want any of your pleasures.' 'Oh, come on,' they said, 'it isn't far!' So I went on. Sure enough, about three miles or so along the road we came across a house in the woods what looked like an inn. Two of the windows were lighted. One of the artisans banged the knocker, the dogs behind the door set up a row, but no one opened. He knocked again; then we heard someone coming out of the house and challenging us; the voice I heard was a woman's. 'Who might you be?' she asked, and the artisan said, 'Friends.' 'What friends?'— 'Just friends from over the hills and far away.' The door was opened. The passage was as black as ink. The woman fastened the door behind us and opened the inner door. In the room there wasn't a single man, only the woman—the one who had opened the door to us—and another, all screwed up and old, who was sitting there, spinning flax. 'Well, how goes it, Chief?' says the artisan to the woman. 'Welcome,' says the woman, and I see her looking at me. And I was looking at her too. A hefty big woman she was, about thirty, I should guess, with milk-white complexion—the Devil take her—and pink cheeks and eyes that sort of commanded. 'Where,' says she, 'did you pick up this lad?' That's me— you follow. 'We'll tell you later,' said they. 'And now we want what makes you stumble and what fills the belly, 'cos our tootsie-wootsies have been lazying it since morning.' She put salt beef out on the table, and horse radish, and a bottle of vodka, and pies. 'Go on, eat!' the artisans said to me. 'No,' says I, 'I don't eat meat.'—'Have a cheese pie, then.' I took one. 'Drink,' they said, 'vodka.' I drank a tot. 'Drink another.' I drank another. 'Do you want to live with us?' they said. 'How do you mean,' I asked—'with you?'—'As you see: we can't manage, the two of us. You come with

us and drink and eat, only do as the Chief tells you—all right?'
Here's a fix, I thought to myself: this is an evil place, this is.
'No,' says I, 'lads; I cannot live with you.'—'Why not?'
They were swilling vodka all the while and plaguing me:
'Go on—have another.' 'Can you fight?' asked one. 'I've
never been taught,' says I. 'Oh, you haven't—well, here is a
lesson for you!'—and with that he fairly lands me one on the
ear. The woman said nothing, and the old hag just went on
spinning. 'What's that for, brothers?' says I. 'That's for
climbing on the seat, for spying at the window'—and with
that he landed me another on the other ear. Well, I reckoned,
if my last hour has come I might as well stand up for myself,
so I just turned and cracked him one on the back of his head.
He simply went down under the table. Then I see him get
up from under that table, fairly snorting. He swept his hair
back with his hand and made a bee-line for the bottle. 'Now,'
says he, 'your last hour has come!' No one said a word, I
noticed, and his pal also says nothing. 'No,' says I, 'I don't
want no last hour.'—'So you don't want no last hour, do you?
Then, drink vodka.' 'And I won't drink vodka either.'—
'Drink! The Abbot won't see you—he won't give you no
penance.' 'I don't want your vodka.'—'Well, if you won't
drink no vodka—to hell with you: pay for what you've had
and go bye-byes.' .

"'How much do I owe for the vodka?'—'All you've got:
our vodka, brother, is dear—known as "the bitter Russian lot",
with water and with a tear, and the heart of a cur.' I sort of
tried to make a joke of it, but it was no good. No sooner had
I pulled out my purse, when the artisan grabs it and chucks it
over the partition. 'Now then,' says he, 'you go to bed,
monk.'—'Where do you think I can go now?' 'That there
deaf one will show you—You take him!' he shouts to the
woman who was spinning. I followed the woman into the
passage, and from there out into the yard. The night was so
good, just as it is now—with the stars burning in the heavens,
and a breeze rustling like a squirrel through the wood. How
my heart ached for that life of mine, and for the quiet monastery.
And the woman she opened a shed. 'Go in,' she said, 'poor

soul,' and off she trotted. Sounded as though she were sorry for me. In I went, feeling about me with my hands—there was something piled up there, but what it was I couldn't make out. I felt a post. Well, said I to myself, I suppose it's all one, and I started climbing up it. I got to the cross-beam, found the rafters and began burrowing my way through the thatch. My hands were bleeding, but I just went on. Then, as I pushed my way through the straw, I saw the stars. I never stopped; just made a hole—pushed my satchel through first—then crossed myself, and tumbled out. And did I run, brothers? —I never ran so fast in my life."

More stories of the same nature would follow, but these narratives seemed in those days so full of absorbing interest that we would scarcely close our eyes before dawn. And there would be Father Ignatii, who would already be prodding us with his stick: "Get up! Time to leave for the lake." Up would get the novices, and stretch and yawn—the wretched lads would be wilting with sleep. They would take the drag-net, remove their boots and trousers, and would make their way to the boats. The clumsy, black, grebe-like monastery boats were always tied up at bunches of poles set in the lake, about fifty feet from the shore, because a sand-bank ran under the water for some distance out, and the black boats sat very deep in the water and could not come inshore. Nevstruev, I remember, would carry me in his arms all the way across the shallows. How well I remember those expeditions—the good-natured, carefree faces. . . . I fancy I see it all now: I see the novices waking up and stepping into the cold water. They are skipping about, laughing and grinning and shivering with the morning chill as they tug at the heavy drag-net, stooping over the surface to splash water into eyes that are sticky with sleep. I remember the thin vapour that would rise from the water, the golden carp and slippery trout; I remember the wearying hours of noon, when we would all drop to the ground as though we had been pole-axed, and would refuse the amber-hued fish broth which the "unlettered" Father Sergii would cook for us. But above all I remember the glum—one might almost have said spiteful—expression in

every face when the tubby little horses were again harnessed
to carry back to the monastery the carp we had caught and our
commander, Father Ignatii, behind whom the "slugs" had to
march back to the protection of their monastery walls.

In these surroundings, which I knew so well from childhood,
I was fated once again to meet, quite unexpectedly, the Musk-Ox,
who had so suddenly fled from Kursk.

CHAPTER THE FIFTH

MUCH water has run under the bridges since the time of
these memories, memories which have little to do with
the relentless fate of the Musk-Ox. I was growing up
and was learning of the sorrows of life; my grandmother
died; Ilya Vasilievich and "Beauty" and "Surprise" were also
no more; the gay "slugs" now walked as dignified monks;
I had acquired a certain amount of book-learning at the Provincial High School, after which I was taken to a University
town nearly three hundred and fifty miles away, where I learnt
to sing a Latin song, read one or two samples of the works of
Strauss, Feuerbach, Büchner and Babeuf, and in the full armour
of my newly acquired wisdom returned to my lares and penates.
It was then that I first met Vasilii Petrovich, as I have already
described. Another four years went by, years which I spent
drearily enough, and again I found myself in the shade of my
own native lime trees. No changes had occurred at home in
the meantime—in habit, outlook or direction. The news was
only of a natural order: my mother had become more aged
and more corpulent, my fifteen-year-old sister had stepped
straight from a school desk into an untimely grave, and—oh—
a few new lime trees planted by her little hand had taken root
and were growing up. "Can it be," I thought, "that nothing
has changed, while I have lived through so much; while I
believed in God, denied Him, and found Him again; while I
loved my country and was crucified with it, and was with
those that crucified it!" My youthful self-esteem felt even
hurt at the thought, and I decided to check up on the position—

to check up on everything—both with reference to myself as well as to everything that had surrounded me in the days when the impressions of existence were new to me.

First of all I wanted to see my beloved Hermitages, and one fresh, fine morning I drove to the P— Hermitage in my racing drozhki. The Hermitage lay some thirteen miles from my house. There was the same road, the same fields, and the starlings were sheltering in the same manner in the thick winter crops, and the peasants bowed as before, from their waist up, and the women were catching fleas, the same as ever, as they lay before their doorsteps. It was all as it had been in the old days, and here were the gates of the monastery, with a new janitor, because the old one was now a monk. But the Father-Treasurer was still alive. The ailing patriarch was well in his nineties. In our monasteries you get many examples of rare longevity. Father-Treasurer, however, no longer occupied himself with his duties, but lived in retirement, although he still called himself "Father-Treasurer". When I was taken to his room, he was lying on his bed and, not recognizing me, began to fidget and asked the lay brother: "Who is it?" Without replying I approached the old man and took his hand. "Good morning, good morning," mumbled Father-Treasurer—"and who would you be?" I bent over him and kissed his forehead and mentioned my name. "Oh, it's you, dear friend, dear friend! Well, well; well, how are you?" the old man broke out, again fidgeting on his bed—"Cyril! Puff up a samovar for us, as quick as you like," he said to the lay brother. "And I—miserable sinner—I can't walk now, as you see. It's nearly a year now since my legs have been just swelling and swelling." Father-Treasurer was suffering from dropsy, with which many monks end their days and which is brought about by lengthy standing in church and by other occupations which predispose one to the illness.

"Well, call Vasilii Petrovich," said Father-Treasurer to the lay brother when the latter had placed a samovar and cups on a little table by the bedside.—"I've got a poor lad staying with me here," he added, turning to me.

The lay brother went out, and a quarter of an hour later

footsteps sounded on the flagstones in the passage outside, accompanied by a kind of lowing noise. The door opened, and, before my astounded gaze, the Musk-Ox appeared. He was dressed in a short *svitka* of Russian peasant cloth, trousers of ticking and rather ancient, high, Russian leather boots. Only, upon his head sat a tall black cap, of the kind worn by novices. The bearing of the Musk-Ox had changed so little that I knew him at once despite his rather weird appearance.

"Vasilii Petrovich! Is it really you?" I said, advancing to meet my friend, and at the same time thinking: "Oh, who but you can tell me how the stern years of experience have passed over the heads of those who are here?"

The Musk-Ox appeared glad to see me, while Father-Treasurer was filled with wonder on seeing that we were old friends.

"Now, that's very nice—now—very nice," he kept on repeating. "Well, Vasya, pour out the tea."

"You know quite well I don't know how to pour out tea," replied the Musk-Ox.

"That's so—that's so. You pour out, guest."

I began to pour out the cups.

"Have you been here long, Vasilii Petrovich?" I asked the Musk-Ox, handing him his cup.

He bit off a piece of sugar, sucked it, and after a couple of sips of tea replied: "About nine months, I should say."

"And where are you off to now?"

"Nowhere, for the present."

"And may I ask where you've come from?" I enquired, smiling involuntarily when I remembered how the Musk-Ox usually answered such enquiries.

"You may."

"From Perm?"

"No."

"Well, then—where from?"

The Musk-Ox replaced his empty cup, and said:

"I've been everywhere and nowhere."

"You haven't seen Chelnovsky by any chance?"

"No—I haven't been there."

"Your mother is alive and well, I hope?"

"Died in a poorhouse."

"What, all alone?"

"Well, who do people die with?"

"When did that happen?"

"About a year ago, I am told."

"You go and have a walk, my children, while I have a snooze before vespers," said Father-Treasurer, who now got tired of the least effort.

"No, I want to drive to the lake," I replied.

"Eh? Well, you go then, God bless you, and take Vasya too. He'll play the fool for you on the journey."

"Come along, Vasilii Petrovich."

The Musk-Ox scratched himself, took his cap, and replied: "Oh, all right then."

We said good-bye to Father-Treasurer till the following day and left. In the grain-yard I myself harnessed my little pony and we drove off. Vasilii Petrovich seated himself with his back to me—back to back—saying that he could not go for a drive otherwise, because he had not enough air to breathe behind someone else's head. During the journey he did not fool at all. On the contrary, he was very silent and merely kept on asking me: Had I seen any intelligent people in St. Petersburg, and what were they thinking? Or, interrupting his questioning, he would suddenly begin to whistle like a nightingale or an oriole.

The entire journey was passed in this way.

By the long-familiar little cabin we were met by a squat, red-haired lay brother, who had taken the place of Father Sergii. The latter had died some three years before and left his tools and materials to the light-hearted Father Vavila. Father Vavila was not in: he was taking a walk—as his habit was—on the shore of the lake and watching the herons swallowing docile frogs. Father Vavila's new companion, Father Prohor, was as pleased at our coming as a Provincial young lady when she hears the tintinnabulation of sleigh-bells. He himself proceeded hastily to unharness our horse, and blew strenuously into the samovar, assuring us the while that "Father Vavila should be back any moment." The Musk-Ox and I hearkened to these assurances, seated ourselves on the raised earth beneath the wall facing the lake, and both were pleasantly silent. Neither of us felt like talking.

The sun had already set behind the tall trees that surrounded the entire monastery lake like a dense screen. The smooth surface of the water appeared almost black. The air was very still, but close.

"We'll be having a thunderstorm in the night," said Father Prohor, dragging the cushions from my racing drozhki into the entrance passage.

"Why bother?" I replied. "Perhaps there won't be a storm at all.".

Father Prohor was smiling shyly, and said:

"Don't mention it—no bother at all."

"I'll take your pony into the passage as well," he began, emerging again from the cabin.

"Why, Father Prohor?"

"There will be an awful storm: she might take fright, and break loose, you know. No—I'd better take her into the passage. She'll be nice and snug there."

Father Prohor untied the horse, and drew her in after him by the rein, talking to her as he did so: "C'mon, mother! What're you frightened of? C'mon, silly!"

"That's better," he said, standing the pony in a corner and filling with oats an old sieve which he had placed before her. "Funny Father Vavila being so late—'pon my word!" he fussed, going round the corner of the cabin. "There! It's getting all overcast now," he added, pointing to a little reddish-grey cloud.

It was getting quite dark outside.

"I'll go and look out for Father Vavila," said the Musk-Ox, and, with a twist of his locks, marched off towards the wood.

"Don't go; you'll only miss one another in the wood."

"I should say so!" and with these words he disappeared.

Father Prohor took an armful of firewood and went inside. Soon the windows of the cabin were lighted up with the fire he had made in the stove, and the water began to boil in the billy-can. Neither Father Vavila nor the Musk-Ox was there. Meanwhile the tips of the trees began to sway from time to time, although the surface of the lake still remained smooth, like hardened lead. Only occasionally would I see its smoothness broken by the white splashes caused by some rising carp, and a chorus of frogs were drawing out their mournful, monotonous note. I was still sitting on the piled-up earth by the wall, staring at the dark lake and reviewing the years that had flown into that darkening distance. Over there, in those days, lay those clumsy boats, to which the Herculean Nevstruev used to carry me in his arms; here I slept with the novices, and everything then was so sweet and gay and full, while now everything seemed the same and yet something was lacking. The carefree days of childhood were gone, there was no more of that warm vivifying faith in much that one believed in so ardently and wholeheartedly.

"I smell the smell of Russ! Whence come ye, dear guests?" cried Father Vavila, suddenly appearing round the corner of the cabin, so that I was entirely unaware of his approach.

I knew him straight away. Only he had become quite white, while that look of childish frankness and the same merry smile had remained.

"Would you be coming from afar?" he asked me.

I named a village twenty-seven miles away.

He enquired: I wouldn't be the son of Afanasii Pavlovich by any chance?

"No," said I.

"Well, it doesn't matter; would you come into our cell, the rain is beginning to drip."

In fact, the rain was beginning to splash down and the surface of the lake became covered in ripples although there was scarcely any wind in this hollow. It had no room to make a proper run; the spot was so quiet.

"And what name might I call you by?" asked Father Vavila when we were well inside the little cabin.

I gave my name. Father Vavila took a look at me and a smile flitted across his genial and sly lips. My little piece of mystification had not succeeded; he had recognized me; the old man and I embraced warmly, kissed one another over and over again and, for no apparent reason, suddenly both burst into tears.

"Let me have a good look at you, properly," said Father Vavila, continuing to smile and leading me to the fire. "Coo—haven't you grown!"

"And you've grown old, Father Vavila."

Father Prohor laughed.

"E-e-eh—they're always trying to look young, they are," explained Father Prohor. "Don't they just try and look young!"

"And how would you have me?" replied Father Vavila, puffing out his chest, but the same instant he sank quickly on a small chair and added: "No, brother! the spirit is willing, but the flesh is weak. High time I joined Father Sergii. I have such a backache to-day—I am not much good nowadays!"

"And has Father Sergii been dead long?"

"Two years it was on St. Spiridon's day."

"He was a grand old man," said I, picturing the dead man to myself, with his bits of wood and his knife.

"Look! You look in the corner: I've got all his workshop now. Oh, do light a candle, Father Prohor."

"And is the Captain alive still?"

"Oh, you mean our cat, the Captain?"

"Yes, of course."

"He was suffocated, brother, our Captain was; got into our kneading-trough, he did; the lid slammed down—we were out at the time. We got home and searched for him high and low—our cat had gone. A couple of days later we opened the kneading-trough, and there he was! We've got another one now. . . . Look at him.—Vaska! Vaska!" Father Vavila called.

From under the stove emerged a large grey tomcat and proceeded to butt at Father Vavila's legs with his head.

"There's a brute for you!"

Father Vavila picked up the cat, turned him over on his lap and tickled his throat. It was like a painting by Teniers: the old white-haired man with a fat grey cat on his knees, with another oldish man pottering about in the corner; various household utensils all round, and the whole illuminated by the warm red glow of the burning stove.

"Oh, do light a candle, Father Prohor!" Father Vavila cried out again.

"Just a minute. . . . Don't seem to get it somehow."

Father Vavila meantime was excusing Prohor and was telling me: "We don't light candles now for ourselves, you see. We go to bed early."

The candle was lit. The room was indeed in exactly the same state as it had been over twelve years ago. Only, in place of Father Sergii, by the stove stood Father Prohor; and in place of the black-and-yellow Captain, Father Vavila was playing with the grey Vaska. Even the knife and the bundle of knotty sticks, which had been prepared by Father Sergii, were hanging where they had been hung by the departed man who had got them ready for something or other.

"There we are; the eggs have boiled and the fish is ready, and Vasilii Petrovich is still out," said Father Prohor.

"What Vasilii Petrovich?"

"The daft one," replied Father Prohor.

"You didn't come with him, did you?"

"I did," I said, guessing that the appellation referred to my Musk-Ox.

"Whoever got you to bring him here."

"Why, we've been friends for years," said I. "But, look here: why do you call him daft?"

"He is daft, brother. Ever so daft!"

"He is very kind."

"I am not saying he is vicious, only it's silliness that's got him: he's a good-for-nothing now: he's against all order."

It was already ten o'clock.

"Well—what about having supper? He may turn up while we're having it," commanded Father Vavila, beginning to wash his hands. "Yes—yes; that's right: we'll have supper and then sing a little requiem . . . All right? For Father Sergii, I say—we'll sing a requiem—eh?"

We sat down to supper, and finished supper, and sang "May he rest with the Saints" for Father Sergii, but still there was no sign of Vasilii Petrovich.

Father Prohor removed all superfluous crockery from the

table, but left on it the frying-pan with the fish, a plate, the salt, the bread, and five eggs. Then he went outside and said on returning:

"No—I can't see him."

"Who is that you can't see?" asked Father Vavila.

"Vasilii Petrovich."

"Well, if he had been here you certainly would not have found him standing behind the door. I reckon he must have decided now to go for a walk."

Father Prohor and Father Vavila were most insistent that I should sleep in the bed of one or the other. I had to be very firm in refusing, and taking one of the soft rush mats —the work of the dead Father Sergii—I lay down beneath the window on one of the seats. Father Prohor gave me a pillow, blew out the candle, went outside again and remained there for some time. He was obviously waiting for "the daft one", but without result, and, coming in, merely said:

"There'll be a thunderstorm, for sure."

"Perhaps there may not be one after all," I said, wishing to set my mind at ease about the absent Musk-Ox.

"Oh yes, there will: it was very close to-day."

"It's been close like that for some time."

"My back's been troubling me all day to-day," Father Vavila chimed in.

"And the flies have been fairly barging into my face ever since morning," added Father Prohor, turning bodily upon his massive bed, and all of us, I think, plunged into a profound sleep that very same moment. It was pitch dark outside, but as yet there was no rain.

CHAPTER THE SIXTH

"GET up!" Father Vavila was saying to me, prodding me as I lay on my bench. "Get up! It won't do—sleeping at such a time. We know not when the Lord's hour may strike."

Not realizing what was happening, I leapt up nimbly and sat up on my bed. Before the ikons flickered a thin wax taper, and Father Prohor, in nothing but his underwear, was on his knees and praying. A terrific crash of thunder that discharged itself over the lake and reverberated through the wood explained the alarm. So, obviously, it was not without reason that the flies had been barging into Father Prohor's face ever since morning.

"Where is Vasilii Petrovich?" I asked of the old men.

Father Prohor, without ceasing to whisper his prayers, turned his face to me and explained by a gesture that the Musk-Ox had not yet returned. I looked at my watch: it was exactly one in the morning. Father Vavila, also in just his underwear and a padded chest-protector, was looking out of the window; I too approached the window and stared out. By the light of the uninterrupted flashes of lightning, which brightly illuminated every corner of the landscape outside the window, one could see that the ground was fairly dry. So there had been no heavy rain since we had fallen asleep. But the thunderstorm was fearful. Crash followed crash, each more deafening than the preceding one, ever more terrifying, and the lightning never ceased. It was as though the sky had been rent asunder and was about to fall upon the earth in a stream of fire.

Thinking of the Musk-Ox, I said involuntarily: "Where in heaven's name can he be?"

"It doesn't bear thinking of," echoed Father Vavila without leaving the window.

"I wonder if anything's happened to him?"

"Don't see how anything can happen to anyone hereabouts. We don't get any large beasts round here. Unless it is some wicked man—but we haven't heard of one for a long time. No, I reckon he's just roaming. He's a queer one."

"As for the view, it is indeed splendid," continued the old man, admiring the lake, which the lightning was revealing right to the farther shore.

At that moment there was such a clap of thunder that the entire house shook; Father Prohor fell to the ground, while Father Vavila and I were flung towards the opposite wall. Something crashed in the passage and fell against the door which led into the room.

"Fire!" cried Father Vavila, who was the first to recover in the general confusion, and ran to the door.

The door could not be opened.

"Let me do it," said I, quite sure that the house was on fire, and took a running leap at the door.

To our intense astonishment, the door this time flew open quite easily and, unable to stop myself, I shot out beyond the doorstep. It was pitch dark in the passage. I returned to the room, took a wax taper from the ikons, lit it, and went back. It was my horse that had been responsible for all the noise. Terrified by the last deafening thunder-clap, she had wrenched at the halter, by which she had been tied to a post, upset a cabbage-press on which the sieve with the oats had been standing, and springing aside had pressed her body against the door. The poor beast was twitching her ears, rolling her eyes fearfully, and shaking in every limb. The three of us put matters right, filled the sieve with fresh oats and returned to the room. Before Father Prohor brought in the little taper, Father Vavila and I noticed a faint glow in the room which was reflected through the window onto the wall. We looked out, and exactly in front of us, on the opposite shore of the lake, an old dry pine, which had for years stood like a solitary sentinel on a sandy hummock, was now blazing like a gigantic candle.

"Ah-h-h," breathed Father Vavila.

"It's been struck by lightning," Father Prohor prompted him.

"And how beautifully it burns!" the artistic Father Vavila said again.

"God has willed it so," replied the pious Father Prohor.

"Well, my Fathers, let us nevertheless go to bed. The thunderstorm has died down."

And true enough the storm had died down completely, and only occasionally could be heard the far-away mutterings of thunder, and across the sky trailed ponderously an endless black cloud which appeared still blacker because of the burning pine.

"Look! Look!" suddenly cried Father Vavila, who was still staring out of the window. "Why, that's our daft one!"

"Where?" Father Prohor and I asked in the same breath, and both looked out of the window.

"Why, there, by the pine."

Sure enough, a few yards away from the flaming pine a silhouette could be clearly seen in which one could recognize at first glance the figure of the Musk-Ox. He stood with his arms clasped behind his back, and with head raised watched the blazing branches.

"Shall I give him a shout?" asked Father Prohor.

"He won't hear," Father Vavila replied. "Hark to the noise —he can't possibly hear."

"And he'll be cross too," I added, well aware of the character of my friend.

We stood for a while by the window. The Musk-Ox did not move. We referred to him several times as "the daft one", and went back to our beds. The eccentricities of Vasilii Petrovich had long ceased to cause surprise even to me; but this time I felt unutterably sorry for my suffering friend. . . . Standing there like a knight of the Image of Melancholy, before the burning pine tree, he presented himself to me as a buffoon.

CHAPTER THE SEVENTH

WHEN I woke up, it was fairly late. The "unlettered" Fathers had already gone out. At the table sat Vasilii Petrovich. He held in his hand a large hunk of rye bread and was taking sips of milk straight from a jug that stood before him. Seeing that I was awake, he glanced at me, and continued his breakfast in silence. I did not speak to him. About twenty minutes passed.

"Well, there's little sense in lying a-bed," Vasilii Petrovich said at last, and put back the jug of milk which he had drained to the last drop.

"And what do you think we'd better start doing now?"

"Let's go roaming."

Vasilii Petrovich was in the best of spirits. I was very mindful of this disposition of his and did not question him about his nocturnal walk. But he himself began to speak of it the moment we left the house.

"What a stormy night it's been!" began Vasilii Petrovich. "I don't remember having seen quite such a bad night ever."

"And yet there's been no rain—has there?"

"It began about five times, but couldn't get going. I do love nights like that."

"And I don't like them at all."

"Why?"

"Well, where's the sense?—Just twisting and smashing everything."

"H'm. That's the beauty of it—everything gets smashed."

"Yes, and quite probably you'll find yourself crushed by something."

"Never mind."

"There's that pine there that got smashed."

"It didn't half burn prettily."

"We saw it."

"And I saw it too. It's a grand life in the forests."

"Too many mosquitos."

"You namby-pambies, mummie's boys. Afraid of being eaten by mosquitos!"

"They even get the better of bears, Vasilii Petrovich."

"And still the bears stick to the forest. I've fallen in love with this life," continued Vasilii Petrovich.

"What—a life in the woods?"

"Yes. What a joy it is in the forests of the North!—So dense and still—even the leaves are blue—fine."

"Not for long, though."

"It's fine even in winter up there."

"Well—I doubt it."

"Oh yes, indeed it is."

"What was it you liked up there?"

"The stillness—and there is such power in this stillness."

"And what are the people like?"

"What do you mean—what are the people like?"

"How do they live and what do they expect?" •

Vasilii Petrovich grew thoughtful.

"You spent a couple of years with them—didn't you?"

"Yes—two years and a bit."

"And did you get to know them?"

"Well, what is there to know?"

"What is hidden in the people there?"

"Silliness—that's what's hidden in them."

"But you didn't think that way before?"

"I did not. But what are our thoughts worth? Those thoughts were built on words. All I heard was: 'Old Believers ','Old Believers—a force—a protest . . .' and that gets you thinking that you'll discover the most wondrous things in them. You reckon they know there the very word you need—everyone needs—and that they won't disclose it to you because they mistrust you, that's why you don't get at it."

"And what is the truth?"

"And the truth is they are a lot of hair-splitters—that's all."

"But are you sure you really got to know them?"

"How could I know them any better? I didn't go there just to play about."

"And how did you go about getting to know them? That's all very interesting. . . . Tell me."

"Oh, it was simple enough: I got there and engaged myself as a labourer, I worked like a Trojan. . . . Let's lie down here, over the lake."

We lay down in the grass and Vasilii Petrovich continued his narrative, as usual in short, jerky sentences:

"Yes—work I did. In the winter I offered to copy their books. I soon learnt the knack of writing in the ancient script and semi-Slavonic characters. Only, all the books they gave me were the Devil knows what. Not the sort I had hoped to see. Life became a bore—just work and intoning prayers, that's all. And nothing more. Then they began to plague me with demands: 'You come,' they said, 'and be one of us for good.' I says: 'What's the difference—I'm one of you as it is.'—'You just take a fancy to a wench and join someone's household.' You know how much I dislike that sort of thing! Still, I thought, that wasn't the sort of thing to chuck up the whole show about. So I joined a household."

"*You* did?"

"Who do you think?"

"You married?"

"Well, I took a wench—that means, I suppose, I got married."

I was thunderstruck with astonishment and asked involuntarily:

"And what happened then?"

"Then a mess-up happened," said the Musk-Ox, and a look of anger and annoyance crossed his features.

"Were you unhappy with your wife, or what?"

"Pooh!—do you think a wife can make my happiness or unhappiness. I cheated myself. I thought I'd find a City there and I found only a chip."

"The Old Believers would not admit you to their mysteries?"

"There was nothing to do any admitting over!" cried the Musk-Ox in disgust. "It is the secret only that matters. You understand—as far as that word was concerned—that 'Open, Sesame', the sort of thing you read of in fairy-tales—well, there just wasn't any of that sort of thing there at all! I know all their mysteries and they only deserve contempt. They would get together, and you'd imagine they are about to produce some great thought, and all you hear—the Devil take them—is: 'Our virtuous honour and our virtuous faith'. Oh, they'll remain in their virtuous faith all right, and as for honourable virtue, that's for those who walk in honour. Mumbling and hair-splitting, and longer whips of leather—that's all that concerns them! If you're not of their Church, they just don't worry about you. And if you are, they'll never give a chap a chance to rise. With them it's—if you're old or infirm, you go to a poorhouse or live on charity in the kitchen. And if you're young, you're made to become a labourer. Your master will see that you don't have too easy a time either. The world becomes a prison. And the damned turkey-cocks strut about and commiserate: 'There isn't enough fear. Fear,' they say, 'is fast disappearing.' And we look to them with hope, we place our faith in them! . . . A lot of sluggards—idiotic sluggards—just fooling everyone with their secrecy."

Vasilii Petrovich spat in disgust.

"So our local simple peasant here is better, I suppose?"

Vasilii Petrovich pondered, then spat again and replied in an even voice:

"Oh, miles better."

"In what way in particular?"

"Because he doesn't know what he wants. A man here speculates one way, and then he speculates another way, while those blokes there can only think one way: always round their own finger. You take a simple mound of earth—or try digging up an old weir. What difference does it make that it has been piled up by human hands? There's brushwood in it—brushwood you'll find. And if you pull out the faggots, you'll find that plain earth remains, and earth that's all been disturbed by a fool at that. So there you are—which do you reckon is better?"

"Then how did you get away?"

"Quite simply: I saw there was nothing doing, so I just left."

"And your wife?"

"Why are you so interested in her?"

"But you did not leave her there all by herself?"

"What would I be doing with her?"

"Why, you should have taken her with you, and lived with her."

"Fat lot of good that would have been. . . ."

"Vasilii Petrovich, do you realize that's being cruel? And what if she's fallen for you?"

"You're talking nonsense, that's what you are! What's all this love business? You read a few lines out of a book to-day, and she's your wife; to-morrow she'll get a dispensation and go and sleep with someone else behind the partition. Besides, what have I got to do with woman—with love—what are all the women in the world to me?"

"But, after all, she's a human being," I said. "You should have some pity on her."

"What—pity a woman in that sense! . . . As though it matters who she'll be going behind the partition with. As though this was the time to worry over trifles of that sort! Sesame, Sesame —who knows how Sesame is to be opened?—that's what's wanted just now!" concluded the Musk-Ox, and began to beat his chest. "A Man—give us a Man who is not enslaved by passion, and him alone shall we nourish in the most secret depths of our soul."

My further conversation with Vasilii Petrovich seemed to

peter out somehow. After taking dinner with the old men I drove him back to the monastery, said good-bye to Father-Treasurer, and left.

CHAPTER THE EIGHTH

ABOUT ten days after Vasilii Petrovich and I parted company, I was sitting with my mother and a sister in the porch of our little house. Dusk was falling. All our servants had gone to supper and there was no one near the house except us. All around reigned the most complete peace of approaching evening, and suddenly, in the midst of all this stillness, two large watch-dogs, who had been lying at our feet, leapt up together, flew to the gate and fell upon someone with fury. I rose and went to find out the cause of their angry attack. By the fence, pressing his back against it, stood the Musk-Ox, who, with some difficulty, was warding off the two dogs with his stick; they were flinging themselves upon him with human ferocity.

"They nearly tore me to shreds, damn them," he said to me when I had driven them off.

"Are you on foot?"

"On Shanks's pony, as you see."

Behind his back, Vasilii Petrovich had the little haversack he usually travelled with.

'Well, come along."

"Come—where?"

"Why, into the house."

"No, I'm not going in there."

"Why on earth not?"

"There are some young ladies there."

"What young ladies? That's my mother, and my sister."

"All the same, I'm not coming in."

"Oh—don't be a fool! They're quite simple folk."

"I'm not going in," said the Musk-Ox definitely.

"Well, where shall I put you?"

"You must put me up somewhere. I've nowhere to go."

I remembered the bath-house. It was empty during the summer and frequently served as sleeping-quarters for visitors, since our house was so small.

Vasilii Petrovich again resolutely refused to walk through our courtyard, past the porch. We could go through the garden, but I knew that the bath-house was locked and the key was with the old nurse, who was having supper in the kitchen. I could not leave Vasilii Petrovich under any circumstances, because he would have been attacked by the dogs again. They had only backed away a few paces and were barking angrily. I leant over the fence, behind which we stood, and called loudly to my sister. She came running towards me and stopped in amazement when she saw the ludicrous figure of the Musk-Ox, in peasant's coat and the headgear of a novice. I sent her to get the key from the nurse, and then, with the precious key, led my guest through the garden to the bath-house.

Vasilii Petrovich and I talked all through the night. He could not go back to the Hermitages—he had come from there—because he had been expelled for discussions which he decided to conduct with some of the pilgrims. He had no plans about going to another place. His set-back had not discouraged him, but for the time being had upset all his calculations. He spoke at great length about the novices, the monastery, about the pilgrims who came there from every quarter, and he spoke of it all quite rationally. While living in the monastery, Vasilii Petrovich had been engaged upon a most original plan. He sought for men "who were not enslaved by passion" among the downtrodden and the disinherited inmates of the monastery, and, with their aid, had intended to open his Sesame by swaying the masses of pilgrims who came there.

"This is a road that no one sees; no one takes any notice of it; the builders despise it, and yet here is the very thing needed for a cornerstone," debated the Musk-Ox.

Recalling to mind the familiar life in the monastery, and the people there of the downtrodden and disinherited kind, I was prepared to concede that the speculations of Vasilii Petrovich were well founded in many ways.

But my propagandist had already shut up shop. The first man who in his opinion was above passions was my one-time friend, the novice Nevstruev, who was now a deacon under the monachal name of Luke. The Musk-Ox confided in him, but he decided to add to his downtrodden and disinherited state : he disclosed to his superior the sort of ideas that the Musk-Ox entertained, and the Musk-Ox was kicked out. Now he was without shelter. I had to leave for St. Petersburg in a week's time and Vasilii Petrovich had nowhere to rest his head. It was impossible for him to remain at my mother's—besides, he did not want it himself.

"You find me a tutor's post—I want to teach," he told me.

I had to find him a job. I got the Musk-Ox to give me his word that he would accept the post merely for the purpose of work and not for any additional reasons, and proceeded to fix up a haven of refuge for him.

CHAPTER THE NINTH

THERE are in our Province large numbers of villages which belong to small landowners. Generally speaking, in our part of the country—to adopt the language of the Politico-Economic Committee of St. Petersburg—small-scale farming is fairly common. Impoverished landowners who used to possess a few serfs, settled down to farm their own lands after these serfs had been liberated; the middling landowners squandered away their cash and sold their peasants for re-settlement in distant Provinces, and their estates to land speculators or their more wealthy neighbours. Near us there were five or six such estates that had passed out of the hands of the landed gentry. About three miles from our farm there was the Barkov Estate, so called after the name of the former owner, of whose indolence and extravagance many stories were current. In his old age this gentleman became a reformed character, married, and got rid of estate after estate. The Barkov Estate, which had once formed a self-contained appendage of a larger estate belonging to the ruined gentleman, now belonged to Alexandr Ivanovich

Sviridov. Alexandr Ivanovich Sviridov was born a serf and had been taught reading, writing and music. As a youth he played the fiddle in a landowner's orchestra, and when nineteen purchased his liberty for five hundred roubles and became a distiller. Blessed with a clear, practical mind, Alexandr Ivanovich managed his business very well. To begin with, he became known as the best distiller in the district; then he started building distilleries and water-mills; then he collected a thousand roubles in cash, went for a year to North Germany and returned such an excellent builder that his renown spread far and wide. Alexandr Ivanovich became known throughout the three neighbouring Provinces and building contracts were thrust upon him. He conducted his affairs with rare precision, and viewed leniently the aristocratic weaknesses of his clients. He knew human nature, and often laughed up his sleeve at many people, but he was not a bad fellow, and he was even a kindly soul, I should say. Everyone liked him, with the exception of the local Germans, at whose expense he was fond of cracking jokes when they began to introduce civilized methods among a semi-savage people. "Look, look," he used to say, "he'll slip up in a minute." And the German would deceive himself in his calculations, exactly as prophesied, and would have no success at all.

Five years after his return from Mecklenburg-Schwerin, Alexandr Ivanovich purchased the Barkov Estate from his former master, got himself enrolled as a merchant of our district town and married off his two sisters and his brother. The family had been redeemed from serfdom by him before he went abroad, and all made their living out of his concern. The brother and brothers-in-law were his salaried employees. He treated them without any nonsense. He did not ill-treat them, but they went about in fear of him. In the same manner he treated his clerks and his workmen. It wasn't that he loved power—it was just that he was convinced that "one has to see that there's no nonsense going on." Having purchased the estate, Alexandr Ivanovich bought from the same landowner a parlourmaid—Nastasya Petrovna—and was lawfully wedded to her. They lived in unbroken harmony. People used to say

58

there was "counsel and love" between them. After her marriage, Nastasya Petrovna "filled out" as the saying goes. She had always been a great beauty, but marriage made her blossom forth like a lovely rose. She was tall, with a milk-white complexion, slightly inclined to corpulence, but graceful, pink-cheeked and with large gentle blue eyes. Nastasya Petrovna was a very good housewife. There was hardly a week that her husband spent at home with her—he was always dashing off to some works contract, and she would be left to manage the estate and pay the clerks, and would even be buying timber and contracting for grain if any of her husband's work needed it. She was the trusted helpmate of Alexandr Ivanovich, and as a result everyone took her very seriously and treated her with profound respect, while her husband put his unbounded trust in her and did not subject her to his stern ways. She could have all she wished from him. Only she never demanded anything. She taught herself to read, and could sign her name. They had only two children—two little girls: the elder was nine and the younger seven. They were in charge of a Russian governess. Nastasya Petrovna referred to herself jokingly as an "unlettered fool". And yet she probably knew just as much as many so-called "women of education". She knew no French, but simply devoured Russian books. She possessed a phenomenal memory. She could recite Karamzin's "History" almost by heart. And she knew a prodigious amount of verse. She was particularly fond of Lermontov and Nekrasov. The latter was especially near and dear to her heart, which had suffered so much in her days of serfdom. In her speech there were often still to be found peasant expressions, especially when she spoke with feeling, but the vernacular somehow fitted her admirably. When, for instance, she would start relating in this vernacular something she had just read, she would make the story so glowing that one had no wish to read it afterwards for oneself. She was a very capable woman. Our gentry would often visit the Barkov Estate, sometimes merely to taste of someone else's supper, but mostly on business. Alexandr Ivanovich enjoyed almost unlimited financial credit, while the landowners were not trusted, because most people knew how

bad they were in meeting their obligations. The reputation of
the aristocracy was an unflattering one. For instance, they
would need grain for their distilleries and the advances had
either been squandered or had gone in payment of old debts, and
they would then come flocking to Alexandr Ivanovich. "My
dear man! My this-that-and-the-other: do please stand surety
for me." They would be kissing Nastasya Petrovna's hands
and would be so charming and unassuming. As for her, she
would run out of the room and split her sides with laughter.
"Seen those wonderful *Girists*?" she would gurgle. Nastasya
Petrovna called all landed gentry "girists" from the time when
a certain Moscow lady, who had returned to her ruined estate,
had taken it into her head to "educate this rough diamond",
and had said to her: "But don't you understand, *ma belle
Anastasie*, that every country has its Girondists!" But, as a
matter of fact, everyone kissed the hand of Nastasya Petrovna
and she had become quite used to it. There were even dashing
fellows who confessed their love for her and invited her to
join them in a quiet spot. A certain Guards Hussar went so
far as to point out that she would be quite safe in doing so,
provided she brought with her the Russian-leather wallet of
Alexandr Ivanovich. But their torments were in vain. Nastasya Petrovna knew how to deal with these votaries of Beauty.

It was to these people—the Sviridovs—that I decided to go
concerning my uncouth friend. When I arrived to plead for
him, Alexandr Ivanovich was away as usual; I found only
Nastasya Petrovna at home, and told her what a helpless infant
Fate had inflicted on me. Two days later I took my Musk-Ox to
the Sviridovs, and a week later went again to say good-bye to them.

"What do you think you are doing, brother, putting ideas
into my old woman's head when I'm not at home?" asked
Alexandr Ivanovich as he met me in the porch.

"What sort of ideas have I been putting into Nastasya Petrovna's head?" I parried, not understanding his question.

"But, goodness, man, what do you want to go and tie her
up in philanthropy for? What's this scarecrow you've landed
her with?"

"You listen to him!" cried a familiar, slightly harsh contralto through the window. "He's first-rate, that Musk-Ox of yours. I'm most grateful to you for him."

"No—seriously—what's this animal you've brought us?" asked Alexandr Ivanovich, when we entered his drawing office.

"A Musk-Ox," I replied, smiling.

"I can't make him out, brother."

"What's wrong with him?"

"Well, he seems quite daft to me!"

"That's only to begin with."

"And supposing he turns out worse in the end?"

I laughed, and so did Alexandr Ivanovich.

"Yes, my lad, it's all very well laughing, but what shall I do with him? Honestly, I've nowhere I can use this specimen."

"Please let him earn something."

"Aw, that's not the point! I don't mind; but what shall I give him to do? You just have a look at him," said Alexandr Ivanovich, pointing to Vasilii Petrovich, who was at that moment crossing the yard.

I watched him as he marched along, with one hand thrust in the bosom of his *svitka*, twisting his lock of hair with the other, and thought to myself: "What, indeed, could he do?"

"Let him supervise the felling," the lady of the house suggested to her husband.

Alexandr Ivanovich laughed.

"Let him work on lumbering," I said.

"Oh, you innocent children! What on earth will he do there? Anyone who's not used to it will hang himself with the loneliness of it. If you ask me—why not give him a hundred roubles and let him go where he pleases and do what he likes."

"No—don't drive him away."

"Yes, you may hurt his feelings that way," Nastasya Petrovna backed me up.

"But what can I possibly do with him? All my men are common peasants. I'm a peasant myself, and he . . ."

"He's no gentleman either," said I.

"Neither gent nor peasant, and no good to anyone."

"But why don't you give him to Nastasya Petrovna?"

"That's right—you give him to me," she chimed in again.

"Take him, take him, mother."

"That's fine," said Nastasya Petrovna.

The Musk-Ox was left in the care of Nastasya Petrovna.

CHAPTER THE TENTH

IN August, when I was in St. Petersburg at the Central Post Office, I was handed a registered letter containing fifty roubles. The letter said:

"BELOVED BROTHER!—I am present here at the destruction of forests that grew for the benefit of all and have passed into Sviridov's ownership. I was handed my first six months' pay of 60 roubles, although six months have not yet passed. I suppose my surety has got round her husband and made him do it, but let this their finesse be in vain: I have no need of this. I have left myself 10 roubles. The 50, enclosed herewith, please send off at once, without any letter, to a certain young female, a peasant's daughter, named Glafira Afinogenovna Mukhina, residing in the village of Duby, —— Province, —— District. See she doesn't know who it's from. That's the one who is supposed to be my wife: the money is for her, just in case there has been a child.

"My life here is just deadly. There is nothing here for me to do, and I console myself with the thought that apparently there is nowhere one can do anything besides what everyone is doing, namely: holding requiems for one's departed relatives and filling one's belly. Here everyone worships Alexandr Ivanovich. Alexandr Ivanovich! There isn't a greater man for anyone here. Everyone dreams of becoming as big as he is, and what is he, this man of the fat wallet?

"Yes, I also have come to understand a few things these days. I have resolved for myself the enigma—'Russia, whither goest thou?', and you need have no fear: I shall not go anywhere from here. There is nowhere for me to go. It is the same everywhere. You can't get past the Alexandr Ivanoviches.

VASILII BOGOSLOVSKY.

"OLGINA-PROIMA, *3rd August* 1858."

Early in December I received another letter. In this letter Sviridov informed me that he and his wife would be leaving for St. Petersburg within the next few days and asked me to find them a comfortable apartment.

About ten days after this second letter Alexandr Ivanovich and his wife were sitting in a charming apartment facing the Alexandrinsky Theatre, warming themselves with tea and warming my heart with stories of the far-away land of my youth.

"And why don't you tell me," I asked, when an opportunity presented itself, "what my Musk-Ox is doing?"

"He's kicking, brother," replied Sviridov.

"In what way do you mean?"

"Behaving crazily. Won't come and see us—disdains our company or something—was always hobnobbing with the workmen, and now apparently he's got tired of that too: he's asked me to transfer him to another place."

"And what about you?" I asked Nastasya Petrovna. "All our hopes were pinned on you. We thought you'd tame him."

"Hopes—hopes. It's her he's always running away from."

I glanced at Nastasya Petrovna, and she looked at me.

"Well, what about it? I'm so hideous, I suppose."

"But how was it? Tell me."

"What is there to tell? There's nothing to tell. It was just that he comes to me and says: 'Let me go.' 'Where?' says I. 'I don't know,' says he. 'Why, don't you like it here?' 'Oh,' says he, 'it isn't that I don't like it, but please let me go.' 'But what's it all about? . . .' He says nothing. 'Has anyone offended you, or what?' He just says nothing—only twists those pigtails of his. 'Why don't you tell Nastya,' says I, 'if someone's done you wrong.' 'No,' says he. 'Will you please put me on another job?' Well, I felt kind of sorry for him—I didn't want to give him the sack—I've sent him to another lumber camp at Zhigovo—that's more than twenty miles away. He's there now," added Alexandr Ivanovich.

"What have you done to upset him so?" I asked Nastasya Petrovna.

"Oh—God alone knows: I didn't do anything to upset him."

"She was like a mother to him," confirmed Sviridov. "She

made him new clothes—looked after him. You know how kind-hearted she is."

"And what happened ?"

"He took a dislike to me," said Nastasya Petrovna, laughing.

The Sviridovs and I proceeded to have a grand time in St. Petersburg. Alexandr Ivanovich rushed about on business all day long, while Nastasya Petrovna and I just frittered away our time. She liked the city very much : but she grew particularly fond of the theatre. Every evening we would be in some theatre, and she never seemed to grow tired of them. Time flew by, rapidly and pleasantly. During this period I had another letter from the Musk-Ox, in which he wrote very spitefully about Alexandr Ivanovich. "Robbers and foreigners," he wrote, "are more acceptable to me than these money-bagged Russians ! Yet everyone is on their side, and my bowels ache when I think that that's how it should be, that everyone sides with them. I see something wonderful : I see that he—this Alexandr Ivanovich—, has always stood in my way in everything, even before I knew him. Here is the enemy of the people—this gorged brute—this brute who feeds with his mites the wandering hordes of paupers, so that they do not die all at once, but work for him.. This particular type of Christian is in keeping with our character, and he will conquer us all until he gets his deserts. With my ideas there is no room for both of us in this world. I will step out of his way, because they love him. He may be of some use to a few, while my ideas, I see, are completely useless. No wonder you call me by the name of some beast. No one recognizes me as his own, and I see no one I can call my own." Then he asked me to write and tell him whether I was alive and how Nastasya Petrovna was. About the same time, some coopers who had been travelling with a consignment of spirits from one of the distilleries came to Alexandr Petrovich from Vytegra. I put them up in a spare kitchen I had. The men were all known to me. We got talking one day on various topics and got on to the subject of the Musk-Ox.

"How's he getting on ?" I asked them.

"Oh, he's all right !"

"Alive and kicking !" commented another.

"And is he working?"

"Well, what work can you expect of him? Why the master should keep him on beats me."

"How does he spend his time, then?"

"Just moons about in the wood. The master gave him the fellings to count—as a clerk might—but there was nothing to be done with him."

"Why?"

"Lord alone knows—the master is too kind to him."

"And he's a hefty lout too," continued another cooper. "There's times he will grab an axe and fairly lam into it—coo!—you should see the sparks fly!"

"And then he'd go as a kind of night watchman, too."

"What kind of watchman?"

"They were saying runaways were snooping round—so we didn't see him for nights on end. Our boys figured he might be in with the runaways, so they kept their eyes skinned. And when he slunk off, the three of them went after him. They saw him go straight to the house. Only it was all right—there was nothing in it. He just sat under a laburnum opposite the master's windows, called Sultanka, the dog, to him, and sat like that till dawn, and at dawn up he gets and back he goes to his place. It was the same another time, and then again. Our boys just didn't worry any more. I reckon he went on like that till autumn. And after Assumption our boys were going to bed one evening and they say to him: 'Isn't it about time, Petrovich, you laid off going the rounds at night? Come and lie down with us.' He says nothing, and two days later we heard he asks the master, and the master he sends him to another lumber camp."

"And did the boys like him?" I asked.

The cooper reflected a moment and said:

"They didn't mind him, it seemed."

"He's very good-hearted, isn't he?"

"Yes, he wouldn't hurt anyone. He'd start telling us all about Filaret the Merciful or something like that, and he'd always talk on kindness, and he'd also speak well against the rich. Many of the boys listened to him."

"And did they like what he told them?"

"They didn't mind. At times he would do funny things, too."

"What sort of funny things?"

"Well, now, for instance, he'd be speaking on God, and suddenly it'd be the gentry. He'd take a handful of peas, and pick out the bigger ones and'd put them all over his *svitka*: now this, he'd say, is the biggest of the lot—a king; and these —not quite so big—his ministers with the princes; and these— smaller still—the gentry, and the merchants and the pot-bellied priests; and here, he'd say, and show the handful—these, he'd say—that's us, the tillers of the soil. And with that he'd throw the tillers at the princes and the pot-bellied priests; all would get mixed up—there'd just be a heap. Well, the boys,—of course they laughed. Natural. 'You do the show again,' they'd say."

"Natural, of course—he's barmy," chimed in another.

I felt I had better say nothing.

"And what had he been? A comedian?" asked the second cooper.

"What makes you think that?"

"There was talk about it. Mironka—was it?—said he was."

Mironka was a quick, nimble little man who had long acted as Alexandr Ivanovich's coachman. He enjoyed the reputation of a singer, story-teller and buffoon. Indeed, he often invented the most absurd *canards* and launched them with great skill among his simple-minded companions, and then revelled in the fruits of his fertile imagination. It was obvious that Vasilii Petrovich, having become an enigma to the men employed in cutting down the forest, also became the subject of many rumours, and Mironka availed himself of this to turn my hero into an ex-comedian.

CHAPTER THE ELEVENTH

IT was Butterweek. Nastasya Petrovna and I obtained with the greatest difficulty some tickets for an evening performance at a theatre. The play was "Esmeralda", which she had wanted to see for a long time. The performance had gone off very well, and, according to Russian theatrical custom, had ended very late. It was a pleasant night, and Nastasya Petrovna and I walked home. On the way I noticed that the distiller's wife was plunged in deep thought and often made replies at random.

"What's on your mind ?" I asked her.

"Why ?"

"You aren't listening to what I'm telling you."

Nastasya Petrovna laughed.

"And what do you suppose : what was I thinking of ?"

"That's rather hard to guess."

"Well, have a guess : for instance ?"

"About Esmeralda ?"

"Yes—you're nearly right; but it isn't Esmeralda herself that's worrying me, but that poor Quasimodo."

"You feel sorry for him ?"

"Very. That's a real misfortune—to be a man no one can love. Yes, you feel sorry for him, and want to lighten his sorrow, and yet it cannot be done. It's dreadful !"

As we sat over our tea, waiting for Alexandr Ivanovich to get back for supper, we had a very long discussion. Alexandr Ivanovich was still out.

"Well, thank God you don't get people like that in real life."

"Like what ? Like Quasimodo ?"

"Yes."

"And what about the Musk-Ox ?"

Nastasya Petrovna struck the table with the palm of her hand, and at first broke into a peal of laughter, but then appeared ashamed of her laughter and murmured softly :

"Why, that's true enough."

She moved the candle towards her and proceeded to stare fixedly at the flame, slightly screwing up her lovely eyes.

CHAPTER THE TWELFTH

THE Sviridovs stayed in St. Petersburg till summer. They kept on postponing their departure from day to day because of all sorts of business matters. They persuaded me to go with them. Together we reached our district town. Here I got into a post-chaise and went to my mother's, and they went home after extracting a promise from me to come and see them after a week. Alexandr Ivanovich intended immediately on arrival to leave again for Zhigovo, where felling was in progress and where the Musk-Ox now lived, and promised to be back in about a week. My mother was not expecting me, and was very glad to see me. . . . I told her I was going to sit tight for at least a week; my mother got my sister and brother-in-law to come down, and there began for me a period of rustic pleasures.

Ten days passed in this way, and on the eleventh or twelfth day, very early at dawn, my old nurse entered my room in a rather agitated state.

"What's up?" I asked her.

"The Barkov people have sent for you," she said.

Entered a twelve-year-old boy who, without bowing, transferred his cap from hand to hand a couple of times, gave a slight cough, and said:

"The missus says you're to go to her at once."

"Is Nastasya Petrovna well?" I enquired.

"What's to come to her will come."

"And Alexandr Ivanovich?"

"The master's not at home," replied the boy, and again coughed into his hand.

"Where's the master, then?"

"At Zhigovo . . . there's doings there."

I ordered one of my mother's horses to be saddled, and dressing hurriedly, rode off at a brisk canter to Barkov Estate. It was only five in the morning, and everyone in our house was still asleep.

But in the house on the estate—when I got there—all the windows except those of the children's and governess's rooms were already wide open, and in one of the windows stood Nastasya Petrovna, her hair tied with a sky-blue silk kerchief. She replied absently to my bow, and while I was tying up my horse she twice waved her hand to tell .me to hurry.

"Here's a fine how-do-you-do!" she said as she met me on the doorstep.

"What's wrong?"

"Alexandr Ivanovich went to Turuhanovka the day before yesterday, and this morning, at three, look at the note he sent me from Zhigovo by special messenger."

She gave me a crumpled letter, which till then she had been holding in her hand.

"NASTYA! [wrote Sviridov]. Send a cart and pair to M— at once to give the letter to the doctor and the district Police Chief. Your freak has got us into a fine mess. Last night he was talking to me, and to-day before supper he's hanged himself. Send someone with a head on his shoulders, tell him to buy all that's wanted and to hurry with the coffin as well. This isn't the moment to waste time on things like this. Please hurry. Make it clear to who goes what to do with the letters. You know how precious every day is now, and here is a dead body.

"Your ALEXANDR SVIRIDOV."

Ten minutes later I was cantering swiftly to Zhigovo. By taking short-cuts down various side-tracks I very soon lost the main road, and it was only at sundown that I managed to reach the Zhigovo woods, where the felling was in process. On emerging in the glade where the watch-house stood, I saw Alexandr Ivanovich. He was standing in the porch in his shirt-sleeves and held an abacus in his hand. His face, as usual, was quite composed, but rather more serious. Before him stood about thirty lumbermen. They were bareheaded, with axes stuck in their belts. A little apart from them was a clerk, Orefyich, whom I knew, and further still—Mironka.

Near by, also, stood—unharnessed—the pair of squat little horses belonging to Alexandr Ivanovich.

Mironka danced up to me, and taking my horse, said with a merry smile :

"Phew—you haven't half got him hot!"

"You walk him about—walk him up and down, properly!" Alexandr Ivanovich called to him without letting go of his abacus.

"Well, lads, then that's right, is it?" he asked, addressing the peasants who stood before him.

"Must be right, Alexandr Ivanovich," echoed several voices.

"Well then, God be with you, if that's all right," he answered the men and held out his hand to me, and after looking me for some time in the eyes, said:

"Well, brother?"

"Well—what about it?"

"What do you say to his latest stunt?"

"He's hanged himself."

"Yes—done himself in. Who told you?"

I told him what had taken place.

"A clever woman she is—sending for you: I confess it never occurred to me. And what more do you know?" asked Alexandr Ivanovich, dropping his voice.

"I don't know anything more. Is there anything more?"

"Sure. He's begun a jolly sort of show here, brother, upon my soul. That's his gratitude for all that was done for him. And I fancy I've to be grateful to you and Nastasya Petrovna too! A fine sort of chap you've foisted on me."

"But what's it all about?" I said. "You tell me plainly."

Yet inwardly I was feeling most uncomfortable.

"He'd started to interpret the Gospel according to his lights, and I might tell you, it wasn't any honest sort of interpreting, but just his own daft notions. All about the publican and poor Lazarus, or who can get through the eye of a needle and all that —you get me?—and he kind of turned it all against me."

"How did he do that?"

"How? . . . Well—you see—I am, if you please, in his reckoning 'a merchant—a money-grabber,' and the tillers of the soil must dot me one."

The matter became clear.

"And what about the tillers of the soil?" I asked Alexandr Ivanovich, who was staring at me with a meaning look.

"Oh, the boys, naturally—there's nothing wrong with them."

"In other words, they all brought it out into the open?"

"Naturally. Wolves, that's what they are!" continued Alexandr Ivanovich with a sly smirk. "They'd pretend they didn't understand: 'There, Vasilii Petrovich,' they'd tell him, 'you must be right. Now, when we see Father Peter we'll ask him about it too,' and then they'd come to me and tell me—joking like—and say: 'That can't be right, what he's saying.' And they'd repeat his own words to his face."

"And what happened then?"

"Well, I figured the best thing was to take no notice, as though I too didn't understand—see? But now, with this trouble, I got them to come and see me on purpose, as though I wanted to check up their accounts with them, and I sort of told them in passing, pretty strongly, that these palavers were just nothing at all and they've got to put them out of their heads now and keep their mouths shut."

"That's all very well if they do it."

"They'll have to. I stand no fooling, you know."

We entered the house. On Alexandr Ivanovich's wooden couch lay a brightly hued Kazan carpet-bag and a red morocco-leather pillow; the table was covered with a clean napkin, and upon it a samovar was bubbling merrily.

"What on earth had bitten him?" I said when I had sat down at table with Sviridov.

"There you are! He was too clever by half—that was his trouble. I just can't stand these Seminarists!"

"You said you had a talk with him the day before yesterday?"

"I did. There was no unpleasantness between us. Some men came here in the evening. I entertained them with vodka, we had a chat, I gave money to those who asked for advances on account, and that's when he slipped away. He wasn't there in the morning, and before supper a little girl came to the men. 'Look,' she says, 'just past the clearing, some man's hanged himself.' The boys went to look, but the poor cove was all stiff and cold already. He must have hung himself that evening."

"And there were no other unpleasantnesses?"

"Nothing at all."

"Perhaps you've said something to him?"

"Get along with you!"

"He hasn't left a letter or something?"

"No."

"You haven't looked through his papers?"

"I don't believe he had any papers."

"Still, I think we'd better make sure before the police arrive."

"Oh, I suppose so."

"I reckon he had a box or something, hadn't he?" Alexandr Ivanovich asked of the cook.

"The dead man? Yes—a little chest."

A small chest was brought in. It was unlocked. We opened it in the presence of the clerk and the cook. There was nothing inside it but two changes of underwear, some dog-eared extracts from the works of Plato, and a blood-stained handkerchief wrapped in a bit of paper.

"What's this handkerchief?" enquired Alexandr Ivanovich.

"That must be when the dead man chopped his hand, when the missus was here; she tied it up for him with her own handkerchief," replied the cook. "That's it—that's the one!" the woman added after a closer look at the handkerchief.

"Well—that's all there is to it," said Alexandr Ivanovich.

"Let's go and have a look at him."

"All right."

While Sviridov was dressing, I carefully studied the bit of paper that the handkerchief had been wrapped in. It was perfectly clean. I flicked over the pages of the Plato—there were no scribbled notes in it anywhere, only some of the passages had been marked off with a finger-nail. I read the passages thus marked:

"The Persians and Athenians lost their balance because the Persians extended the rights of Monarchy too much, and the Athenians extended too far their love of liberty."

"An ox is not made chief among oxen, but Man. Let genius rule."

"The power nearest to nature is the power of Force."

"When the old men are shameless, the young men must of necessity be shameless too."

"It is impossible to be immensely good and immensely rich. Why? Because he who acquires both by honest and by dishonest means acquires twice as much as he who acquires by honest means only, and he who does not make sacrifices to

Virtue does not expend as much as he who is prepared to make noble sacrifices."

"God is a measure of all things, and a measure most perfect. To be like God one must exercise moderation in all things— even in desires."

Here, written in the margin with some rusty liquid, were some words in the handwriting of the Musk-Ox. I could make out with difficulty: "Vasilii, thou fool! Why art thou not a Priest? Why hast thou clipped the wings to thy utterances? Thou art not a cassocked Teacher—a clown to the people, a curse unto thyself, a killer of ideas. I am a thief, and the farther I go, the more I shall steal."

I closed the book of the Musk-Ox.

Alexandr Ivanovich put on his long-skirted coat, and we went to the glade. From the clearing we turned to the right and continued through a dense, dark pine forest; we crossed a clearing where the felling had begun, and again emerged in another big glade. Here stood two large ricks of last season's hay. Alexandr Ivanovich stopped in the middle of the glade, and filling his lungs with air, emitted a loud "Ghop! Ghop!" There was no answer. The moon illuminated the glade brightly and cast two long shadows from the ricks.

"Ghop! Ghop!" Alexandr Ivanovich bellowed again.

"Ghop-pa!" came an answering call from the wood on our right.

"That's where it is!" said my companion, and we went to the right.

After a ten-minute walk Alexandr Ivanovich shouted again, and he was answered at once, following which we saw two peasants: an old man and a young lad. Both of them, on seeing Sviridov, took off their caps and stood leaning on their long poles.

"How goes it, Christians?"

"Good evening, Alexandr Ivanovich."

"Where's the deceased?"

"Here he is."

"Where? You show me; I hadn't noted the spot."

"Why—here."

"Where?"

"Here—here he is."

The peasant gave a laugh and pointed to the right.

A couple of yards from us hung the Musk-Ox. He had hanged himself by means of his thin peasant's belt, after attaching it to a branch no higher than the height of an average man. His knees were bent and just cleared the ground. He appeared to be kneeling. Even his hands were, as usual, thrust into the pockets of his *svitka*. His figure was completely in the shadows, while upon his head, through the branches, streamed the pale light of the moon. That poor head! Now it was at peace. The two locks upon it stuck upwards in the manner of a ram's horns, while the bloodshot, dilated eyes stared at the moon with the expression which is left in the eyes of a bull who has been struck several times on the head with a bludgeon, and then straightway has had his throat slit. It was impossible to discern in them the dying thoughts of the voluntary martyr. Neither did his eyes express what his passages from Plato had revealed, or the tell-tale handkerchief with the red mark.

"That's all there is to it; once he was a man, and now it's as though he had never lived," said Sviridov.

"He's for the worms, while it's a long life we are wishing you, *batyushka* Alexandr Ivanovich," the old man wheezed in a sweet, ingratiating voice.

He also went on to say that his own time to die would soon come, while Alexandr Ivanovich would live.

It was stifling in this dark woodland nook in which the Musk-Ox had picked upon to put an end to his torments. In the glade all was so light and peaceful. The moon rode serene in a clear night-sky and the larches and pines were heavy with sleep.

PARIS, *27th November* 1862.

KOTIN AND PLATONIDA

NO INHABITANT OF STARY GOROD EVER ENJOYED
a renown and respect equal to that commanded, even in our
irreverent time, by a very humble personage who has cultivated
the barren soil of the now fertile town eyot. This person belonged, by descent, to the Old Believers' clan of the merchant
Deev. But it was not his family or his stock, but the life and
works of this man, that won for him the renown and the respect
of his fellow-citizens.

The merchant Semen Dmitrievich Deev was only the cause
of the misfortunes of the subject of the following narrative.

It is not a very long tale.

Having become the head of a group of people who refused
to be united with the Church, old Deev built himself a timber
house "in the offing", on the very fringe of the town. Nowadays no one lives there, and it stands alone, bleak and forbidding.
And yet this grey, two-storeyed edifice, with its double row
of small windows, was just as uninviting in the days when it
was inhabited and when its windows reflected the sombre flicker
of countless burning cressets. The house wished to have nothing
to do with anyone, and punished unmercifully those of its inmates in whom was noted the least desire, on any occasion
whatsoever, to approach the new world outside. Very few of
the townspeople had any idea of the kind of life that went on
inside the house of the Old Believer, merchant Deev. In the
streets, the citizens of Stary Gorod met only Deev himself, but
they saw him always bad-tempered, morose, given to anger and
spite; and if by chance they happened to come across any of
the other inhabitants of the house anywhere, they regarded them
as denizens of the Kingdom of the Dead. Of the women of
Deev's household still less was known; they were born there,
or came there to cohabit, and there they died. The gates of the
house of Deev would close behind them only after death. There
were but two occasions when this established rule was broken.

Fifty years back, one exceedingly stormy, dark and abominable night, the gloomy house of Deev ejected into a friendless world a very young girl.

It seemed the house had only woken up to spit out this child, and then it had once more snapped to its surly lips.

CHAPTER THE SECOND

THE girl who had thus been driven from the house was an orphan and niece of Semen Deev, Aksinya Matveevna. She was only eighteen at the time; yet, in spite of the strictly secluded life that she had led hitherto, she knew where to turn her footsteps on this howling night. She followed street after street, lane after lane, leading straight towards a small grey cabin in the churchyard, and here she tapped timidly at the little crooked window. A few minutes later she tapped again—more insistently—and at the same time there ran towards her a young man, dressed only in his underclothes and wearing a pair of very decrepit shoes. This was the sexton, Iona Pizonsky.

"Ksyusha! Sweetheart!" he cried in amazement when he saw the girl in front of him.

The girl merely whispered dejectedly:

"I've been turned out."

"Turned out?"

"Turned out; beaten and thrown out."

The young man, highly delighted, flung wide the gate, and clasping the girl to him, barred the gate again, and carried his trembling guest into his tiny room.

The entire abode of Iona Pizonsky, to which Ksyusha had come, consisted of this tiny room and a still tinier spare room. Iona Pizonsky was a single man, and young. He led a most carefree existence, and, as a rule, hunger caused him to sing the gayest of songs. These songs, his beauty and dashing manner, enthralled the town girls and won for him the ardent little heart of the outcast from the house of Deev. The scene which had just been enacted was the epitome of their secret passion, when this passion, obedient to the laws of nature, ceased to be a secret to the inmates of the house.

The dispossessed orphan, meek as a lamb, followed her sweetheart without question : she joined his faith, took his name, accepted his position—became the sexton's wife, and five months later bore him a son, Konstantin.

"Slipped a bit—hence the premature arrival," Sexton Pizonsky explained jocularly; but a year later he himself slipped accidentally as, late in the autumn, he was cutting bracken on the steep bank of the river Turitsa, crashed head-on, and in lonely solitude gave up his merry ghost to the One God in Heaven.

The sexton's widow, with her year-old infant, was left alone in the world.

The gates of Deev's house, at which the widow knocked during that wretched year, opened only to load her with curses.

Finding herself without kith or kin, without a roof beneath which to rest her weary head, the widow Pizonsky sought shelter as a servant in a convent. Into the same convent she introduced her son, declaring him untruthfully to be a little girl, Makrina.

CHAPTER THE THIRD

THE ruse which the widow was driven to adopt in her desperate situation was completely successful. Thanks to the unremitting watchfulness of the mother, the real sex of the child was never discovered; on the other hand, the child himself was ignorant of it, and regarded himself as a little girl. However, when Konstantin Pizonsky, under his adopted name of Makrina, reached the age of twelve, Widow Pizonsky, faced with the problem of her son's education, led him out of the convent, changed his attire in a near-by gully from one that consisted of a skirt and black calico dress to a yellow nankeen coat, and entered him at the local parochial Church School under his real name of Konstantin Pizonsky. But bookish wisdom did not come easily to him. The unfortunate child straightway became the butt of general ridicule. Having cast off his female name, he could not at first manage to regard himself as a boy, and constantly spoke as if he were a girl; and this provided an inexhaustible source of amusement from the moment he made his appearance. He had a great aptitude for learning. But the harsh traditions which obtained in the schools of that day, and the endless torments to which he was subjected by his school-mates, robbed him of every chance of success. His terror-inspired timidity developed to an incredible degree, and in the end he was relegated to being among the backward children. One day—this was soon after he first went to the school—Pizonsky, in writing his name in an exercise-book, put down Kinstintin instead of Konstantin. The master caught him in the act, and flipping him over the head with a cane enquired:

"What's your name?"

"Konstantin," replied the child.

"Write it on the board."

The child, with trembling hand, took the chalk, and suddenly felt that his hand was racing, racing, racing, without his being able to stop it, and it was fashioning row after row of letters. All over the board stretched Konstantintintintintintintin . . . and still there was no end to it, no finality, no limit. The child felt there was something wrong here—that all was not well—he went hot and cold, his limbs shook—and yet he continued to scrawl syllable after syllable: "tintintintin."

"Oi!—bit long, aren't you, whippersnapper?" the teacher remarked with dry sarcasm. "Keep to your 'pleportion'!"

Pizonsky hastily wiped the endless chain of syllables from the board, and with a firm, decided hand, wrote a brief "Kotin".

Greatly puzzled by this rapid contraction of such an expansive and complex word, the teacher thought it an offensive piece of impertinence; once more he cut Pizonsky across the ear with his cane, and once more, in sterner accents, he reminded him to keep to his "pleportions".

"I can't," the child replied firmly.

"What is it you can't?"

"I can't write in 'pleportion'."

The teacher jerked back his head, and the child, knowing what the sign meant, made his way with impassive docility to the form by which there always stood a bucket with birch twigs.

"Well, Makrina, make yourself comfortable," the executioners on duty invited him; and the execution duly took place.

And over and over again the same gibes and entertainment were repeated at his expense, and every day, to the accompaniment of a chorus of laughter, he fashioned for hours his endless Konstantintintintintin, and then, driven to despair, suddenly wrote a curt "Kotin" and walked to the execution bench. Every day he was thrashed over the still fresh weals, and still he could not accommodate himself to his "pleportion" and either crawled into infinity or frantically dashed off a brief "Kotin".

Pizonsky's education was ended by his schoolfellows breaking the bridge of his nose—which made it crooked—while the school authorities expelled him for being over age and for backwardness and permitted him to choose any mode of life recognized by the laws of the land. To Pizonsky all permitted modes of life were the same, and therefore he never took the trouble to choose any particular one as his very own. He thought, first of all, about his daily bread, and became an apprentice to an encyclopaedic artisan, who was also coppersmith, mechanic, bookbinder, astronomer and poet. Together with his eccentric master he was all and nothing: the two of them bound books, painted houses, mended pans—and did it all with equal zest— cheaply and badly. Their meagre daily earnings were hardly enough to buy them the sustenance of paupers; but they were not worried by that. During the frequent spells when there was no work and no food in the house, they would forget their hunger as they pored in an ecstasy of delight over some old work on astronomy and poked their fingers into a greasy star map. The approaching evening would only drive them to the window, through which, all night long, they would stare at the sky and pick out constellations, or would quote by heart passages from "Manfred", or "The Monk" by Kozlov; or, perhaps, seating themselves on the steps of their cabin, they would sing in duet:

"O mortal man!
Think of thy span.
Look at the tombs,
They're eternal homes."

It is impossible to say how long this sweet and poetic existence of our Makrina would have lasted, had she not—as a man who, in his allotted term, hadn't chosen any recognized means of livelihood—been conscripted for military service.

CHAPTER THE FOURTH

FOR three years Konstantin Pizonsky was sexton in the regimental church, and at last, on the petition of his mother, was allowed to return home to support her. But when he got back he found that his mother had departed for a better world. He arrived in Stary Gorod and presented himself at his uncle's, the Old Believer Markel Deev. Markel Semenovich Deev admitted Pizonsky into his presence, heard all he had to tell him, called all the members of his family together, and then said to his nephew:

"Well—now turn!"

"How, uncle?" asked Pizonsky.

"Just like that—sideways."

The other made a half-turn.

"Good. Now turn your back on me."

Pizonsky obeyed again.

"Isn't he grand?" Markel Semenych enquired of his family.

A burst of laughter—loud in places, restrained in others—greeted this remark from every corner of the room.

It was indeed hard to contemplate Pizonsky without laughter: his bald head—shaven in the army style at that—his crooked nose, his rounded bird-like eyes, blue lips and long nankeen coat, which was purchased in the town where his military career had ended—all this taken together presented a most amusing and ridiculous sight.

"For three years, if you please, he's been a gallant warrior and has now earned three brass buttons. Good enough. And now, my lad, you needn't worry any more; don't bother to turn, but, as you're facing the door, just go where you came from," his uncle concluded, firmly and finally expelling from his house the son of heretics.

Pizonsky went out.

Forgetting in his abstraction to put on his cap, with head bared he marched right across the town, his baldness occasioning surprise among the passers-by, who laughed at him more cruelly than the children did at the prophet. But Pizonsky proved more patient than the prophet: he cursed no one—he only had a quiet cry under a laburnum beyond the town boundary. He had nowhere to go, and sat by the roadside like a plucked owl. It is usual to think that a man in such a plight is within a short step of crime, but this is not always so. At any rate, Pizonsky was not contemplating any evil deed; he only felt very heavy at heart and very hurt, and he sat and wept merely to relieve his feelings. Still, he could not sit for ever by the roadside; he had to go somewhere, and look somewhere for some kind of shelter.

CHAPTER THE FIFTH

PIZONSKY remembered that in a village that lay not very far from the town there lived a niece of his mother's—his cousin —who had married a small landholder of the name of Nabokov, and he decided to look her up. He set out on foot, and by dint of hard slogging and diligent enquiries he arrived the following evening at the village, where he hoped to find his relative and where he learnt that neither she nor her husband was in the land of the living, but that there remained her two little girls—Glasha, aged about five, and Nilochka, in her third year. But they too—the orphans—were not there, because they had been taken away to be brought up by a blind beggar woman, Pustyricha. So that's how things were with his last relations!

"At least I'll go and have a peep at the children," Pizonsky said to himself, feeling more and more an orphan, and he ascertained the whereabouts of Pustyricha and found the children there.

His meeting with the children occurred late in the afternoon. Both the little girls—dressed in the most fearful rags—were sitting on the dusty earthwork outside the cottage: the elder one was playing at tossing little stones into the air, while the younger was sulking and watching her sister's hand listlessly.

Pizonsky suddenly appeared from round the corner and stopped before them like an ugly genie from a fairy-tale.

After taking a good look at the children, he seated himself on the grass and put his arms about them both.

"Dearies," he said, "you are not happy with granny?"

The children leapt up in alarm and clasped each other tightly. Then, after staring at one another for some time, both at once burst into silent tears.

Pizonsky dived into his pocket and produced a slightly crushed baked onion, blew off the crumbs that stuck to it, broke it with his nails and gave half to each orphan.

Whether it was the mysterious call of blood, or only the tempting taste of the sweet baked onion, the children suddenly felt confidence in Pizonsky. They crawled off the earth-mound, seated themselves opposite one another on his knees and sucked at the onion, fingering meanwhile the shining brass button that was sewn to the collar of their uncle's nankeen coat.

"Does granny beat you, children?" Pizonsky began directly, stroking the little girls' heads.

"Yes," softly murmured the children.

"And hurt you?"

"Yes," they admitted more nervously, and blinking away their tears, continued to gaze intently—their eyes full of heart-rending childish despair—at the same silly, shiny button.

Pizonsky began to sigh. Tears streaming down the cheeks of a cowed, broken-spirited child are unbearable to see. A great love and tenderness filled Pizonsky's heart at the sight of these tears. He was prepared to do anything to wipe them away. But what could he do for anybody—he, a beggar, cripple, a deformed clown? Most people, had they considered his own circumstances at that moment, would probably have decided that he himself was doomed to perish.

And most people would have forgiven him had he turned a deaf ear to sorrow, because the poor monster could do nothing for the two orphans. They at least had a home with Pustyricha, be it never so wretched, while Pizonsky was quite homeless.

And to carry off someone else's child—this, we are told, is so grave a matter, that fear of the consequences might have excused his leaving everything to blind chance.

Happily Pizonsky was a bad philosopher, but he felt things on the right lines, and therefore he acted differently.

He hung about till Pustyricha returned, and asked her to let him spend the night in the cottage. During the night he kept on getting up to have a look at the children, and towards morning vague and lovely visions began to flutter in his mind, and when he arose next morning, forgetting his own helplessness and homelessness, he begged the old woman to let him have the orphans.

"I'll bring them up, grandma. I'll teach them, granny," urged Pizonsky.

The old woman refused to listen to him. She wanted to send the children out to beg, and therefore ordered Pizonsky himself out of the cottage and slammed the door in his face.

"To go to law with her," argued Pizonsky, "is a long business; also I have no money, and by the time they order her to give me the children she'll blind them." But to abandon the children and again go God knows where, alone, Pizonsky now thought impossible, and during the following night he decided upon a different course.

CHAPTER THE SIXTH

NOTICING near a peasant's threshing-shed a rush basket, such as is used for carrying straw, Pizonsky took it behind a barn, tipped out the cornstalks with which it was filled, lined the bottom with fresh hay and hid it in Pustyricha's kitchen-garden. (He committed a crime—he stole the basket.) The following morning, as soon as the sun rose, and Pustyricha, with the help of a guide, sallied out on a begging expedition, as usual, Pizonsky grabbed the girls, who had been left at home, put them in the basket, hitched it onto his shoulder with his belt, and, a long staff in hand, strode off, on his long legs, in the direction of the town. Fear of pursuit and apprehension about the fate of the children, who, like a couple of unfledged chicks, slept in the basket on his back, drove Pizonsky on at such a rate that he did forty miles without a rest that day and in the evening was back in Stary Gorod. Here he had no corner he could call his own, and here he now came with two children for whose welfare he had accepted responsibility.

Anyone would have been justified in calling the man a fool.

"What's he going to do now? Where will he go with them?"

"Fool!"

CHAPTER THE SEVENTH

THE two orphans who, swinging rhythmically, travelled in the basket on Pizonsky's back, slept all that day; but the coolness of the evening awoke them, and they began to shiver and whimper with the cold. But by then Pizonsky was already approaching the landing-stage which lay on the river-bank just outside the town. He turned off into the hempfields near the town boundary, where he carefully lifted both girls out of the basket, shook onto the ground the hay which he had placed at the bottom of it, arranged both children on the hay, and, squatting over them like a broody hen, pressed them to his bosom and thus all through the brief summer night kept them warm with the heat of his own body, while he himself wept— wept gently with happiness.

"Why should I worry?" he thought. "And why this blessing? Thou, O Lord, didst want to gather the children of Jerusalem as a hen gathers her chicks, and they would not. They hurt Thee—they came not, and mine have come to me. . . . I took them . . . stole them. . . . I am warming them; Lord, forgive me for stealing them! . . . Let me shield them from evil; and forgive me . . . forgive me, please, for stealing the basket also!"

And he gave a sob as he finished this prayer, and immediately fell asleep, still warming the sleeping orphans with his body.

The tall hemp screened this nest and it could only be seen from the sky.

Early next morning, the moment the sky had been flushed by a bright sun, Pizonsky got up, covered the sleeping children with the basket, and, to prevent them throwing it off when they woke, tied four bunches of hemp crosswise over it, and then emerged from his hiding-place. After a careful look round, he sighed, crossed himself, and without entering the town, set off towards the town allotments. The town was still asleep, lazing in the tawny mist that rose from the river. The district through which Pizonsky was now walking obviously was not very familiar to him, because he scrutinized and recalled to mind various landmarks, and only after a long cogitation, his eyes having located a large kitchen-garden surrounded by a tall wattled fence of wild hazel, did he make straight for this kitchen-garden and climb over the ditch that surrounded it and then over the wattles. Finding himself right in the garden, Pizonsky bent double, darted quickly along the edge of the beds and concealed himself in a bed of feathery peas. Here he went down on his haunches and proceeded to look out for someone. For a whole hour he squatted among the peas, now and again poking out his head above the plants, and then again dropping down hastily at the least sound. Why had Pizonsky come here —when only a few days before he had been driven from this house with singular harshness and ridicule—and whom did he expect to meet here now? No one would have guessed. One thing only could be assumed with every reason, and that was, that Pizonsky was not waiting for Markel Semenych.

CHAPTER THE EIGHTH

PIZONSKY was indeed waiting for the appearance of quite a different member of the Deev family, and he was greatly put out when the gate of the back-yard creaked and a tall, curly-headed young man strolled into the kitchen-garden. This was not Markel Semenych, nor his son, Marko Markelych, nor, to all appearances, was it the person Pizonsky wished to see.

As the young man came in, Pizonsky not only didn't rise, but bobbed down as low as he could.

The young man who had entered the kitchen-garden took a few steps along the narrow path that divided the beds into two equal parts, propped up his left side with his hand, and taking in with a merry glance the wide expanse of dewy vegetables, slowly yawned, stretched himself, and paused, rubbing one booted leg with the other. The boy was the picture of youth—freshness incarnate. Pizonsky studied him not without pleasure, forgetting, it seemed, his own impatience. But presently the gate creaked again. This time there appeared in the kitchen-garden a tall young woman with merry pink cheeks and fine dark eyebrows. She was dressed in a dark woollen skirt and a well-worn, trimmed, sleeveless jacket, and on her head she wore a white handkerchief with pink borders.

On seeing the woman, Konstantin Ionych blushed to the tips of his ears with pleasure, and began to hop about in his hiding-place.

It was clear that she was the very person he had hoped to see, and that now only one thought possessed him, and that was how to attract her attention without at the same time revealing his presence to the boy who stood near. But such a manœuvre was quite impossible, and Pizonsky again squatted down and began hurriedly to part the bluish tendrils of the peas.

CHAPTER THE NINTH

MEANWHILE the plump beauty, on entering the kitchen-garden, lifted her skirt with one hand as a protection against the dewy grass, and walked straight to the bed of young beet-root. Pizonsky fancied that on seeing the boy standing on the path the young woman reddened slightly, but smiled to herself immediately after. Reaching the bed with a firm step, she deposited in the furrow a large wooden bowl painted in gold lacquer, and began quickly to pick the young beetroot-leaves and put them in the basin. Meanwhile the youngster approached the beauty with a slow, swinging step and said with a merry smile:

"Good morning, sister-in-law!"

She to whom this greeting was addressed took not the least notice of it.

The young man grinned again; he walked round his sister-in-law, and coming up from the other side said much more boldly:

"Platonida Andreevna, good morning!"

"Good morning to you, Avenir Markelych," Platonida Andreevna replied without raising her eyes from the ground.

Avenir made a low bow to his sister-in-law, and proceeded to help her pick the beetroot-tops and fill the basin.

"Helping me is something I did not ask you to do," said Platonida Andreevna.

"Why, does it worry you?"

"No, it does not worry me, but I don't want it."

"Will you allow me, then?"

"No, I don't allow it."

And with these words she threw out of the bowl the bunch of beetroot-leaves that Avenir had picked.

"Why are you so cross, sister?" asked the boy, straightening himself to his full height.

"Just because—I don't want you hanging about here."

Avenir gave a smile, again picked a handful of greens and placed them in the painted bowl.

"Listen, Avenir! I wish to goodness you would take yourself off with your help, please!" cried the beauty, and, unable to restrain herself, burst out laughing and flung the leaves that Avenir had picked into his face.

Avenir appeared to have been waiting for just that change.

"There, sister, you are laughing now and you have become a beauty again!"

"You think of some new lie to tell!"

"God's truth, may God strike me dead on the spot—a beauty, and there isn't a queen in the world as beautiful as you!" he broke out, gazing at her with hands folded on his bosom.

"Shoo!" cried Platonida Andreevna, but without much heat, and again began to pull the tall beetroot-tops with her white hands.

Avenir walked away, took a few turns, and again approaching his sister-in-law, spoke softly:

THE TALES OF LESKOV

"And why were you crying yesterday evening, sister, and what was it about?"

"How do *you* know I was crying?"

"Do you think I didn't hear?"

"Umph! Where could a fool like you hear, I wonder?"

Platonida Andreevna smiled and continued:

"No—I see truly that I'll have to complain about you to Marko Markelych, so that you are locked up at night."

"Why should I be locked up?"

"So that you don't snoop round under windows, where you shouldn't."

"Who cares—I've a collapsible ceiling in my room, for that matter," retorted Avenir.

"A collapsible fool, that's what you are, and nothing else," said Platonida Andreevna. "Don't you get enough hidings on my account as it is, fool that you are? You want your father and brother to thrash you still more, it seems. They'll thrash you all right."

"Let them thrash me while they have a chance. Only I reckon I'll soon be starting to give as good as I get."

"Ho, yes! give as good as you get! No, you listen to me, Avenir: you mind, father-in-law Markel Semenych, the other day, said before all the elders in the prayer-house that he will write a will so that everything will go to Marko Markelych alone, and you, silly, for your disrespect to your parents, will get nothing—nothing at all."

"I don't worry! You and that husband of yours will be the richer. I'll be all the happier."

"Mmm! . . . No, honour bright, what do you reckon you are thinking about, Avenir?"

"I don't think anything, sister. There isn't much for me to think."

"Oh! And you like being pummelled and walloped on my account, do you?"

"How do you know I don't?"

"Silly fool!"

"Fool, maybe, but devoted to you."

88

δ   "Then I don't want you to be bashed about on my account, and made a pauper too. What's bitten you?"

Avenir stood silent, with folded arms. Platonida Andreevna, her brows knitted, was saying impressively:

"You good-for-nothing scallywag, you should get into that thick head of yours that I am, after all, your brother's wife; sister-in-law, as they say."

"D'you think I don't remember that?" rejoined Avenir warmly. "I remember all that right enough, and don't think anything bad."

"Bad! Good or bad, or whatever it is, only I'll have you know I am sick of you and won't have you mooning after me. You hear that, Avenir? You hear it? Don't you ever dare to meet me here again . . . and don't dare to stick up for me at home either, and don't pester me about my being beautiful . . . because I don't want it; don't want it or wish it . . . and . . . if it comes to that, I'll have you know I don't like you—so there!"

"Oh, steady there. . . . Why not be truthful, sister? There's no cause—"

"What d'you mean, no cause? What's no cause? Where did you get that?"

Avenir waved his hand in a hopeless gesture, and placing a beetroot-leaf to his lips sucked it in, till it burst with a loud pop.

Platonida Andreevna laughed derisively and remarked with a shrug:

"Look at that fool, now, good folks."

"Oh, stow it, sister; don't keep calling me a fool," retorted Avenir.

"What?"

"Why have you been kissing me, then?"

"When was that? When was it I kissed a fool like you? That's a lie, fibber you, I've never kissed you."

"Never?"

"Never."

Platonida Andreevna blushed, and, bending down, began to pull at the beetroot-tops and to fling them into the bowl.

"And have you forgotten how when the people were all out last year . . . ?"

"Well?"

"And when you and I were playing hide-and-seek and wrestling in the hay . . . don't you remember?"

Platonida Andreevna raised herself and, looking firmly into Avenir's eye, demanded:

"Well; and what if we were wrestling?"

"Well, that's when you tickled me . . ."

"Well?"

"Well, you kissed me, you can't get away from it; you did kiss me."

"Pshaw! Fancy remembering a trifle like that!" retorted Platonida Andreevna, hiding her face in her sleeve. "Maybe I did kiss you by chance, because you are only a boy—why shouldn't I have kissed you? You are my husband's young brother. I could kiss you like that a hundred times more, if you like."

"Go on, then, kiss me."

Avenir took a step towards his sister-in-law, and touched her white piqué sleeve lightly.

"Clear off, fool!" Platonida Andreevna replied sternly, shaking off her brother-in-law's hand.

"To think of it," she continued. "I kissed him! Living in this gaol of a house you'd kiss Old Horny himself!"

"There again, sister, you are not telling the truth; you're not too fond of kissing my brother."

"Avenir!" cried Platonida Andreevna, rising and trying to speak as incisively as she could, "you good-for-nothing wastrel; d'you want me to snap your head off? I can deal with a brat like you so that you'll never forget it."

"Don't keep calling me a boy, and brat, and whatnot. I've had enough. About time you stopped calling me a brat."

"I shall call you that because you are nothing more than a boy."

"Because I'm twenty-one—well, you're only that. You haven't lived in this world any longer than I have."

"I am a woman."

"And I am a man."

"A fool, that's what you are—not a man. Call yourself a man. Look at yourself."

"Well, then, what d'you reckon a man *should* be like?"

"What? . . . Now, I don't care a button if you're a man, I'll give you such a box on the ears in a moment."

"Go on, then, do it!"

"God's truth, I will."

"Go ahead then, won't you."

"That I will, and I'll give you such a talking-to, you'll look pretty small then," said Platonida Andreevna, raising her voice and growing angry in real earnest. "Of all the pests! All day long he just wastes his time; there's no dragging him to the sawmills; he won't learn business, just waits for a chance to snoop off from the quay; and now if you please, what's he taken into his head? Any honest man's head would have burst with the thought of it. Get out of my sight, wretch!" she shrilled, raising her basin threateningly. "Get away, or I'll call your brother!"

"Platonn-id-aa!" came at that moment a dry, tremulous voice from behind the barn in the back-yard.

At the first sound of the voice, Avenir quickly began to hop across the beds like a goat, and leaping over the dividing furrow into the bed of peas, he found himself exactly face to face with the hidden Pizonsky.

Both sat on their haunches, facing one another, as young rabbits sit on the fringe of a copse in the early morning, and both were rubbing their astonished eyes.

CHAPTER THE TENTH

MEANWHILE Platonida Andreevna, who was watching the leaping Avenir with an amused smile, calmly called back to her husband:

"Coming!"

"Do you happen to know where that Avenir has got to?" continued the same voice, now sounding a little nearer.

"No, Marko Markelych, I don't," answered Platonida Andreevna.

In the opening of the gate appeared a squat, dark man, aged

about forty-five, who reminded one of a hedgehog, with greying hair, a peevish face, and cold, suspicious eyes under lowering brows.

"He's not here, by any chance?" he enquired, pausing in the gateway and spreading his arms across the top of the gate.

"No."

"And hasn't been here?"

"And hasn't been here."

"Honour bright?"

"Why—what should he have been doing here?"

"Where the hell has the slinking little dog got to?"

"I thought I saw him going to the jetty early in the morning," replied Platonida Andreevna.

"Drat him—he's always doing things at the wrong time."

"He seemed in a hurry, apparently, there's a lot of work for him."

"Too hard-working he is! Now, how about leaving him without his tea again to-day, for his diligence? Father and I are going to the weaving-shop, and if he should get back, don't you dare boil another samovar for him. Do you hear me?"

"I heard you."

"He's not to have any tea when he can't do things on time."

"I won't give him any."

"Those are my orders: no tea!"

"But I said I won't give him any—I won't, Marko Markelych. Do you reckon I would disobey you? You can ask Darya afterwards," Platonida answered her husband.

The gate slammed on its spring, and from the bed of blue peas immediately emerged the frightened head of Avenir. He started again to hop over the beds like a goat, and as he ran he was silently drawing Platonida Andreevna's attention to the bed of peas by jerking his hand towards it.

"Oh, leave me alone, you hateful nuisance!" Platonida Andreevna said, advancing to meet him, and looking around apprehensively. "What do you want to go hopping about the beds like a goat for? Go away, I tell you!"

But Avenir ignored the order, gently took his sister-in-law by the sleeve, and silently, his face serious, pointed with his hand at the peas behind which Pizonsky had until then secreted himself.

Platonida Andreevna no sooner cast her eyes in that direction than she gave a wild shriek and let fall from her hand the bowl of beetroot-tops. Among the peas, a few feet away from the scarecrow that had been put there to frighten the sparrows, stood the long, ridiculous figure of Pizonsky, on which, as on the scarecrow, hung the remains of a wet calico robe tied about the waist with a bunch of flax.

"Dearie! Wait! Dear Platonida Andreevna, wait!" Pizonsky began rapidly, emerging from his fort. "I haven't come to you with evil intent, dear girl!"

In silent wonder Platonida Andreevna studied the queer figure before her: it seemed that it was the scarecrow itself that had come to life to tax her with the sin of Herodias—in other words, with her childish but genuine weakness for her husband's brother.

Konstantin Ionych, shattering her impression that he was identical with the scarecrow, hastened to inform her of their relationship, then reminded her of how three days previously he had been received by Markel Semenych and her husband, and finally, bowing to the ground before Platonida Andreevna, he proceeded to beg her to help him find shelter for the children he had hidden in the hempfield.

It is well known that to no one is a woman readier to extend greater sympathy and help than to the person who has by chance become a witness of her sentimental weakness.

Platonida Andreevna confirmed the truth of this fact: without questioning Pizonsky any further, she at once turned to Avenir and asked:

"Well, what's to be done? What are we going to do, Avenir?"

Avenir made a puzzled gesture with his hand.

"Perhaps this is what we can do," continued Platonida Andreevna. "Avenir, perhaps you'd better go from me to Granny Rochovna; though she doesn't belong to the Church, she isn't fussy; perhaps she will take pity on them."

And Pizonsky proceeded meantime:

"And there's something else I must tell you, my clever one: they have no clothes now, the poor chicks—none whatever;

one has a shift of sorts, but the other—the smaller one—is quite
naked. I wrapped my trousers around her, she doesn't look
very decent in them, but her rags have all dropped off—yes,
completely dropped off."

"That's soon mended," replied Platonida Andreevna. "I'll
fetch you some rags presently. Only Darya, the thief, mustn't
catch me at it," she added, looking at Avenir and placing a
finger on her lip. "She's following me everywhere nowadays,
watching every step of mine."

"Well, sister, you pretend you're taking some cast-offs for
the scarecrow: make a parcel and bring it here," Avenir told
his sister-in-law.

"Only it will have to be something of my own—I haven't
any children's things, because there are no children in the
house—I don't have them," said Platonida Andreevna, running
towards the gate.

Five minutes or so later she was heard to emit a loud "shoo"
in the yard and leapt into the kitchen-garden with a tightly
made up bundle, from which dangled calico, and linen, and the
hem of a quilted overcoat.

Thrusting this parcel at Pizonsky, she jerked Avenir's elbow
and said:

"You look in at a *traktir*, and have some tea"—and with this
she pushed a fifteen-kopeck piece into his hand.

Avenir gently turned away her hand and remarked:

"Put it away, sister, put it away; you need it yourself; I'll
be all right without it."

With these words Avenir, with the agility of a monkey,
vaulted over the wattles and ran after Pizonsky, who, holding
with both hands the cast-offs that had been given him, had nearly
reached the fields already, with his big stride.

CHAPTER THE ELEVENTH

GRANNY Fevronya Rochovna, an ancient Old Believer
and local medicine-woman and midwife, was a very kind old
dame and, in the words of Platonida Andreevna, was "not

fussy". She allowed Pizonsky and the two children he had brought in the basket to take up their abode in a little wooden closet where her medicinal and pseudo-medicinal herbs and roots were hung. Here Pizonsky found shelter until the autumn, so that at least neither rain nor night-frosts presented any terrors for him and the children; while about twice a week Avenir brought him from Platonida Andreevna all sorts of baked and boiled food, milk, and fresh vegetables. Pizonsky was settling down. He sat constantly on the floor by the bed, on which his children were, and either amused them with home-made toys, or plied a needle, fashioning for them, from the clothes that Platonida Andreevna sent him, various little shifts, caps, vests and rompers. He sewed excellently, like an experienced woman. He had been taught to do so at the convent when he was still a little girl. As yet, scarcely anyone in Stary Gorod knew of Pizonsky's existence; and those who did, either thought nothing of him, or thought he was one more beggar, one more pauper by the church-gate. Old Rochovna herself, as she watched him bustling about and absorbed in his work, foretold no other future for him, and mentally reproached him for having taken the little children.

"How are you going to manage with them, Ionych?" she would say to him now and again, pointing at the children.

"Grandma," retorted Pizonsky to the old woman, "the prophet Elijah sat alone in a deserted steppe; before his eyes was a blue sea, and behind him a sharp rock of stone, and he should have perished of hunger by that wild crag."

"That's so, father," assented Rochovna.

"But God sent a raven to him"—Pizonsky spoke with rising earnestness—"and ordered the bird to feed his servant, and it fed him. Consider: a bird, granny, a bird fed him! *A bird!*"

"That's so, father. It did, indeed."

"Yes, mother, Fevronya Rochovna, it did. And God sent me two birds: the raven Avenir flies to see me, while the white swan Platonida Andreevna takes care of me, and they will keep me and my chicks until I shall have clothed the children and shall have got on my feet."

"That's something you can never do," old Rochovna told

95

herself as she left; but soon she changed her opinion. Konstantin Ionych, in receiving the help of Avenir and Platonida, did not sit with folded hands and let grass grow under his feet. His encyclopaedism soon proved of greatest use to him and saw him through. Pizonsky showed Granny Rochovna that neither he nor his chicks would perish of cold and hunger.

Having clothed the little girls, Konstantin Ionych entered into negotiations with the old dame to obtain permission to fit out her closet at his own expense as a living-cubby, on condition that, when God mended his poverty, he would hand it back to her in good order, and meanwhile he would live there and pay her fifty kopecks rent per month.

Old Rochovna saw nothing in it but profit for herself, and agreed. And Pizonsky, taking advantage of the hours when the children slept after their games, brought into the old woman's back-yard sacks of clay, carefully plastered the closet, stuffed earth under the floor, built a tiny stove, and finally grunted contentedly.

Ou-u! How rich and happy was Pizonsky now, and what a practical example he could be to a great number of people who pore over questionable tracts about happiness.

CHAPTER THE TWELFTH

THE fixing up of his closet drove from Pizonsky's mind all cause for worry. Now he had only one immediate problem, and that was to teach the elder girl, five-year-old Glasha, to look after her younger sister Nilochka, or, as he called her, Milochka, while he was out.

When this was achieved, and little Milochka could safely be left in Glasha's charge, Konstantin Ionych began to absent himself for short periods, and after each such expedition always returned home with purchases, on which he spent the last two roubles he had brought back from the Army. First of all, Pizonsky came home with a large glazed pot; then, by gradual stages, he accumulated a collection of various discarded jars, flagons and bottles, and, finally, he arrived with some nut-galls, honey and Dutch soot. With these preparations and materials Pizonsky settled down before the stove and became absorbed in chemical research. About two days later he emerged from the house with a large bottle of ink and a wooden box full of black shiny boot-polish. With the ink Pizonsky failed signally, because the watchman in the Government offices manufactured ink at the Government's expense and therefore could sell this commodity to outsiders considerably cheaper, but his fresh boot-polish proved far superior to the blue, dry polish obtained from Moscow in tablet form, and this branch of his business saved him. Konstantin Ionych's spirits rose no end and he grew more daring and enterprising. Soon Stary Gorod beheld him constantly popping in and out of houses with a wooden box full of polish and very strong home-made brushes. Pizonsky and his wooden box flitted from house to house, called at shops, official buildings, taverns; quietly and unhurriedly he won everyone's good opinion wherever he went, made friends, and proved of service in various ways. For nearly twenty years the clock in the district Law Court had been striking so rapidly that no one could possibly tell whether it had struck twelve or one. Pizonsky took down the clock, fiddled about with it, banged about inside, and it began to strike clearly—one, two, three, as it should do. For the Archpriest, the Very Reverend Father Tuberozov, he fixed up a tin ventilator in the window. Father Tuberozov praised him and said: "Yes, you are not much to look at, but you are not without talent." For the Mayor, Pizonsky made a wooden leg on which his jack-boots could be polished, and the Mayor also did not fail to praise him. For Deacon Achilla, at his request, he fixed a pair of spurs to the boots in which the Deacon intended to ride out to the villages to visit friends. True, they did not survive long, because Father Tuberozov met Achilla in spurs and ordered him to break them off on the spot; nevertheless, even the spurs spoke in Pizonsky's favour. Then Pizonsky repaired an umbrella for someone, tinned a pan for someone else, mended some broken brass fittings for another person and some broken china for a fourth, and in no time Stary Gorod came to regard Pizonsky as one of its most useful inhabitants. It seemed now that if

Pizonsky decided for some reason to leave Stary Gorod of his own accord, there would have been a chorus of protest: "No, no, how on earth shall we manage without Konstantin Ionych?" The postmaster's wife, who had a great reputation for domesticity and sharpness of tongue, went so far as to anticipate such a possibility and publicly voiced her opinion that without Pizonsky life in Stary Gorod would become impossible.

Taking their cue from the postmaster's wife, others very soon began to say the same thing about Pizonsky.

"No, no, no!" said these others: "God forbid that we should be left without Konstantin Ionych! Even to think now of the time when he was not here, when for every trifle we had to send into the Provincial centre; we just can't think how we managed then."

Perhaps the time had come for Pizonsky to take care that he did not excite ill-feeling and envy against himself, but Pizonsky behaved quietly and evenly, without becoming inflated with success or exciting anyone's jealousy.

His reputation and everyone's goodwill towards him continued to grow. This friendliness expressed itself not only in words, but also in deeds. Several townspeople suddenly became seriously exercised with the question of arranging on a more permanent basis the existence in their town of so useful a person.

The first to display this concern was the wife of the postmaster.

This large, purposeful woman, whom the postmen feared more than the Greek Fire, and who was especially feared by her husband, went so far in her good disposition towards Pizonsky that she made it her husband's imperative duty to give Pizonsky a job at the post office.

"Mammy!" began the postmaster in pleading tones, folding his hands on his chest and desiring by this gesture of submissiveness to convey to his spouse how difficult it was to create such a job for Pizonsky.

"Wha-at?" the formidable lady bellowed at her husband. "I demand it; you hear me—*demand it*!"

"My angel!" the postmaster began to whine in a lower key: "but if it is impossible?"

The postmaster's wife transfixed her husband with a cold, disdainful look.

"Darling Desiderii Ivanych," the postmaster appealed to his sorter next day, "be an angel and think how we could fix up Pizonsky in the office. Agafia Alexeevna demands it without fail."

"Oh dear me!" sighed the sorter, and both he and the postmaster plunged into thought.

"Perhaps this is what we could do," began Desiderii Ivanych, tugging at his lower lip with two fingers. "What about getting him to sign in the Receipt Book?"

"God's truth, you're a regular Cabinet Minister," cried the delighted postmaster, and at once sent the watchman to fetch Konstantin Ionych.

Thus summoned, Pizonsky felt pleased, and yet upset, by his good fortune: on the one hand, the idea of earning regular money, by signing for the illiterates, appealed to him; on the other, he remembered the degree of his own illiteracy, and took into account his lack of practice in the art of writing, and he felt he dared not take upon himself so complicated a responsibility.

"I am a timid girl with the pen," he informed the postmaster.

"Desiderii Ivanych will practise with you, Konstantin Ionych; he'll teach you, he will."

Pizonsky pondered a moment, and swayed by a sinless self-interest, replied: "Naturally . . . if he teaches me . . ."

Pizonsky was appointed to the post of "signer"; only this job, obtained through influence, proved to be a failure. The very first day on which he had to sign for an illiterate payee was the last of his postal career.

"Write, Konstantin Ionych," the sorter told him.

Pizonsky took a quill, sucked it, then dipped it in the ink, then placed his hand on the paper and pressed on the hand with his right cheek, then for some time he drew various squiggles with the pen, and finally said: "Ready!"

The sorter proceeded to dictate clearly and slowly: "The said seven roubles and ten kopecks in silver received and signed for by so-and-so, and in his stead, owing to illiteracy, by ex-private Konstantin Pizonsky."

Pizonsky pressed his cheek still harder against his hand and began to twist and turn.

This time he laboured on and on; his round eyes bulged as he watched unblinkingly the hand that drove the quill; on his brow gathered beads of cold perspiration and all his face expressed unbearable alarm.

This lasted a good fifteen minutes, at the expiration of which, Pizonsky suddenly threw himself back in his chair, then leapt up and began to shake, staring at his handiwork. At that moment he looked simply terrible: he reminded one of a medium who had conjured up a hideous ghost and was aghast at its apparition. The sorter and postmaster took a peep at the fatal page and were also struck dumb. On the page, in Pizonsky's handwriting, stood: "Thes skilbures and tencock peaks in roubles reved and sisted experd ad Konstantintintintintintin."

The name—so fatal for expressing with the pen—aroused in Pizonsky's soul all the forgotten sufferings of his orphaned childhood, each "tintintintin" that oozed out of the preceding one rose before him as a fresh, cruel, mocking nightmare or gnome, till he could bear it no longer, and leaping up in his seat, he shook with terror.

"There, my angel, this is how he signed," the postmaster was saying a minute later, as he presented the damaged Receipt Book to his wife.

The postmaster's wife could not suppress a smile on beholding the "skilbures" of Pizonsky.

"And 'experd ad'," the postmaster pointed out, encouraged by the smile.

"Well, I don't see what there's to point out in particular."

"But, gracious, my love—'experd ad'." Whoever heard of such a thing? It simply has no sense."

"Yes, I see that, but I shall nevertheless have the highest opinion of him," the postmaster's wife replied in a tone that seemed to imply that she had the highest opinion only of people who were incapable of postal service.

This new story about Pizonsky spread all over the town, but it did not in the least harm his unshakable reputation.

On the contrary, it seemed it was from that time on that he

began to be received in the houses of the officials, not as an artisan, but as a free-lance artist who stood on a higher plane than the wretched official quill-pushers. He was now no longer given his food in the kitchen, but a special chair would be placed for him by the doors of the main room; he was no longer presented with a glass of vodka between two fingers, but on a slice of bread, and he was addressed to his face, not as "you", but "you, Konstantin Ionych". He rose so much above the status of a labouring artisan that even the Mayor himself began to send him his tea, not into the hall, but to the servants' quarters, and permitted him to carry on conversation with himself standing by the door jamb. And scarcely a year went by but all the notables of Stary Gorod, quite imperceptibly, found themselves friends and partisans of the miserable outcast Pizonsky, and the time came for him to become a property-owner and citizen.

CHAPTER THE THIRTEENTH

WHILE rendering all the service he could to those around him, and rising, without fawning and servility, in everyone's esteem, Konstantin Ionych never complained of his lot and never brought up the subject of his orphans. Only if someone else happened to enquire about them first—"Well, Konstantin Ionych, and how are your children ?"—then only would Pizonsky say : "Oh, they're getting on all right, my love—little by little."

"Shouldn't you give a thought, Konstantin Ionych, to having them educated ?" the ladies suggested.

Pizonsky would either say nothing or reply briefly :

"Why, of course, dear girl, I'm thinking."

"Why not send them to me for some schooling ?" offered the postmaster's wife.

But Pizonsky put even her off :

"They're very wild, my friend, they are—very lonesome— don't see many people. What should they be a-doing with the gentry ?"

Concerning the upbringing of the orphans Konstantin Ionych

had his own plans, which he discussed with no one, but which he was firmly set upon, down to the smallest details.

His conscience, which forbade Pizonsky to cut across anyone else's interest in any way, turned his thoughts towards those unwanted means of livelihood which lie idle, which no one covets anyway and which attract no one. The collapse of his postal career convinced Pizonsky that his was not the path of influence. He felt that only straight roads were open to him—that he should occupy himself with that which others did not want and thus avoid an ignoble struggle, new enemies, and jealousy.

Pizonsky saw that in our vast country, on our broad lands—ungarnered and unploughed—there were enough riches for all manner of men who were prepared for sweat and toil, and he made a new move to assure a future for his orphans. One summer's day Pizonsky appeared at a meeting of the Town Council and said:

"Would it please you, Your Honours, Sirs, to let me and my orphans find a pittance on the empty eyot under the bridge?"

"That's an idea," said the members of the Council. "Let them settle on our empty eyot. Anyway, that empty plot is no use to anyone—why not let a decent man at least live on it?"

And Pizonsky—rent-free and rates-free—received on a long-term lease the ownership of the empty island—a wilderness of thistle, grass snakes and nettles.

This acquisition was such a tremendous source of joy for Pizonsky that he could not imagine now anyone in the world more happy than he. The very first year he got this island as his property, he erected a cabin on it, excavated a little dug-out, surrounded it with a ditch, and put up a pair of little gates. The following year the once derelict island was already a melon plantation which provided Pizonsky and his orphans with bread and butter and all they needed. In the winter, Pizonsky even began to feel somewhat of a gentleman. He obtained where he could a number of different books and taught his charges to read and write, and the progress of the two intelligent little girls was a source of untold consolation to Pizonsky. In this blissful felicity, in idyllic surroundings, our modern Crusoe saw four whole years go by: nothing upset the peaceful run of his family life; his children were growing up and learning; he became the possessor of a horse and buggy, which, owing to his love of the arts, he painted a different colour every year; the harvests were good—there was nothing more to wish for. Pizonsky was respected by everyone as an all-round useful person, and indeed the only thing he could not do was to be a Government clerk.

Thus arose Pizonsky—without influence or protection—who now himself acted as protector of those who have every right to protection—the children. But . . . When we come to think of it, there always lie in wait for us all sorts of unpleasant *Buts*.

CHAPTER THE FOURTEENTH

IN that memorable year when in many parts of Russia, in the autumn, cherry and apple trees suddenly burst into blossom for a second time, and the people on that account foretold a great plague, Marko Markelych, the husband of the plump Platonida Andreevna, whom we met that morning in the kitchen-garden, passed into eternity. In an enormous oaken coffin, to the burning of ponderous candles and the wreathing of incense, accompanied by the nasal chanting of the Old Believers, he was borne to the cemetery and, according to custom, his grave was levelled with the earth he had trodden for half a century with his heavy boots. No one was particularly heartbroken at the graveside of the defunct Marko. His widow, Platonida Andreevna, cried a little, and old Markel Semenych shed a few tears. This was the extent of the outward expression of grief over this death. The brother of the dead man remained quite unmoved by the end of his hard-hearted elder brother, particularly as during the three preceding days, while the corpse had been laid out in the house, old Markel Semenych, who from fear of cholera had begun lifting his elbow freely, had attempted to thrash Avenir on at least five occasions with whatever happened to be at hand, reproaching him, while doing so, with insensibility, and snarling: "Of course, it would be your brother and not you, you lout, that's lying there now." Markel Semenych, having become thoroughly wrought up by his bereavement, by the fear of death, and the wine of consolation, was quite unable to return to his senses, and continually fortified himself with a glass. After his son had been trampled down under the soil, he even drank a silver cup at the cemetery, for the repose of his soul, distributed with his own hand a bagful of coppers for orisons, and sat astride his ancient drozhki to which was harnessed a fat black horse; at his feet, and sideways to him, his widowed daughter-in-law, Platonida Andreevna, timidly seated herself. The clear eyes of the young widow, with their expression of smouldering languor, were very little affected by her tears, and no sooner had she and her father-in-law emerged from the cemetery into the field that lay between the graveyard and the town than those clear eyes dried completely and looked out from beneath the thick lashes clearer than they had ever gazed hitherto. It seemed as though they had merely been washed by the tears, or as though they had now, for the first time, beheld the world about them. Yes, one was sooner led to suppose that they actually did see this world for the first time. This could be gathered, not only from the eyes of the beauty, but also from her bosom, which now heaved freely and deeply, swaying beneath the crimson jacket.

Who would have dared now to remind this luxuriant rose: "You are a widow!" Whose hand would have attempted by such a reminder to cut this lovely flower, that protested so vehemently for its right to bloom, gladden the eye and spread its aroma? No, the most fiery idealist would never have urged her to spend her days sighing for those who had crossed to eternity; she would not have been condemned to be burnt on her husband's funeral pyre by the most fanatical of Hindus.

Even the crusty old Deev did not chide her on account of the fewness of her tears, and on the way back from his son's funeral he forgave his daughter-in-law her earthly beauty, and after contemplating her said merely:

"You are not comfortable like that, Platonida; move up, my swan—nearer." With this the old man moved his daughter-in-law away from the driver's back and towards his knees, and again said: "You sit like that."

"No, father, I am all right; I'm ever so comfortable," Platonida Andreevna replied.

"You move closer; you'll be even more comfortable then."

To please her father-in-law, Platonida Andreevna moved up a little. Markel Semenych stared for a long time at her nose and forehead and eyebrows, and finally said:

"Young woman, you should, of course, weep for your husband, because he was, after all, your husband; but don't fret yourself overmuch; you won't be forgotten or come to harm in my house."

Platonida Andreevna bowed slightly to her father-in-law.

This meek gratitude so pleased Markel Semenych that on climbing down from the drozhki by his gate he squeezed his daughter-in-law's arm near the elbow and said again:

"Don't you fear, my swan; don't you be afraid of anything."

Over the funeral-meal Markel Semenych began several times to say that, although his son had died childless, yet he, honouring the widow, and his daughter-in-law, wished to endow her, and intended to leave her an equal share with Avenir.

"And perhaps, even," he declared, glancing askance at Avenir —"perhaps I'll be of a mind to leave her the lot, as she deserves it, because I have nothing to reproach her with, and I am pleased with her all round, and the wealth is my own, and I can give it to whom I choose."

Platonida Andreevna was covered with blushes and did not know what to say or think, and in her confusion made deep and awkward bows across the table to her father-in-law.

All through dinner Markel Semenych was fortifying himself and continually dashing down cup after cup, and finally grew quite fuddled. After somehow seeing off his guests he collapsed on the sofa and merely muttered incoherently:

"Daughter-in-law!"

Platonida Andreevna and Avenir took the old man under his arms and led him to his bedroom.

"Daughter-in-law," he said again, with difficulty, when he was put on the bed.

"What is it?" Platonida Andreevna enquired. But Markel Semenych was already asleep and made no reply.

Avenir and Platonida left the old man to sleep off the effects of his cups and went their respective ways.

CHAPTER THE FIFTEENTH

AVENIR, after a stroll in the kitchen-garden, went into town, and the young widow seated herself mournfully at her window. She was not sorry for her harsh, unfriendly husband, because she had never heard anything from him all her life but threats and reproaches, and had never expected anything better from him in the future. But what lay before her now? What awaited her—a lonely widow, without riches—in her present young life? Life was so alluring, she so much wanted to live— life called to her and seemed to whirl round and round before her eyes.

"Oh, tut, what am I thinking of?" Platonida Andreevna said with annoyance, and scratched angrily at her elbow and leant on it on the window-sill and proceeded to watch how, on the cornice of the warehouses that faced her, a number of bluey-grey pigeons were billing and cooing.

All was empty and tedious about her; tedium and emptiness were in Platonida Andreevna's heart.

"It would be better if I aged the sooner; it would be better if I had never married; it would be better if they had sent me to a convent . . ." she thought, as she wiped the tears which welled in her eyes with her gauze sleeve, and with a sigh transferred her head from one hand to the other. In this way an hour went by—two hours—and the oppressive day burnt up before her.

In deepest twilight Avenir entered her room. He looked round him, hung his cap on a nail, seated himself in a chair opposite his sister-in-law and offered her a bunch of grapes on his open palm.

"Where did you get them?" Platonida Andreevna asked him.

"Lyalin's got groceries in, so they got these too; only they say it doesn't do to eat them now, with the sickness about."

"Why not? You give them to me, I'll see how it doesn't do."

Platonida took the bunch, nibbled all the grapes off, wiped her red lips with her sleeve, flung the bare stalk out of the window onto the verandah, and laughed softly.

Both Avenir and the widow were quite composed; yet both, for some reason, felt in no mood for talking.

"Where have you been?" Platonida asked her brother-in-law with an effort.

"Oh . . . just having a little stroll," Avenir answered.

"It's so deadly dull here—it fairly gets you."

"Well, what can one do?"

"What's that you said?"

"I said, What can one do if it's dull?"

"If you ask me, I'd say it'd be all right to go to bed," said Platonida Andreevna.

"Well, why don't you?"

"Only that father will be up, I'll have to be getting his tea."

"Well, you get up when he wakes; only he's sozzled—I doubt if he's going to wake now."

"Well, I think I'll do as you say and sleep a little in my dress for the time being. You leave me now."

The young man rose and took his cap from the nail. Platonida Andreevna rose with him from her seat and remarked with a yawn:

"Oh, my elbows are itching; I wonder what that means."

"That means sleeping in a new place."

"Get along with you! What new place would I be sleeping in? My elbows are itching for sorrow," she added, manœuvring her brother-in-law out of the door and shutting it after him on a hook.

On finding herself alone in the locked room, Platonida walked over to a coffer covered with a rug, placed near it a candle, and an iron box with tinder, sulphur sticks and flint, crossed herself, lay down on the coffer, and, exhausted with the excitement of the past three days, fell fast asleep the very same instant.

Platonida Andreevna did not dream; only in her deepest

slumbers she continually wanted to wake up because she knew that she still had to give her father-in-law his tea, and she even fancied her father-in-law was calling her and saying: "There you lie, Platonida, like a boiled cod! Get up then, give me some tea, please!" She kept on hearing it—twice, three times, four times, and finally, the fifth time, she heard it so clearly that she sat up on the coffer and cried:

"All right! Just a minute, father, just a minute!"

CHAPTER THE SIXTEENTH

PLATONIDA ANDREEVNA rubbed her eyes and looked round the room; all about her was pitch blackness; even the black wardrobe was indistinguishable from the yellow wall. But on the stove the yellow, shining samovar could just be discerned, and the long towels on a string seemed a patch of grey, like a corpse standing in its winding-sheet.

Platonida Andreevna puffed up some light, then put her hand under the coffer and brought out a cleaver, while from a corner she took a dry birch-log, intending to cut some shavings. But before chopping the log with the cleaver she thought: "What if I only thought I heard it all in my sleep? Supposing father is not yet awake?"

This thought made the young woman pick up the candle and go into the main room.

The big clock on the wall said half-past twelve. Platonida Andreevna tiptoed to the door of her father-in-law's room and pressed her ear to the jamb. All was quiet in the old man's bedroom.

"I must have been imagining it all," the widow decided, and with a yawn went back to her own room.

Again putting her door on the hook, Platonida Andreevna placed the candle on the table next to the window and began to undress.

"Well, I shouldn't grumble even at this bit of luck! I ought to be grateful for being able to live in my own room alone, without him, the pesterer," she thought, and, with an impatient gesture, throwing onto the floor the two pillows which were now superfluous, she loosened her skirt and sat down on the bed with an abandon she had never dared to display before in her life.

This tall, plump beauty, with the soul of a child and the strength of a man, with breasts that could have weaned a paladin, now reminded one of an innocent schoolgirl who, making up for years of restraint, thoroughly enjoyed a day's holiday.

The novel sensation of independence and freedom so filled her being and her thoughts that she no longer wanted to sleep; besides, she had had her sleep. Now she wanted to sit and think, think of heaven knows what, but only think. For so long she had not dared to take a step or say a word for fear of being pulled up and lectured, and here she was alone, there was no one to see her on that bed, no one to say: "What do you want to go hopping about for? Keep still, don't fidget."

She changed her position again and again; then she lay across the bed and raised herself again and, smiling at the two pillows which lay on the floor, she leapt up, stood quite still for a while, clasping her hands behind her head, shut her eyes, and a minute later, opening them, darted in a fright to a corner of the bed and trembled. On the top pillow of the dead Marko, which the light-hearted widow had flung on the floor—right in the middle appeared a little dip, as though someone unseen was resting his head there. Over that dip, at the spot where a picture of the Saviour is placed on the crown of a corpse, sat a grey night-moth. It sat raising itself on its thin legs, and alternately opened and shut its wings like a monk who, by flapping the sleeves of his gown, was blessing an unseen open grave.

Platonida shuddered. The dusty grey moth had, in the twinkling of an eye, annihilated her selfish joy. Meanwhile, the moth again, and for a third time, softly touched the pillow with its wings and just as softly detached itself and disappeared noiselessly out of the window and into the blackness of the warm night.

The widow rose quickly from the bed, closed the window after the departed moth with a hurried hand, and said: "Woe is me! It's a sin; I should not have thrown his pillows on the floor."

With the words she picked the pillows up and placed them on the empty ledge of the stove.

Just then she fancied she heard someone heave a sigh outside her door.

Platonida, in still greater haste, seized the pillows again, and placing them on the sofa under the ikon, quickly walked away from them and stood by her bed.

"O Lord, rest his soul," muttered the widow, feeling a warm gratitude towards her husband, because with his death he had left her mistress of at least this corner and the bed—"Well, I've sat up long enough."

And Platonida went on undressing.

CHAPTER THE SEVENTEENTH

BUT no sooner had the widow thrown off her clothes than in the utter stillness of the night she again fancied that someone had tinkled a glass by the cupboard in which her departed husband had always kept his wines and spirits under lock and key. Platonida Andreevna, having half pulled off her stocking, waited, and, hearing the sound no more, said to herself: "Probably mice gallivanting."

Having reassured herself with this thought, the young woman pulled her stockings off and approached the little parquet table that stood in front of the window; on it she placed the candle, and stretching lazily, began to change her day-chemise. But just as she unbuttoned the yoke and let it drop from her shoulder, she suddenly thought she saw something flit like a dark shadow along the verandah under her very window. She fancied it was a human shadow. Platonida Andreevna was impressionable, but she guessed that it was a living creature that had gone by, and not a denizen of another world, and quickly blowing out her candle she threw on her nightdress and thought:

"No—but what a swine that good-for-nothing Avenir has become! There's only one thing for it after that—to spit in his face."

And she determined firmly not to overlook this latest piece

of cheek on the young bounder's part. Platonida covered her bare shoulder with the old worn jacket in which we had seen her talking to Avenir in the kitchen-garden, and crept stealthily alongside the window-frame. On the verandah all was now still, and not a noise or rustle could be heard; but Platonida distrusted this stillness. She remained motionless, firmly resolved, at the first reappearance of the nocturnal prowler under her window, to wrench open the window and spit in his face.

CHAPTER THE EIGHTEENTH

THE deductions of Platonida Andreevna proved correct: the night-visitor did not keep her waiting long.

The partly-clad beauty had not been at her post by the window two minutes, when from the direction of the verandah, across the dark pane of glass, softly crept, first only the palm of a human hand, then an elbow appeared, next a shoulder, and finally the entire top half of a man's form. . . .

Dark as the moonless night was, illuminated only by occasional clusters of stars, yet the room grew darker still as its only window became entirely blocked by the form that had approached.

Platonida continued to stand stockstill, her hands pressed to her bosom, in which her impatient heart beat violently, and fluttered, despite herself, with terror and indignation. Notwithstanding her rage, however, the widow kept herself in hand, and with bated breath wondered how it would all finish.

The nocturnal Paul Pry stood and listened cautiously for a long time, then, encouraged by the complete stillness, softly touched with his finger the window-flaps, which closed from inside. He did this very cautiously, yet very clumsily. His fingers slipped repeatedly and the nails grated on the painted frame. Platonida quietly pushed her head towards the window and could now hear that the person who was scratching on it was breathing heavily and shaking all over. The more Platonida Andreevna, mastering her fear, held herself in hand, the more audacious did the other figure become. He was now beginning to shake the frame without fear of being heard.

"Why, if he goes on like that, the blackguard might wake father-in-law," thought Platonida Andreevna, and, overcome by her indignation, darted to the window, and became rooted to the spot.

It was not Avenir at all. By the window stood her white-haired father-in-law, Markel Semenych himself.

Platonida checked her outburst and her arms dropped in amazement.

On seeing his daughter-in-law before him, Markel Semenych for a moment appeared confused, but then muttered something dully and began to tap the glass gently with the knuckle of his middle finger.

"What do you want, father?" Platonida Andreevna forced herself to say, trying to keep her voice under control.

The old man whispered something softer still; but of this speech not a sound penetrated into the room.

"Can't hear you," said Platonida Andreevna, placing her ear to the joint of the window.

Markel Semenych proceeded passionately to kiss the glass where the elbow of Platonida Andreevna was pressed against it.

The daughter-in-law stared in horror at her relative and did not recognize him. The snow-white head of the old man, which resembled the noble head of Avenir, was dishevelled like that of a hoary Jupiter; his eyes were burning, and the white cotton shirt heaved and trembled on the quaking chest.

"Swan! My swan!" gasped the demented old man, clawing at the window like a greedy cat at a covered jug of milk.

"Father, I'll boil up a samovar for you in a minute," said the bewildered Platonida Andreevna, moving away from the window.

"No, don't boil any samovar . . . I don't want any samovar . . . you open the window . . . let me in . . . I've got a word to tell you . . . just a word . . ."

"Well, wait, father, I'll be dressed in no time."

"No, no, no, why should you dress? . . . you don't want to dress; don't dress; you hurry up and open . . . open."

"But, father, I've only got my shift on!"

"Well, why worry about a shift! . . . We aren't strangers, you and I, are we? . . . open for a minute," insisted the old man, fidgeting nervously.

Platonida became frightened, and darted aside, but no sooner had her white shoulder flashed in the blackness of the night before Markel Semenych's gaze, than the brass hook that held the window-frame clattered onto the sill as the result of a strong push, and the window opened with a crash, and the father-in-law's two arms seized the body of the daughter.

"Father! Father! Lord, what's this?" cried Platonida Andreevna, struggling desperately; but for answer her father-in-law, with a fierce movement, wrenched her arms apart and pressed his hot lips on her bare breast.

"Lecher! Get away!" Platonida gasped in disgust, as she felt on her bosom her father-in-law's dry, shaking beard.

Realizing now, at last, the true object of his visit, she plunged both her hands frantically into the old man's white hair and held his head away from her breast. The same instant she felt his strong sinewy hands tear her linen nightdress, and Platonida, almost naked, found herself in the arms of the love-demented patriarch.

"Avenir!" she cried, but the old man seized her throat and began to cover her lips with kisses.

He was very strong, and Platonida implored in vain:

"Father—mercy! I couldn't bear it from you!"

Markel Semenych only held his daughter's waist more firmly, and whispering hoarsely, "with me—not with a stranger"— swung his legs across the window-sill into the room.

Platonida Andreevna took advantage of this movement—she slipped to the floor between her father-in-law's arms, and in her hand there suddenly flashed the cleaver with which a little earlier she had intended to split the log of wood. Instantly the cleaver twanged and buried itself in the wooden support of the verandah, while Markel Semenych crashed heavily on his back and groaned. . . .

CHAPTER THE NINETEENTH

HAVING hurled the chopper at her father-in-law, Platonida Andreevna was positive that she had killed the old man. In speechless terror she leapt out of the room, ran across the yard, paused by the back gate, and, breathing heavily, clutched at her heart. In the stillness of the night a gasping rattle reached her ears. Platonida Andreevna was trembling; her head was filled with harsh, whistling noises, as though quite close to her a countless multitude of partridges was flashing past; the roofs and walls of the houses were swaying, and somewhere blood was dripping; prison, horrible, inhuman punishment, penal servitude for life, all passed in a whirl before the mental gaze of the widow—who only such a short time back had dreamt of life—and caused her to pull herself together with the energy of desperation. She folded her jacket over her bosom, crawled stealthily under the gate into the kitchen-garden, from the kitchen-garden she made her way over the wattles and behind the kitchen-garden, and breaking into a run beyond it, disappeared into the darkness of the night.

Meanwhile, Markel Semenych breathed heavily as he lay on the verandah. Platonida Andreevna's blow had missed his white head—but had missed it only because, a fraction of a second before the blow, Avenir's two strong arms had seized his father from behind and thrown him to the ground, just as the axe, after slightly grazing the old man's shoulder, buried itself deep in the woodwork. Markel Semenych felt neither his guilt nor his shame and disgrace. There was no longer any lust in his blood now, nor indignation in his heart, nor strength in his muscles. His old flesh, fired by wine and excited by the passion of desire, had suddenly become weak and impotent. Thus, a mountain-stream, lying dormant under the snow, will sometimes leap into life with the warmth of the March sun, will roar in a wild torrent under the mantle of snow, and reaching a rocky ledge, will crash with all its force to the ice-covered bed down below.

    .   .   .   .   .

Seeing no attempt at a struggle on his father's part, Avenir held him for a time on the floor, and then let him go and himself made off in silence. The old man, on finding himself alone, took some time to come round, and did not realize at once the shameful situation in which he now found himself.

As for Platonida's escape, neither he nor Avenir knew any-thing about it that night. They both thought that she had locked herself in her storeroom in the turret. The first in the house to think of her next day was Avenir. He searched for her high and low, and could not find her anywhere. Old Markel Semenych kept to his room and did not show himself.

Platonida Andreevna had vanished. Nowhere were any traces of her to be found, and her disappearance became the cause of great misfortune to one who, in the entire affair, was the least guilty of all.

Compelled to explain somehow the disappearance of his daughter-in-law, and not being certain what she herself would tell when she was found, Markel Semenych crowned his night of madness with perjury to the effect that Platonida and Avenir had wanted to kill and rob him, and showed his wound. In this way the old man revenged himself on his son and daughter-in-law and rid himself of both at once. Avenir was taken to prison, while police investigation established that some water-men, who had been working that night on a barge that was being overhauled, saw how someone, all in white, either a woman, or, more likely still, a witch, had run rapidly along the bank and suddenly vanished. Two of the watermen main-tained that the witch turned into a fish and jumped into the water, but two others swore, on the contrary, that they saw clearly how she swam across the river in a white shift and emerged on the melon plantation of Konstantin Pizonsky.

Pizonsky fell under suspicion of harbouring Deev's daughter-in-law; his place was searched and he was questioned and lodged in gaol and threatened with transportation. Although Konstantin Ionych, to all the questions put to him by the investigating magistrate, replied only that: "I never knew or connived at anything like that, dearie," it was as clear as daylight that, in all the world perhaps, Pizonsky alone knew where Deev's vanished daughter-in-law had got to. The judges, as well as the townspeople, felt keenly that, to clear up this mysterious affair, all that was needed was that Konstantin Pizonsky should unlock his silent lips. The judges maintained that the Robinson Crusoe of Stary Gorod was lying when he denied all share in the disappearance of Platonida Andreevna, and that perhaps he himself had had a hand in the attempt on the life of old Deev. The people, too, did not deny that Konstantin Ionych was lying when he repeated his "don't know; I've no idea"; but the townspeople were certain that Pizonsky was lying to shield someone else's sin. Whether this is right or wrong, the people are not very clear, but they believe that "there is a lie unto salvation".

CHAPTER THE TWENTIETH

IN connection with the case, Konstantin Ionych was kept in prison for some time and eventually released under suspicion, but nothing was learned from him that could shed any light on Platonida's whereabouts. Later it was said, and firmly believed, that Platonida did not go far, but was given shelter by the nuns, and that the "Seer", the Venerable Nun Ioyl, who appeared just about that time at the convent, was the same Platonida. She had "wept out her eyes", and was blind, and found her way about with a stick, and in her empty eye-sockets she carried little ikons. As for Avenir, it was said that, having been conscripted into the Army, he became "a great warrior in the Caucasus", had earned for himself "an officer's rank and a cross", and thanks to his handsome appearance had married a General's daughter. Once, it was maintained, he even visited Stary Gorod and went to the convent and saw the Venerable Ioyl, but she could not see him, but recognized him by his voice and gave a start, and passed her hands over his head and asked:

"Has this head repented yet?"

Avenir replied:

"It has repented."

"That is good," said the Venerable Ioyl: "fortify with your mind your path to the haven of blessing," and then added:

"And now farewell, with the blessing of God, for ever."

THE SPIRIT OF
MADAME DE GENLIS

THE QUEER INCIDENT WHICH IT IS MY INTENTION
to relate occurred several years ago and may now be published
with impunity, especially as I reserve the right, in doing so,
not to mention a single real name.

In the winter of 1862 there came to settle in St. Petersburg
a very wealthy and distinguished family, which consisted of
three persons: the mother—a middle-aged lady and a princess,
who was held to be a woman of refined education, and who
possessed the most excellent connections in Russia and abroad;
her son—a young man who had just been launched upon a
career in the diplomatic service; and a daughter—the young
princess, who was barely in her seventeenth year.

The newly arrived family had, until then, usually resided
abroad, where the late husband of the elder princess occupied
the post of Russian representative to one of the minor courts
of Europe. The young prince and princess were born and had
grown up abroad, where they received an entirely foreign yet
very careful upbringing.

CHAPTER THE SECOND

THE princess was a woman of exceedingly rigid rules, and
justly enjoyed a blameless reputation in Society. In her opinions
and tastes she adhered to the views held by Frenchwomen who
had won fame and prominence by their wit and talent during
the heyday of feminine wit and talent in France. The princess
was considered very well read, and it was declared that she
read with the greatest discrimination. Her favourite writings
were the letters of Mme Sévigné, Lafayette and Maintenon, as
well as Coclus and D'Ango Coulenge, but above all she respected Mme de Genlis, towards whom she entertained a weak-

ness that amounted to a cult. The little volumes of the work of this intelligent writer, published in Paris, and bound with restrained elegance in sky-blue morocco, always rested upon a handsome wall-bracket hanging above a large armchair which was the princess's favourite seat. Over the mother-o'-pearl incrustation surmounting the bracket itself, and depending from a cushion of black velvet, was an excellently fashioned replica in terra-cotta of the little hand that Voltaire was wont to kiss in the seclusion of Ferney, never suspecting that it would let fall upon him the first drop of delicate yet mordant criticism. How often the princess re-read the little volumes penned by this dainty hand I could not say; but they were always at her elbow, and the princess maintained that they held for her a particular, so to speak, mysterious significance, the nature of which she would not permit herself to divulge to all and sundry, inasmuch as it was not everyone to whom understanding had been vouchsafed. Judging from her utterances, one was inclined to believe that she had not been parted from these volumes since "as far as she can remember", and that they would rest with her in her grave.

"My son," she would say, "has been instructed by me to place the books beside me in my coffin, and I am certain that I will find them useful even after death."

I expressed a cautious wish for some elucidation of this last remark, and obtained it.

"These little tomes," said the princess, "are impregnated with the spirit of Felicity" (thus she referred to Mme de Genlis, as an indication, no doubt, of their intimate friendship). "Yes, holding a sacred belief in the immortality of the human spirit, I also believe in the capacity of the spirit to create a contact from beyond the grave quite freely with those who require this contact and who prize it. I am certain that the thin fluid of Felicity has chosen for itself a pleasant spot beneath the morocco that protects the leaves upon which her thoughts have come to rest, and if you are not a complete unbeliever, I hope that this will be clear to you."

I bowed in silence. The princess was to all appearances pleased that I did not argue with her, and as a reward she added

that all that she had just told me was not only her belief, but a
real and complete conviction so deeply rooted that no powers
could shake it.

"And the reason for that is," she concluded, "that I possess
masses of proof that the spirit of Felicity lives, and lives precisely there."

With these last words the princess raised her hand above her
head and pointed a bejewelled finger at the bracket upon which
stood the sky-blue volumes.

CHAPTER THE THIRD

I AM, by nature, a little superstitious, and always listen with
pleasure to stories that contain a modicum of the supernatural.
For this, I believe, the omniscient critics, who classify me according to various unpleasant categories, suggested at one time that I
was a spiritualist.

It may not be inappropriate to mention here that all this, of
which we are now speaking, took place precisely at a time
when, from abroad, a spate of reports about spiritualist
phenomena began to spread in Russia. They excited
curiosity, and I did not see any reason why I should not
take an interest in what some people began to accept quite
seriously.

The "masses of proof", of which the princess spoke, she would
refer to constantly. The proof consisted in the fact that the
princess, for many years past, had formed a habit, during
moments when her mind was perplexed by divers problems
that required a decision, of resorting to the writings of Mme de
Genlis as to an oracle; and the sky-blue volumes, in their turn,
displayed an invariable gift for replying with great wisdom
to her mental questions.

This, according to the princess, became with her a "habitude"
to which she remained ever true, and the "spirit" that dwelt
in the books never once told her anything inappropriate.

I saw that I was confronted with a convinced follower of
spiritualism, and one who lacked neither brains, experience,

nor education, and so I found myself growing highly intrigued by it all.

I was already familiar with one or two characteristics of the nature of spirits, and on the occasions when I happened to have witnessed them I was always struck by a peculiarity common to all spirits, namely, that when they rose from the grave they behaved with far greater skittishness and, truth to tell, stupidity than they had ever displayed during their earthly existence.

I already knew of Kardeck's theory about "mischievous spirits", and I was now very interested to see how the witty spirit of Marquise Sillery, Countess Brusslar, would deign to manifest itself in my presence.

The occasion was not long in arriving; but since in a short story, as in a small household, one should not disturb an established order, I beg another minute's patience before coming to the supernatural moment that exceeded all expectations.

CHAPTER THE FOURTH

THE persons who composed the small but very exclusive circle of the princess knew, of course, about this oddity of hers. But as they were all people of good breeding and impeccable manners, they were accustomed to respect other people's beliefs even when those beliefs diverged sharply from their own and were not worth their criticism. And so nobody ever argued with the princess about her strange theories. True, this may partly have been due to the fact that the friends of the princess were not quite certain that she really considered her sky-blue volumes an abode of the "spirit" of their author in a direct sense, but thought her words were a rhetorical form of expression. Or again, perhaps it was all very much simpler, and they really treated the whole matter as a joke.

The only person who could not view the situation from such an angle was, unfortunately, myself; and I had my own reasons for this, which were, perhaps, to be found in my credulity and my impressionable nature.

CHAPTER THE FIFTH

THE good graces of this Society lady, who had opened to me the doors of her very respectable home, I owed to three circumstances. Firstly, for some reason she liked my story "The Sealed Angel", which, shortly before, had appeared in "The Russian News"; secondly, she became interested in the fierce persecution to which I was subjected for so many years and on so many occasions by my dear literary *confrères*, who, of course, wished to correct my lack of understanding and my delusions; and thirdly, I was very well recommended to the princess by Prince Gagarin, a Russian Jesuit who lived in Paris—the kindliest of old gentlemen, with whom I had many pleasant talks and whose opinion of me was not of the worst.

This last circumstance was especially important, because the princess was very anxious to obtain a clear picture of my views and mental outlook. She had designs upon my services, or fancied that she might have need of them. This may seem strange for a man of so modest a station as mine, but it was so. These calls upon my services were dictated to the princess by her motherly concern for her daughter, who was almost completely ignorant of the Russian language. In bringing this delightful young girl to the land to which she belonged, the mother wished to find a person who could to some extent instruct the young princess in Russian Literature—only Good Literature, of course, i.e. genuine literature, that was not infected with "current problems".

Concerning these latter the princess had some very vague ideas, and, it seemed, very exaggerated ones. It was rather difficult to follow what it was exactly that she feared from the contemporary giants of letters—whether it was their strength and audacity or their weakness and pitiable self-confidence. But by catching somehow, with the aid of intuition and guesswork, the "head and tail" of the princess's own thoughts, I concluded—the only correct conclusion, to my way of thinking— that she most definitely feared "impure suggestions", with which, according to her, our immodest literature was irretrievably ruined.

It was no use trying to make the princess alter her views, because she had reached that stage of her life when opinions become set and fixed, and it is not often that anyone at her age is capable of subjecting them to a revision and revaluation. Certainly she was not one of these exceptional beings, and to make her doubt that in which she had absolute faith was beyond the power of an ordinary mortal; the only being who might prove capable of working a change in her would be some spirit that came for the purpose from hell or from heaven. But could such a worldly matter occupy the insubstantial spirits of the unknown world? Would not all the wrangles and concern about literature appear as petty to them as they do to a great many of the living, who deem them a senseless occupation of idle minds?

However, circumstances soon showed that in arguing in this way I was very much mistaken. The urge for literary indiscretions, as we shall presently see, does not desert literary spirits even beyond the grave, and it will be for the reader to decide to what extent the spirits act successfully and remain faithful to their literary past.

CHAPTER THE SIXTH

OWING to the fact that the princess held definitive views on everything, my task of helping her to select literary works for the young princess was strictly circumscribed. The requirement was that the young princess should, from her reading, obtain a knowledge of Russian life, and yet in doing so should come across nothing that could offend her chaste ear. The maternal censorship of the princess never accepted completely a single recommendation—not even Derzhavin or Zhoukovsky. They all seemed to her suspect to some degree. Of Gogol, of course, there could not even be any mention—he was damned, lock, stock and barrel. Of Pushkin's works the following were reprieved: "The Captain's Daughter" and "Eugene Onegin" —the latter considerably bowdlerized by the hand of the princess herself. Lermontov—like Gogol—was also banned. Of the later authors, only Turgenev was undoubtedly approved of, but even then with the exception of passages that "spoke of love", while Goncharov was rejected, and although I championed his cause stoutly, it was no use, and the princess replied:

"I know that he is a great artist, but that makes it all the worse. You must know that he contains inflaming subjects."

CHAPTER THE SEVENTH

I FELT I *had* to know precisely what the princess meant by her "inflaming subjects", which she had discovered in the works of Goncharov. How could he possibly, with all his mild attitude towards humanity and the passions that ruled them, offend anybody's susceptibilities?

I was so curious that I mustered my courage and asked her point-blank what Goncharov's "inflaming subjects" were.

To this direct question I received an equally direct and very brief answer, delivered in a strident whisper: "Elbows".

For a moment I thought I was mistaken or had not understood her.

"Elbows, elbows," repeated the princess, and, noting my puzzled air, she appeared annoyed. "Don't you remember . . . what's-his-name—that hero of his, somewhere . . . peers at the elbows of his . . . very common woman?"

Now of course I remembered the well-known scene from "Oblomov", and was struck speechless. Perhaps it was just as well I said nothing, because I was in no mood to argue with a person incapable of being converted to any other view, and whom, truth to tell, I found myself more interested to study than to serve with my views and advice. And what could I say after the disclosure that she considered the idea of "elbows" a piece of indecency, and when all our latest literature had gone far beyond these indelicate allusions?

Courage was indeed required—knowing all this—to mention a single contemporary work in which the screen of beauty is raised with a much greater determination.

I felt that in the circumstances my role of adviser should come to an end, and I decided not to offer any more advice, but to fight out the question.

"Princess," said I, "I think you are being unfair: in your demands on artistic literature there are exaggerations."

I put before her all that, in my opinion, had any bearing upon the matter.

CHAPTER THE EIGHTH

WARMING up to my task, I delivered not only a critical lecture on false prudery but quoted the well-known anecdote of the French lady who could not bring herself either to write or utter the word "calotte", and then, when she was once obliged to use the word in the presence of the queen, faltered, which caused an outburst of laughing. I could not at the time recall the name of the French author who described this distressing Court *contretemps*, which would not have taken place had the lady uttered the word "calotte" as simply as the queen herself pronounced it with her august lips.

My object was to show that excessive diffidence may be harmful to modesty and that too strict a choice of reading was, therefore, scarcely necessary.

The princess, greatly to my astonishment, heard me without manifesting the least sign of displeasure, and, without leaving her seat, raised her hand above her head and took down one of the sky-blue volumes.

"You have arguments," she said, "while I have an oracle."

"I am most interested to hear it," I said.

"It will not take long: I call upon the spirit of Genlis, and it will answer you. Open the book and read."

"Will you be good enough to show me where I must read?" I said, taking the little volume from her.

"Show you? That is not my business: the spirit itself will show you. Open at random."

I was beginning to feel a bit ridiculous and even slightly embarrassed on the princess's account; nevertheless I did exactly as she wished, and no sooner had my eyes alighted on the first passage on the page that opened, than I experienced a feeling of annoyed surprise.

"You are confounded?"

"Yes."

"Yes: that has happened to many people. I would ask you to read."

CHAPTER THE NINTH

"READING is an occupation too serious and important in its consequences for the tastes of young people not to be guided. There is reading which is liked by the young, but it makes them casual and inclined to superficiality, following which it is difficult to improve the character. All this I have experienced myself." That is what I read, and stopped.

The princess, with a gentle smile, made a circular motion with her hands, and delicately enjoying her triumph, murmured:

"In Latin, I believe, this is known as *dixi*?"

"You are quite right."

From that day on we argued no more, but the princess could not deny herself the pleasure of expatiating occasionally in my presence upon the ill-breeding of Russian authors, whose works, she held, "it is quite impossible to read aloud without a preliminary perusal."

Of the spirit of Mme de Genlis I naturally did not think seriously. One hears so much of these things nowadays.

But the "spirit" lived all right, and was quite definitely active, and further, strange to say, was on our side, i.e. on the side of literature. The literary nature in it got the better of mere dry reasoning, and the impeccable "spirit" of Mme de Genlis, speaking suddenly *du fond du cœur*, let fly (indeed "let fly") in the prim *salon* such an unseemly sally that its consequences involved us in profound tragi-comedy.

CHAPTER THE TENTH

ONCE a week, in the evening, the princess entertained "three friends" to tea. They were all worthy men in an excellent position. Two of them were senators, and the third a diplomat.

Naturally the time was not spent over cards, but in conversation.

As a rule the talking was done by the seniors, i.e. the princess and the "three friends", while the young prince, princess and I very rarely put in a word. We were more in the position of learners, and to give our elders their due, there was much we could learn from them—especially from the diplomat, who surprised us by his shrewd remarks.

I enjoyed his good graces. He was most friendly towards me, though I do not know why. Actually I was led to think that he did not rank me any higher than the rest, for, in his view, all writers were "sprung from the same root". He maintained jokingly that "the best of serpents is still a serpent".

It was this opinion of his that gave rise to the distressing occurrence that follows.

CHAPTER THE ELEVENTH

THE princess was staunchly loyal to all her friends, and she did not wish this general opinion to be extended to Mme de Genlis and the female "Pleiad" which that author had taken under her protection. And so, when we happened to be gathered in the house of the worthy princess for a quiet New Year's celebration, and the conversation turned, shortly before midnight, to the usual subjects, in which the name of Mme de Genlis was mentioned, and the diplomat recalled his remark that "even the best of serpents is still a serpent", the princess said : "There are no rules without exceptions."

The diplomat guessed *who* the exception should be, and said nothing. But the princess could not restrain herself, and, casting a glance in the direction of de Genlis' portrait, said :

"Who can maintain she is a serpent ?"

However, the diplomat, with his experience of life, insisted that he was right. He gently wagged a finger before him and was smiling gently—he did not believe in flesh or spirit.

To decide their difference of opinion, proof was obviously required, and here reference to the "spirit" was quite appropriate.

Our little group was excellently disposed for an experiment

of this nature, and our hostess first reminded us of what we already knew about her belief, and then proposed a test:

"I can vouch for it," she said, "that the most exacting person will not find in de Genlis anything of a nature that may not be read aloud by the most innocent girl, and we will try it out straight away."

Again, as on the previous occasion, she threw back her hand over her head towards the bookcase that hung above her settee, took down a volume at random, and turned to her daughter:

"My child! Open and read us a page."

The young princess obeyed.

We all assumed attitudes expressive of the most profound attention.

CHAPTER THE TWELFTH

IF a writer begins to depict the outward appearance of his characters at the end of his tale, he is deserving of censure; but I wrote this trifle in such a way that no one may be recognized. So I disclosed no names and painted no portraits. Besides, the portrait of the young princess would have been beyond the powers of description, because she was in every respect what is known as "an angel incarnate". As regards her perfect purity and innocence—it was such that she could even have been trusted to solve the insuperably difficult theosophical problem which was debated by Heine's "Benardiner und Rabiner". Surely for this soul, untainted by any sin, something that stood above this world and its passions should speak. And the young princess, with precisely that innocence, with a most attractive purl peculiar to the French tongue, read de Genlis' interesting recollections of Mme du Deffant in her old age "when she became feeble in the eyes". The record spoke of the bloated Gibbon, who was introduced to the French diarist as a famous author. De Genlis, it will be remembered, soon saw through him and bitingly ridiculed those compatriots of hers who were carried off their feet by the inflated reputation of the foreigner.

Further, I quote from a translation of the French original

THE TALES OF LESKOV

which was read by the young princess, who was capable of deciding the argument between "Benardiner und Rabiner".

"Gibbon is small of stature, exceedingly fat, and has a most surprising face. In this face it is impossible to distinguish a single feature. Neither nose nor eyes nor mouth can be seen at all: two fat, puffy cheeks that look like heaven knows what swallow up everything. . . . They have become so inflated that they have lost even such respectable proportions as would be permitted for the largest cheeks: anyone seeing them must have been puzzled to know why this region had been put in the wrong place. I would have described Gibbon's face in one word if it had been possible to utter the word. Lauzun, who was on intimate terms with Gibbon, once brought him to du Deffant. Mme du Deffant at the time was already blind, and had a habit of using her hands to feel the faces of the remarkable people who were presented to her for the first time. Thus she acquired a fairly correct idea of the features of the newcomer. To Gibbon she applied the same method of touch, and it was dreadful. The Englishman approached her armchair and with a particular *bonhomie* presented to her this extraordinary face of his. She searched diligently for something to get hold of, but it was impossible. Then the face of the blind old lady expressed astonishment first of all, then anger, and finally, quickly jerking back her hands with disgust, she cried: 'What a dirty joke'."

CHAPTER THE THIRTEENTH

THIS was the end of the experiment, and of the gathering of friends and the awaited arrival of the New Year, because when the young princess, closing the book, asked, "What was it that had appeared to Mme du Deffant?" the face of the old princess was so terrible that the girl gave a shriek, clapped her hands to her face and rushed into another room, from which we at once heard her weeping with a sound like hysterics.

The brother ran to his sister, and at the same instant the old princess quickly strode thither with a majestic step.

The presence of strangers was now inappropriate, and therefore all the "three friends" and I at once slunk out, and the bottle of Veuve Cliquot that had been got ready for greeting the New Year remained wrapped in its napkin, unopened.

CHAPTER THE FOURTEENTH

THE feelings with which our party broke up were oppressive, but did not redound to the credit of our hearts, because, though our faces were set in an expression of forced seriousness, we could hardly keep back the laughter with which we were exploding, and we bent down with unnecessary diligence to search for our goloshes,—which we were forced to do because the servants had also stampeded on account of the alarm occasioned by the sudden illness of the young princess.

The senators got into their sleighs, while the diplomat decided to join me in a stroll. He wished to get a breath of fresh air, and I think he was curious to know my humble opinion about what could have presented itself to the mental gaze of the young princess after reading that passage from the writings of Mme de Genlis.

But I positively dared not make any conjectures about this aspect of the affair.

CHAPTER THE FIFTEENTH

SINCE that unfortunate day on which the incident took place I never again saw either the princess or her daughter. I could not bring myself to go and wish her a Happy New Year, but merely sent round to enquire after the health of the young princess, and this with great uncertainty, lest it should be taken the wrong way. On the other hand, visits of "condolence" appeared to me quite out of place. The position was of the silliest nature : I felt it was rude to cease visiting a friendly house so abruptly, yet to appear there also seemed inept.

Perhaps I was wrong in my conclusions, but they appeared

correct to me. And I was not mistaken: the blow the princess had experienced on New Year's Eve from the "spirit" of Mme de Genlis was very serious and had serious consequences.

CHAPTER THE SIXTEENTH

ABOUT a month later I ran into the diplomat in the Nevsky. He was very friendly, and we had a chat.

"Haven't seen you for a long time," he said.

"There's nowhere we can meet now," I answered.

"Yes, we have lost the charming house of the worthy princess: she was obliged to go away, poor thing."

"What do you mean—go away?" said I. "Where?"

"Do you mean to tell me you don't know?"

"I don't know anything."

"They have gone abroad, and I am very happy that I was able to fix up her son there. There was nothing else to do after what happened that night. What a deplorable occurrence! The unfortunate lady, you know, that same night burnt all her volumes and broke the terra-cotta hand into atoms—though, I understand, one finger, or rather, a knob, escaped as a memento. On the whole, a most unfortunate business, and yet it serves as an excellent illustration of one great truth."

"To my mind—of two or three."

The diplomat smiled, and looking at me fixedly, asked:

"How?"

"Firstly, it proves that books we venture to speak of should first be read."

"And secondly?"

"And secondly, that it is unwise to keep a young girl in such a state of childlike ignorance as the young princess had been in prior to this incident; otherwise she would certainly have stopped reading about Gibbon much earlier."

"And thirdly?"

"Thirdly, that you can't rely on spirits any more than you can on living beings."

"And all that is not the point. The spirit confirms an opinion of mine that 'the best of serpents is still a serpent'; and further, 'the better the serpent, the more dangerous it is, because it carries its poison in its tail'."

Had we possessed a satirical school, this would have been an excellent subject for it.

Unhappily, since I possess no satirical talents, I can relate this tale only in the form of a simple narrative.

THE STINGER

(A TALE OF PRE-REFORM RUSSIA)

UNDER THE LATE GOVERNOR WE WERE NOT allowed to smoke in the Chancellery. The senior officials usually smoked in a little room behind the Assistant-Governor's office, and the juniors in the watchman's room. This smoking accounted for more than half the working time of our officials. My colleagues and I, who worked on Special Missions, were not obliged to stick to the office, and therefore had no need for official smoking corners; nevertheless we all felt in duty bound to come in regularly for the purpose of adding our smoke to that of the others in the room behind the Assistant-Governor's office. This room was our meeting-place, to which we were all anxious to slink off for a chat, for gossip, fun and advice. The sessions here sometimes lasted till the commissionaire, Kuzmich, opened the door and proclaimed: "The Assistant-Governor has left, gentlemen."

One day, after a spell of hard work going over an investigation I had just concluded, I went out for a stroll. The weather was lovely—it was warm, the roofs were dripping, and pools of water lay in the streets. Step by step I reached Bolkhovsky Street and decided to drop in at the Chancellery for a smoke. The Assistant-Governor had gone to the Governor with a report. In the room behind his office I found his two assistants, the Chief of Police, and one of my colleagues just back from an investigation in a distant area. After shaking the hands that were proffered me, I lit a cigarette and sat down on the window-sill, without interrupting the conversation that had been begun before my arrival. The young official who had just returned from his Special Mission was relating with some heat the abuses he had discovered in the M— Police District. There was really nothing of particular interest in his narrative, and the person most interested in it was the speaker himself, who believed that, in our administrative organization, to discover abuse meant advancing a step towards its extirpation. Of the two Assistant-Controllers, one looked as though he was listening, while the other unceremoniously drummed upon the window-pane with his fingers, and the Police Chief, sitting astride his cavalry sword, blew smoke-rings from under his moustache and looked as though he was on the point of saying: "You are a silly young man!"

While we were thus engaged, the door leading to the Assistant-Governor's room was thrown open and the Assistant-Governor said to someone inside his room:

"This is our Club. Would you like to have a smoke in here? I'll be free in half a second and will be at your service."

In the doorway appeared a tall gentleman, aged about forty, with glasses, a small bald patch on his head and a kindly expression on his face.

"Mr. Dane," said the Assistant-Governor, introducing the newcomer to us. "Mr. Dane has come, gentlemen, with a Power of Attorney from Prince K— to manage his estate. Allow me to introduce to you. These are my assistants— Mr. N, Mr. X, Mr. Y, Mr. Z," continued the Assistant-Governor, presenting us to Mr. Dane. There followed a shaking of hands and muttered "Pleased to meet you", "How do you do", etc. The Assistant-Governor and the Chief of Police went out into the office, while we settled down again to our interrupted *dolce far niente.*

"Have you been in our part of the country long?" enquired my young colleague of Mr. Dane with an amiable smile.

"This is my first visit to the Orel Province, and I only came here yesterday," Mr. Dane replied with a no less amiable smile.

"Oh yes; that wasn't what I asked. I meant to say—are you already familiar with our Province?"

"I don't know how to put it: yes and no. I am familiar with the Prince's estates from reports I used to get at the Head Office and from what the Prince told me. But . . . I suppose the Orel Province is the same as the Voronezh Province and Poltava Province, where I have managed the Prince's estates."

"Well, not quite," put in one of the Assistant-Controllers, who enjoyed with us a reputation as a politico-economist.

"In what respect is the Orel Province especially peculiar?"
Mr. Dane turned to him. "I shall feel greatly obliged to you
for your experienced views."

"Oh, in many ways."

"Oh, I dare not presume to argue; but I am most interested
to know exactly in what way. I may come a cropper if I keep
in the Orel Province to the system of management I adopted
since I first came to Russia."

The politico-economist made no reply, because the young
official chipped in with a question:

"And have you been in Russia long?"

"Over six years," Dane replied.

"You are . . . if I am not mistaken . . ."

"I am an Englishman."

"And yet you speak such good Russian."

"Oh yes. I studied Russian while I was still in England, and
now, getting on for seven years, I've been hobnobbing with
the peasants daily: there's nothing surprising in that!"

"You've got used to our people and our way of living?"

"So I believe," Dane replied with a smile.

"The Prince's estates are not doing too well in our Province."

"No, so I've been told."

"You'll find it very hard here."

"As everywhere."

"Perhaps harder than in any other place."

"Why do you think so?"

"You know, our Province is famous throughout Russia."

"Yes. But I've already had some experience of the people
from here. About two years ago I had to deal in Nizhni with
two hundred families of Orel peasants and accompanied them
down the Volga as far as Syzran, where I settled them on the
lands that had been granted to the Prince. It wasn't so bad. All
you need is system. You mustn't be a brute with them, or a
softie, but do the thing systematically, firmly, with insistence,
yet intelligently. You need system in everything."

"And where do you intend to take up your residence?" asked
the politico-economist.

"I think at Soltykovo."

"Why not at Zhizhki? That's where the late princess lived; there's a house all ready there, and servants; I believe there is nothing at Soltykovo," remarked the young official.

"I have certain reasons of my own for that."

"Your own system," interposed the Assistant-Controller, with a laugh.

"Precisely."

The Assistant-Governor, his hat on his head, opened the door and said to Dane: "Let's be going!"

We shook hands all round again, and the meeting broke up.

Soltykovo is quite near the Gostomelsky Farmsteads. The distance, they reckon, between them is not more than six miles, and one always hears in one about the goings on at the other. When my duties took me to the Kromy District, I usually seized the opportunity of calling at the Farmsteads and looking up my mother and seeing how her little farm was doing. My mother made the acquaintance of Stuart Yakovlevich Dane and of his wife, and every time she saw me she couldn't stop praising her new neighbours. She was especially delighted with Dane himself. "There," she would say, "is a real man for you: clever, full of common sense and orderly. He's meticulous in everything he does: he knows how much he can spend, how much he must put aside—in other words, you can see he's not suffered from our idiotic upbringing. If our gentry could only understand and appreciate people like him, things would have been different long ago."

The other neighbours were also full of Dane: "Dane says you've got to do it this way"; "Dane's advice is to do it that way"—that's all you heard. There were endless stories about him. We heard how everything was changed on the Prince's estates from the moment Stuart Yakovlevich came—everything, we were told, was going full swing; he'd found employment even for the out-and-out thieves with which our part of the country is so thick. And that wasn't all: he'd made supervisors of the most outstanding ne'er-do-wells; while as for thieves who had several prison sentences behind them—why, he made them stewards and storekeepers and accountants, and everything with him seemed to go like clockwork, and he was the envy of the

District. "There," I thought to myself: "the Kromy peasants seem to have met their match at last."

I was very keen to have a look for myself at these Soltykovo marvels, but somehow the opportunity never presented itself. And meanwhile about eighteen months went by, and it was winter again.

On the evening of December 4th a gendarme brought me a note in which the official on duty asked me to see the Governor at eleven that same evening.

"I believe you are a local man?" the Governor asked when I presented myself before him as requested.

I replied in the affirmative.

"You have lived in the Kromy District?"

"I spent my childhood there."

"And you have many friends there?" the Governor continued to question me.

"What's he after?" I wondered as I faced this examination, and replied that I knew nearly everyone in the District quite well.

"I have to ask a favour of you," began the Governor. "Prince K— writes to me from Paris that he sent to his estates here an Englishman named Dane, a very experienced man, whom the Prince has known very well for years as a first-rate person, and yet he's inundated with complaints against him. Will you be a friend and—quite unofficially—will you go to the Kromy District and find out the rights and wrongs of this business, so that I can act with justice in the matter?"

I went to Kromy the same night and was at my mother's in time for morning tea. There nothing was known about any complaints by the Kromy peasants against Dane. I asked my mother whether she had heard anything about the Soltykovo peasants?

"No, I have heard nothing," she said. "But what could be wrong, when they have Stuart Yakovlevich?"

"Perhaps he's hot-tempered."

"Of course he makes demands, as he should do."

"Perhaps he's too fond of birching?"

"Good heavens! Gracious! Why, he doesn't have any

birchings at all! The only birchings people get is by sentence
of the *mir*. . . ."

"Perhaps he . . ."

"What?"

"Likes other people's girls?"

"You are a fool! Fool—that's what you are!" cried my
mother with feeling, and spat in disgust.

"But why are you so angry, mother?"

"What are you talking nonsense for?"

"Why nonsense? You know perfectly well things like that
happen."

"Do use your brains: he's married, isn't he?"

"But your nephew Iosaph Mikhailovich is a married man too."

"Get along with you!" my mother cried again, scarcely able
to suppress a smile.

"Well, he must have put the peasants' backs up somehow."

"But what are you to do with our peasants? Tatterdemalions
they ever were and tatterdemalions they'll remain. Mischief
and thieving—that's all they want."

I called at one or two neighbouring houses—the result was
the same. On St. Nicholas' Day there was a fair at our village.
I dropped in at the priest's house for a chat with the Churchmen,
trying in my conversation to find out the reason why the peasants
were dissatisfied with Dane, but everywhere the answer was
the same: Stuart Yakovlevich was a manager the equal of
whom you could not find anywhere. "He's like a father to the
peasants," I was assured. What was I to do? The peasants
must simply be lying, I told myself. I felt I would have to go
back to Orel without having achieved anything.

At Kromy I called—without any particular object—on an
old friend of my father's, a merchant called Rukavichnikov. I
only wanted to warm myself with some tea at the old man's
while the post-horses were being brought, but he refused to let
me go till I had had some dinner. "It's my youngest son's
birthday to-day," he insisted. "There's a *pirog* sitting in the
oven right now, and you talk of going! No, you mustn't
dream of it. Else I'll call my old woman and the girls and get
them to prostrate themselves before you." I had to stay.

"Meanwhile, let's go and have some tea," said Rukavich-nikov.

A pot-bellied samovar was brought to us to the mezzanine, and my host and I settled down to tea.

"Well, lad, have you been here on pleasure, business or of your own free will?" Rukavichnikov asked me when we sat down and he had brewed the tea and covered the teapot with a white towel.

"Well—on business and pleasure and of my own free will, Petr Ananyich," I replied.

"I guess your Big Noise is starting something about the Old Believers again?"

"No, it isn't that, thank God."

"What sort of a business is it then?"

I knew that Petr Ananyich was very well disposed towards me and that he was a man of brains and tact, and knew the District intimately.

"This is what I am on now," I said—"a fiddling sort of business, and yet a queer one," and I told him of my mission.

Petr Ananyich listened to me with rapt attention, and during my recital smiled to himself several times; and when I had finished he merely remarked: "There's a problem for you, lad."

"And do you know Dane?"

"Of course I knows him, sir! Very well too."

"Well, and what have you to say about him?"

"Well, what can I say about him?..." said the old man, making a circular motion with his hands.

"Is he a decent sort of chap?"

"Must be a decent sort."

"Honest?"

"It would be a sin to think otherwise."

"Is he too strict, or what?"

"Haven't heard anything about that."

"Well, then, what's wrong—why are they complaining?"

"I suppose—put it this way... the mouzhiks somehow just can't digest him—so they grouse."

"But why can't they digest him?"

"They say his methods are too burdensome."

"Does he overload them with work, or what?" I persisted, trying to draw out Rukavichnikov.

"Overload them! Why, they're doing half the work they used to before. . . . Ah! Wait a moment.—Filat! Filat!" Rukavichnikov cried, opening a small pane in the window.— "Now we'll hear a tale of woe," he added, closing the window and resuming his seat at the table.

Into the room crawled a small, wizened, myopic man, with diseased eyes, who proceeded to cross himself before the ikons.

"Greeting, Filat Yegorych!" said Rukavichnikov, after the peasant had finished his devotions.

"Greeting, Father Petr Ananyich."

"How's life?"

"Eh?"

"How's life, I said."

"Eh, praise be to God, we're alive."

"All well at home?"

"Seems all right."

"Happy all round, then?"

"Eh?"

"Happy all round, I said."

"E-e-e-e! What've we to be happy about."

"Well, what's the trouble?"

"Just seems—the Lord knows—as though we're all tied up."

"The boss again, is it?"

"And who else would it be?"

"Done you wrong, has he?"

"Seems so."

"What's he done now?"

"Started building a distillery."

"You don't say so!"

"And won't let us go to earn money in the Ukraine."

"None of you?"

"Hasn't allowed a single carpenter to go."

"Too bad."

"Well, it isn't good enough! We've complained to the master—sent him two petitions, but we've had no decision as yet."

139

"There's bag full of trouble for you!" remarked Rukavich-nikov.

"Yes. So there we are, plagued by that hell-hound there."

"There—you see what a scoundrel that Dane is!" said Rukavichnikov, turning to me.

The peasant fixed me with a long, pleading look.

"And now I'll tell you," continued my host, "the kind of scoundrel this Filat Yegorych is."

The peasant remained entirely unmoved.

"Mr. Dane, their manager, is a man of the kindliest disposition and of the straightest principles . . ."

"That's so indeed," agreed the old man.

"Yes. But this Mr. Dane can't get on with them. He's always introducing his own rules and what not: and as I see it, he's not bringing order—he's just a weak man."

"That's so indeed—he's weak," the peasant repeated.

"Yes. He's been there more than a year, and you ask them: has he ever touched anyone? Is it the truth I'm telling, or am I lying?"

"That's the truth."

"Now, if you please, they don't like it. His punishments are mild, and then he doesn't often punish them; the work is piece-work, and easy; get your work over and go where you please."

"Yes, go."

"What?"

"Do what you've got to do and go, I said, where you please," repeated the peasant.

"Yes. And they, you see, spend their time writing complaints."

The peasant was silent.

"Well, and why doesn't he let them go and earn money outside?" I asked.

"'Won't let them—won't let them go.' Will you ask Filat Yegorych here how much his sonny brought him back after two years away from home? You tell us, Filat Yegorych."

The peasant was silent.

"What he brought home for him, sir—this son of his—was

140

a Ukrainian satchel, and in it a broken jack-plane, and for his young wife, and the children, a French present from which they all but lost their noses. Am I lying now?" Rukavichnikov again turned to the peasant.

"No, that did happen."

"Yes, that did happen. Well now, Stuart Yakovlevich has decided to build a distillery. I think he's very wise, because he's not building a showpiece or something, but only a distillery for his own grain, to make spirits and to feed the cattle with the by-products. He's seen all sorts of contractors; they asked 5000 roubles for the job, but he wouldn't pay that. Why not?"

"We can't know that," Filat Yegorych replied.

"No, brother, you lie—you *do* know. He's worked out what the others asked of him for the work, and how much the contractors would be paying you a month, and he's given you a rouble a month more, so that you do the work and don't spend your time idling about."

"I've heard that said—it's true."

"That's just it—it isn't 'can't know'. And now I suppose they've gone and written that he won't let them earn money outside and they're made to slave on the distillery. And not a word about the pay. Is that so?"

"I know nothing about that."

"Well, that's as it should be. So there's my old friend Filat Yegorych for you! My friend—your friend—a grand specimen."

The peasant grinned.

"You should have me for boss!" Rukavichnikov continued jocularly. "Eh? Would you have me for boss?"

"Why not?"

"And we'd never fall out; all would go smoothly with us. Because we'd have a heart-to-heart kind of order. You, now, Filat Yegorych, say you'd miss a day—I'd have you put on double work; a lad, say, has been stealing or something—I'd give him such a drubbing; anyone gets anything in the Ukraine, like Filat Yegorych's sonny; well—it would be the hospital for him, and the birch then, and then I'd let him go off again. Is that right, Filat Yegorych?"

"According to our lights, yes."

"There you are! I know, of course."

We let the peasant go.

"But what is it all?" I asked Rukavichnikov, wondering what he'd say about Dane.

"Well, there you see, my good sir. Mr. Dane is a good man, but he's not one of us; my advice to him would be to take himself off from here or they'll explode a mine under him yet!"

I related the matter to the Governor in detail. The Governor was beside himself with delight: he was so pleased that in his Province he'd got such a first-class land administrator in Stuart Yakovlevich Dane.

On Friday of Butterweek the Governor invited a number of people to eat pancakes. Nearly the entire town was there. While we were at table the official on duty handed the Governor an envelope. The Governor broke the seals, read the paper, and dismissed the official with a "Very well". But it was clear that something was not at all well. On rising from table, the Governor had a brief conversation with some of the guests, and then he and the Assistant-Governor slipped out quietly to his office, and a quarter of an hour later I was also summoned there. The Governor stood leaning against his high desk, while the Assistant-Governor was writing something at the Governor's table.

"There's a nasty bit of trouble," the Governor said, turning to me: "there's mutiny at Soltykovo."

"A mutiny?"

"Yes, there you are—read this."

The Governor took from his desk the paper he had received during dinner and handed it to me. It was a report by the Captain of Police of the Kromy District, who wrote that the previous day the Soltykovo peasants had mutinied against their manager, had burnt his house, the distillery and the mill, and had beaten up the manager himself and driven him out.

"I am sending you to Soltykovo," said the Governor, when I had read the report. "In a minute you'll get a warrant to the Officer Commanding the Invalids; take some men with you; do what you like, but see that the mutiny is stopped and the ringleaders found. Get ready as quick as you can, so as to be on the spot by morning, and act while the trail is hot."

"If I may, I'd rather not take soldiers with me," I said to the Governor. "I know everyone there and hope to carry out your orders without any soldiers; soldiers will make my work so much more difficult."

"That's as you please; but—just in case—take a warrant with you, to the O.C. the Invalids."

I bowed and left, and four hours later was already drinking tea with the Captain of Police at Kromy, with whom I had to go on to Soltykovo. From Kromy to Soltykovo it is only about ten miles, and we got there after dark. There was nowhere we could put up: the manager's house, the office, the men's quarters, the laundry and the workshops—they had all been burnt with the distillery and the mill, and here and there over the hot and blackened ruins smudges of blue smoke were still rising from the smouldering timbers. We took up our abode in the cottage of the headman Lukyan Mastakov and sent for the local Police Superintendent. Very early in the morning the Superintendent came bustling in, bringing with him a Soltykovo peasant, Nikolai Danilov, whom he had arrested the previous day on suspicion of having set fire to the distillery and of inciting the peasants to mutiny.

"What have you found out?" I asked the Superintendent.

"This is a case of arson."

"What makes you think that?"

"Fire broke out in uninhabited buildings, and all at once."

"Whom do you suspect of having caused the fire?"

The Superintendent made a motion with his hands, and his face expressed complete bewilderment.

"On what grounds have you arrested this man?"

"What—Nikolai Danilov?"

"Yes."

"Well, just in case. . . . He had been punished by Dane that day, was insolent to him, and besides, he remained during the night in the neighbourhood of the distillery, which was about the first place to catch fire."

"And is that all?"

"Yes, that's all. There is no other evidence. The peasants—they deny everything."

"Have you examined anyone?"

"I made an investigation."

"Found out anything?"

"Nothing so far."

The headman entered and stopped by the door.

"What is it, Lukyan Mitrich?" I asked.

"Your Honour."

"And what is it my Honour can do for you?"

"The peasants have got together."

"Who told you to get them together?"

"They've got together of their own accord—they want to speak to you."

"Where are they?"

"Just here," the headman pointed to the window. Outside the window stood an enormous crowd of peasants. There were old men there, and youngsters and middle-aged peasants; all stood quite still, their caps on their heads; some carried sticks.

"Oho! what a lot of them," I said, keeping quite calm.

"The whole estate," remarked the headman.

"Well, you go, Mitrich, and tell them I'll just put my coat on and come out."

The headman went out.

"Don't go!" said the Superintendent.

"Why?"

"Doesn't take long for accidents to happen."

"Well, it's too late now. The cottage door won't save us: if they've come with a purpose they'll find us in the house if need be."

I put on my overcoat and, accompanied by the Police Captain and the Superintendent, went out into the porch. The crowd began to sway, the caps began to tumble off the heads, but unwillingly—not all at once—while a few men in the back rows kept theirs on.

"Good morning, boys!" I said, and took off my cap.

The men bowed and boomed: "Wishing you good health!"

"Put your caps on, boys; it is cold."

"Doesn't matter," boomed the peasants again, and the remaining caps vanished.

"Do put on your caps."

"We're all right as we are."

"We're used to it."

"In that case, I order you to put your caps on."

"Order—is it?"

One or two of the men put on their caps—the rest followed suit. I felt easier. I saw that I was right in not bringing any soldiers.

Right up by the porch stood a sleigh and pair, and in it sat Nikolai Danilov, his feet thrust in a birch stock. He was wearing a black coat, with a belt about the waist, and a fur cap on his head. He looked about thirty-five, had goldish hair, a long narrow beard, and seemed nervous and timid. His face wore a peculiar crushed look, but it was placid and quite respectable-looking, despite a broken lip and a bruise on the left cheek-bone. He sat motionless, and kept looking first at me and then at the crowd.

"What is it you want of me, boys?" I asked the assembly.

"Is it you that's from the Governor?" a middle-aged peasant in the front row asked.

"It's me."

"Are you an official?"

"An official."

"Of the Governor?"

"Yes."

"Then it's you we want to talk to."

"Very well—I'm listening."

"No, you come down from off that porch. We want to speak to you alone."

Without a moment's hesitation I plunged into the crowd, which opened, received me into its depths and immediately closed again, thus cutting me off from the Police Captain and Superintendent.

The man who had invited me to come down stood before me.

"Well, what are we going to talk about?"

"You're Marya Petrovna's boy, aren't you?" the same man continued to cross-examine me.

"Of course. Don't you know?"

145

"We know. That's why we got you to come here, because you're of our parts, local, as one might say."

"What did you want to speak to me about?"

"Just all about this business."

There was a burst of sighs from various parts of the crowd.

"That's your doing, boys?"

"God's doing, sir—God's—not ours."

"Why did you throw the manager out?"

"He went of his own accord."

"Naturally—when you nearly killed him."

The crowd was silent.

"What's going to happen now?"

"That's just why we wanted you here, so that you'd tell us what's coming to us."

"Penal servitude—that's what's coming."

"For the boss?"

"Yes, for the boss, for arson, for mutiny; for all together."

The men hung their heads.

"There wasn't any mutiny," said someone.

"Oh, what's the use, boys? Don't try to deny it," I said. "The facts are there; they speak for themselves. If you try to deny it there'll be questionings and examinations, you'll start saying different things and will get all mixed up. Hadn't you better think how you can best get out of this mess?"

"That's right," muttered several voices again.

"That's just it. And now good-bye. There's nothing more we can talk about."

I touched one of the men, he stood aside, and, following him, others also allowed me to pass.

The examination then began. The first to be questioned was Nikolai Danilov. Before examining him I ordered his stock to be removed. He seated himself on a bench and watched with indifference how the wood of the stock was eased by wedges, and then as stolidly got up and approached the table.

"Well, uncle Nikolai: that's a fine hole you've got yourself into!" I said to the prisoner.

Nikolai Danilov wiped his nose with his sleeve and replied not a word.

"What've you got to say for yourself?"

"What've I got to say, Mikhaila Ivanych?" he said, his voice quavering considerably.

"You tell me, brother, how it all happened."

"I know nothing about the business, I don't, and I had nothing to do with it."

"You lie!" roared the Superintendent.

I looked coldly at the Superintendent, and without altering my voice asked again: "Well, tell us what you know."

"I only know what was done to me."

"Well, what happened to you?"

"The boss was fairly taking it out of me, he was."

"In what way?"

"Well, just as he pleased."

"Did he knock you about?"

"No, he didn't."

"What did he do to you, then?"

"He shamed me."

"How did he shame you?"

"Oh, he's a great hand at it, he is."

"Now, Nikolai, you talk sense, or I'll have nothing more to do with you," I said with a wave of my hand.

Nikolai pondered, hesitated, and then said:

"Could I please sit down? My legs hurt from the stock."

"Sit down," I said, and ordered a form to be brought for the accused.

"I asked him to let me go out on jobs," began Nikolai Danilov. "I asked him with the other boys, as early as last autumn it was; well, he wouldn't let us go then. And I just had to get to the Chernigov Province."

"Anyone owed you money there, or what?"

"No."

"What was it, then."

"Something else."

"Well!"

"Well, he wouldn't let me go—made me work on the distillery. I worked for a week and went off."

"Where?"

"Where I told you."

"To the Chernigov Province?"

"Naturally."

"What sort of business had you got there?"

"Drinking cheap vodka," interposed the Superintendent.

Nikolai said nothing.

"Well, what happened then?"

"Well, then I was arrested at Kirilevets and marched back to our town, and there handed over to the boss."

"Without being punished?"

"Oh, I was punished right enough, and then handed to him. He straightway puts me to work again, and I—ten days back it would be—ran off again, but called at my village, and the bailiff nabbed me there, and back I went to the manager."

"Well, and what did he do when you were brought back?"

"He told me to sit on a corner!"

"What corner?"

"A corner—see? The boys would be working and I would be sitting on the corner of the frame of the wooden house, in view of everyone, with my hands folded."

"And did you sit?"

"I went off again."

"Why?"

"Well, I begged him—I said to him: 'Let me work!' He wouldn't. 'You sit there,' says he, 'so that everyone can see you. That's your punishment.' 'If you want to punish me,' I said, 'you punish me as you please; thrash me,' I said; 'better than sitting there to be laughed at.' He wouldn't. When the dinner-bell went, the boys went to dinner, and I walked off, but I was caught outside the village."

"Well?"

"Well, that's when he about finished me."

"How?"

"Tied me on a thread."

"How?"

"Just as I say," said Nikolai Danilov, flushing to the tips of his ears, his voice rising on a sing-song note. "He brought me to the distillery, got a flunkey to bring a soft chair from the house, put the chair before the men, put me in it, stuck a pin in the back and tied me to it by a thread, just as if I was a sparrow."

There was a burst of laughter, and one could not help laughing when one looked at this hefty peasant who was telling the story of how he had been kept on a thread.

"And did you sit for long on that thread?"

Nikolai Danilov sighed and wiped his face. He was sweating at the very thought of the thread.

"All day I sat there like a sparrow."

"And in the evening the fire broke out?"

"In the night—not the evening. At third cockcrow it must have started."

"And how did you hear of the fire?"

"There was shouting in the street, I heard it—that's all."

"And till all this shouting," I asked him, "where were you?"

"At home—sleeping under the shed."

He was quite composed as he said this, but avoided my eyes.

"Well, and how did you turn out the manager?"

"I know nothing about that."

"But you must have seen him beaten up in front of the distillery?"

He made no reply.

"Everyone must have been there, I reckon."

"Everyone was there."

"And everyone must have been beating him."

"That's how it must have been.".

"And you helped?"

"No, I didn't beat him."

"Well, who was beating him, then?"

"Everyone beat him."

"And you noticed no one in particular?"

"No one."

Nikolai Danilov was led aside, and we examined the night watchmen, the supervisors, Nikolai's family, the neighbours, and many many others. In three days we collected something like a hundred depositions. Had we written down all these statements we would have used up a whole ream, but there was no need to take them down in writing—they were all

identical. Whatever the first man said was repeated by the
rest. And the first witness explained that he did not know the
cause of the fire; that maybe it was indeed a case of arson, and
maybe it was just something God alone knew; but that he
himself took no part in the arson and had no suspicions against
anyone, except perhaps against the manager himself, because
he was a stinger and even tied peasants by a thread as though
they might be sparrows. As for the manager, no one drove
him out, and he had left of his own free will because of an unpleasantness with the peasants: they beat him up at the fire.

"Who beat him up, then?"

"Everyone beat him."

"And you beat him too?"

"No, I did not beat him."

"Well, did you notice anyone in particular?"

"No—the *mir* beat him up."

"Therefore you deserted the *mir*?"

A long silence, and then in a decisive tone: "I did not beat
him."

"Who beat him, then?"

"The *mir* beat him up."

"Why?"

"He's plagued us so much—got to tying us on a thread, as
you might a sparrow."

The following ninety-nine statements were a word-for-word
repetition of the first, and were written down thus: "Ivan
Ivanov Sushkin, aged 43, married, goes to Confession, no
previous convictions. Showed the same as Stepan Terekhov."

I realized what a mountain would be made of it all. I had
a good think, and ordered Nikolai Danilov to be kept under
observation, and told the Police Captain and Superintendent
that I was going to Orel for three days. When I got there, I
had a talk with the Assistant-Governor, and together we went
to the Governor. The latter was having his evening tea, and
was in good spirits. I related the affair to him, and by painting
it all in as naïve colours as I could, I persuaded him that, strictly
speaking, there had been no mutiny at all, and that if the Prince
would only agree to forgive his peasants, the matter of arson

could be dropped, and then there would be no investigation, no thrashings, no lashes, no penal servitude, and order and peace would be restored.

The words "order and peace" so appealed to the Governor that he began to pace up and down the room, thought a little, stretched his lower lip towards his nose, and wrote out a telegram of sixty words to the Prince. The same evening the telegram went off, and two days later a reply came from Paris. The Prince telegraphed that he granted his peasants an amnesty, provided the entire commune obtained Mr. Dane's forgiveness and never again wrote any complaints against him.

I went to Soltykovo with this amnesty, got the men together, and said: "Boys! The situation is this: the Prince forgives you. I pleaded for you before the Governor, and the Governor before the Prince, and here's the Prince's forgiveness, on condition you obtain forgiveness of the manager and do not in future make idle complaints against him."

They all started bowing and thanking me.

"Well, what about it? You'll have to choose delegates and send them to town to the manager and they'll have to say you are all sorry."

"We'll choose them all right."

"You'll have to be quick about it."

"We'll send them off to-day."

"And no fooling afterwards."

"We never did it for fun. We don't mind him so long as he keeps away from us."

"What d'you mean—away from you? The Prince means that you'll now live in peace with Dane."

"Does that mean that he's coming back?" cried several voices simultaneously.

"Yes. What did you think I was telling you?"

"So-o-o-o! No: that we don't agree to."

"But you yourselves wanted to send representatives to him to-day to ask his forgiveness."

"Oh, we'll ask his forgiveness all right, but we can't let him come here again."

"Well then, they'll institute proceedings against you."

"What's to be can't be helped; we can't get on with him, can't possibly."

"What are you talking about? Think: half of you will be deported."

"No-no! We can't live with him. We've nowhere to put the hell-hound."

"But why is he a hell-hound?"

"Well, what else is he? Tying a man—a householder—to a thread, as though he were a sparrow. Isn't that enough?"

"Oh, forget the idiotic thread! All that fuss! Were you better off when the Prince himself was here? Didn't you sweat away weeding paths, and brushing down the horses in the stables?"

"We may have done. But he's the master, it was his will, and he never did what this manager's been doing. Christ!—on a thread, as one might a sparrow. . . . Never seen such a thing."

"Think, boys."

"What's there to think about? We've thought it all out. We'll find ourselves in worse sin with that hound."

"But he won't tie you on any more threads. I promise you that"

"He'll think of something worse to do to us."

"Why should he invent anything?"

"He's that sort of man—a stinger."

"Now stop it, boys. We've got to give an answer to the Governor."

A pause.

"Well. . . . We're prepared to beg his pardon."

"And will you take back the manager?"

"Noa—we can't do that."

"But why can't you?"

"He's a stinger."

.   .   .   .

I could get no further with the Soltykovo peasants, and there was nothing for it but to let the Law take its course.

A FLAMING PATRIOT

OF FOREIGN RULING CELEBRITIES, THE LATE
Napoleon III I saw at the opening of a new boulevard in Paris;
Prince Bismarck, at a Spa; MacMahon at the changing of the
Guard; and the present Emperor of Austria, Francis Joseph—
over a jug of beer.

The most lasting impression produced upon me was by
Francis Joseph, even though the occasion led to a profound
quarrel between two women, compatriots of mine.

It is well worth recording.

．　　．　　．　　．　　．　　．　　．

I have been abroad three times, and on these journeys I
travelled twice along the Russian "High Road", from St.
Petersburg to Paris direct, while the third time, owing to
various circumstances, I made a detour and called at Vienna.
I also wanted to take this opportunity of paying my respects
to a most worthy Russian lady.

It was then the end of May, or early June. The train I had
taken brought me to Vienna about four in the afternoon. I had
no need to look for lodgings; in Kiev I had been furnished with
letters of recommendation which relieved me of all bother. I
got fixed up as soon as I arrived, and an hour later had already
made myself presentable and sallied out to visit my compatriot.

Vienna, too, had just finished her toilet: a heavy summer
shower had passed over her, and then, quite suddenly, a bright
sun had sparkled out from a sky of vivid, uniform blue. The
lovely city, after the brief ablution, looked still lovelier.

All the streets along which my guide led me seemed most
graceful, but as we neared Leopoldstadt their elegance became
even more striking. The buildings here were larger, more
solid, and grander. Before one of these my guide stopped
and said it was the hotel for which I was looking.

Through an imposing archway we entered a lofty hall,

decorated in the Pompeian style. To right and left of this hall were heavy doors of dark oak; the opposite wall was richly draped with reddish hangings. In the middle of the hall stood a brougham to which were harnessed two living horses, while a coachman sat on the driver's seat.

This splendid hall was nothing more than the gateway. We were in a gateway the like of which I had never seen till then, either in St. Petersburg or Paris.

To the right was the doorkeeper's lodge. It, also, was a remarkable piece of work, and so was the doorkeeper, who looked as though he was, in fact, a Court Chamberlain: he sat there like a golden beetle in a showcase of enormous sheets of plate-glass. He could see all round him; while at his side— to lend importance to him, or for some other reason—stood three assistants, each with a shoulder-knot. Should occasion have arisen to deny entry to someone, or to show a person the door, such a doorkeeper would, of course, disdain to sully his own hands over such an indecorous incident.

To my enquiry whether my friend was staying there, one of the assistants replied: "She is here," and when I asked: "Can I see her?" the assistant conveyed my question to the keeper of the door, and he, with a diplomatic movement of his eyebrow, *himself* explained:

"I venture to think that the Princess will not find it convenient to see you now; her horses are ready, and Her Highness is about to leave for a drive. But if it is very urgent . . ."

"Yes," I interrupted, "it is important."

"In that case I must beg you to wait a minute."

It was clear that I was dealing with a true diplomat, and an argument concerning a wait of a minute was out of place.

We exchanged bows.

The doorkeeper pressed an electric button on his desk, before which stood his Papal High Chair with a carved Gothic back, and placing his ear to the tube, he enlightened me a second later:

"The Princess is already descending the stairs."

I proceeded to wait.

Presently my friend appeared on the white marble steps, accompanied by Anna Fetisovna, her middle-aged Russian maid, whom I had known for many years and who has a part to play in this short narrative.

.   .   .   .   .   .

The Princess greeted me with the charming friendliness that had always distinguished her, and telling me that she was on the point of going for her afternoon drive, invited me to accompany her.

She wished to show me the Prater. I had no objection, and accordingly we started off, with myself seated in the back, next to the Princess, and Anna Fetisovna facing us on the seat in front.

In contradiction to those who assert that, abroad, it is usual to drive much more slowly than in Russia, we sped along the Vienna streets at an exhilarating pace. Our horses were spirited and dashing, our driver—a high priest of his art. The Viennese handle a pair in shaft-harness with that beauty and skill which the Poles also possess. Our coachmen at home cannot drive like that. They are too heavy, and jerk the reins—there is not that ease with them in the movement of the ribbons, none of that *haute école* one sees so much in a Pole or a Viennese.

Before you could say Jack Robinson we were on the Prater.

I shall not try at all to describe this park; I shall only mention enough to complete the picture of what presently occurred.

Let us remember that it was about five in the afternoon and immediately after a heavy shower. The cooling moisture was everywhere in evidence: the coarse gravel of the paths seemed brown; crystal-clear drops glistened on the leaves of the trees.

It was fairly damp, and I do not know whether it was this dampness or the early hour that made all the main walks of the park, along which we were driving, quite empty. We passed a solitary gardener in a short jacket with a rake and spade on his shoulder, and no one else; but my kind hostess recalled that there was another part of the park: besides this show part, so to speak, there was the less exclusive Kalbs-Prater, or "Calf Park", where the Viennese people went for their relaxation.

"I am told it is quite interesting," the Princess said, and at once told the driver to go to the Kalbs-Prater.

The driver bore left, emitted his throaty "oi", cracked his

whip, and it seemed as though the ground began to give beneath us. We appeared to be descending somewhere; we were dropping, as though born to a lower sphere.

The situation was in perfect keeping with social prejudices.

.   .   .   .   .   .

The scene changed rapidly: the walks grew narrower and were not so immaculately kept; here and there scraps of paper could be seen on the sand and the edges of the herbaceous borders. But human beings also made their appearance—pedestrians all—first the sellers of the well-known Viennese sausage, and then the general public. Some were trudging along with their children. Obviously the public here was not afraid of the damp, and only seemed anxious not to waste a moment of precious time.

A poor man, when he marries, finds the night all too brief: briefer still are the hours of leisure of such hard-working and frugal people as the Southern Germans, whose thirst for pleasure is nevertheless almost as great as that of the French.

There was no traffic to meet us—we were overtaking everyone. Everyone's goal was obviously ahead. It was the place we too were hurrying towards, and from which now, steadily increasing in volume, could be heard some strange sounds. They were like the buzzing of a bee trapped between the window-pane and the curtain. Presently between the tree tops we caught a glimpse of the tall front of a large wooden building; the brougham again bore left and stopped abruptly. We were at the crossing of two walks. Before us opened a fairly large clearing, at the opposite end of which stood a large wooden house, in the Swiss style; while in front of it, on the grass, stretched long rows of tables, and before them sat a large number of all sorts of people. Before each guest stood his pot of beer, and on the open gallery four musicians were playing and a Hungarian man and woman were whirling in a dance.

"That's the Tchardash they are dancing: I would advise you to look closely," the Princess remarked. "It's quite a rare sight. No one can do the Tchardash like the Hungarians. Driver! will you get nearer."

The driver moved the reins, but no sooner had the horses taken two steps forward than he pulled them up again.

We had of course got nearer, but were still too far to be able to study the dancers, and so the Princess told the driver again to get closer. He appeared not to have heard this new command, but when the Princess told him the same thing for the third time, the driver not only moved the reins, but cracked his whip loudly and straightway brought the brougham right into the middle of the clearing.

We could now see everything in detail and could ourselves be seen by everyone present. Several people sitting at the tables glanced up at the crack of the whip, but at once turned back to the dancers. Only a fat waiter was looking at us from the bottom step of the terrace as though awaiting some appropriate moment when, between him and ourselves, there would occur an exchange of appropriate relations.

I tried to follow the advice of my companion as conscientiously as I could and settled myself to watch the Tchardash closely, but a casual circumstance drew my attention to something else.

No sooner had we stopped than the driver half turned to our carriage and said:

"Kaiser!"

"Wo ist der Kaiser?"

For reply the driver moved the little finger of his gloved hand to the left, towards the opposite end of the clearing, and there at the crossing of two walks, similar to the one from which we had advanced, I could now see two horses' heads, of a goldenish, light-bay colour.

Only these two gorgeous heads with tassels at the snaffles and with the plates on the cheek-pieces picked out in turquoises could be seen; the carriage itself remained on a line with the spot where our driver had wished us to stop first of all.

"That," thought I to myself, "is indeed most tactful of him, but he won't see much from where he is, and he won't let us see him either. Most annoying, this."

But there was no reason to feel disappointed; the same instant, glancing towards the spot where the horses were standing, I perceived without difficulty a tall, slightly round-shouldered but vigorous man, in a blue Austrian jacket and a plain forage cap.

This was His Apostolic Majesty, the head of the House of Hapsburg, the Emperor Regnant, Francis Joseph. He was quite alone and was walking straight towards the tables standing in the clearing, where sat the cobblers of Vienna. The Emperor approached, and at the nearest table seated himself on the end of a form, next to a tall labourer in a light-blue blouse, while the waiter at once placed before him a mat of black felt and stood upon it a jug of beer which he had skilfully frothed.

Francis Joseph took the jug in his hand but did not drink; while the dance lasted he continued to hold it, but when the Tchardash was over, the Emperor, without a word, held out his jug to his neighbour. The latter immediately understood what was expected of him; he clinked jugs with his Sovereign, and straightway turning to his other neighbour, passed on the salute. With this, everyone present simultaneously clinked tankards with one another, and a unanimous chorus of "Hoch!" swept the valley. This "hoch" is here emitted not very loudly and without that familiar roll, but rather as though it were more a sigh from an overflowing heart.

The Emperor drained his tankard at one gulp, bowed and walked away.

The bays rushed him off along the road which we too presently followed. But we now carried with us a considerable force of the impression produced upon us by this incident, and most of it lodged with Anna Fetisovna. The girl, to our considerable astonishment, was *crying*! . . . She sat before us with a white pocket-handkerchief covering her eyes, and she was pressing it down with her hands.

"Anna Fetisovna! What's the matter?" exclaimed the Princess, turning to her with gentle and kindly concern.

Anna Fetisovna continued to weep.

"Why are you crying?"

Anna Fetisovna opened her eyes and said:

"Oh, nothing—it's nothing."

"No, but really?"

The girl heaved a profound sigh and replied:

"It's their simplicity I find so touching."

The Princess gave me a wink and said jokingly:

"Toujours servile! C'est ainsi que l'on arrive aux cieux."

But this quip somehow failed to penetrate the heart. Anna Fetisovna's emotion lent a different character to this trifling incident.

.   .   .   .

We returned to the hotel, and there found yet another visitor waiting for us. He was an Austrian baron who was thinking of going to Russia and was learning Russian. We drank tea, while Anna Fetisovna served us. We talked of a great many things: of Russia, and the people we knew in St. Petersburg, of the rate of exchange, and of who had proved our champion embezzler, and finally of our afternoon's meeting with Francis Joseph.

The entire conversation was carried on in Russian, so that Anna Fetisovna could not help but hear every word of it.

The Princess recounted to me not entirely "permissible" anecdotes of Court bucolics and political rhapsodies. The baron sat and smiled.

I don't want to record it all, but there is one thing I think I should mention, and that is that my hostess tried to represent many traits in the Austrian Emperor's character as being due to a hankering after popularity.

This dissertation on popularity, or rather publicity-mongering, was developed in a particularly detailed manner, and with instances, among which the afternoon's mug of beer again made its appearance. And—I am sorry if I'm wrong—but it seemed to me that this was done not so much for our benefit as for the benefit of Anna Fetisovna, who kept going in and out, bringing various things required by her mistress.

It was seemingly some female caprice which spurred my compatriot onwards, till she passed from the Emperor to the people, or peoples, to the Austrians and the Russians. She was pleased with the manner in which "the Vienna cobblers" behaved "with dignity", and then switched rapidly over to our own country, to the Russian people, their jollifications and

pastimes, the drinking, and then again to the emotional outburst of the impressionable Anna Fetisovna.

This was now said in French; nevertheless, the baron merely
continued to smile.

"We must still ask my worthy Jeanne for her opinion," said
the Princess, and when the girl came in to fetch a cup, her
mistress said:

"Anna Fetisovna, you were very struck with the Emperor
here to-day, weren't you?"

"Yes, I liked him very much," Anna Fetisovna answered
shortly.

The Princess whispered to me: "She's piqued," and continued aloud:

"And what would you think if he suddenly came to Moscow,
to where all our swings and roundabouts are?"

The girl was silent.

"Don't you want to talk to us?"

"Why should he come to our Moscow?"

"Well, supposing he suddenly took it into his head to come?
What do you think—would he go and sit next to our mouzhiks?"

"Why should he go and sit with our people when he's got
his own?" replied Anna Fetisovna, and hurried out of the room
with her empty cup.

"She's positively fuming," the Princess said in French, and
added that Anna Fetisovna was a flaming patriot and had a
passion for generalizations.

The baron was still smiling and soon left. I followed an hou
later.

When I had said good-bye, Anna Fetisovna, candle in hand,
went to show me the way to the stairs, along the unfamiliar
corridors of the hotel. On the way she said suddenly:

"And you, sir: you agree that people of our nature are all
without dignity?"

"No," I said, "I don't agree."

"Then why didn't you say something?"

"I didn't want to start an idle argument."

"Oh no, sir, it wouldn't have been idle. . . . And with that
foreign baron there too. . . . Why is everyone always so unfai

about our people! As though we liked what's wrong, and not
what's good."

I felt sorry for her and rather ashamed of myself.

.   .   .   .   .   .

My foreign wanderings did not last long. In the autumn I
was already back in St. Petersburg, and one day, in one of the
galleries of the *Gostinny Dvor*, I suddenly met Anna Fetisovna
carrying a basket of worsted knitting.

We shook hands, and I enquired after the Princess, to which
Anna Fetisovna replied:

"I know nothing of the Princess, sir—she and I have parted."

"Indeed! What, out there—abroad?"

"Yes. I came back by myself."

Knowing of their many years' association, one might almost
say friendship, I expressed my unfeigned surprise and asked:

"Why did you part company?"

"You know the reason: it was while you were there. . . ."

"Good gracious—not on account of the Austrian Emperor,
surely?"

For a minute Anna Fetisovna said nothing, and then burst
out suddenly:

"There's nothing to tell, really: you saw it. . . . He is very
courteous, and all honour to him, and I felt hurt for the Princess
—because of her ignorance."

"But what had the Princess's ignorance got to do with it?"

"Well, this. *He* was Emperor, and yet he knew how to
bring it off—got out and sat with the others, as an equal would;
and we in our carriage barged in ahead and sat there like a pack
of dummies, showing off, for everybody to stare at us. So
everybody just laughed at us."

I said: "I saw no one laughing at us."

"Oh, it wasn't there: at the hotel. The commissionaire,
and all the servants."

"Well, what did they say to you?"

"There's nothing they said to me, because I don't understand
their talk; only I saw it in their eyes, how they had no respect
for us because of our ignorance."

"I see. And you felt that was enough to make you leave the Princess?"

"Yes . . . after all . . . do you wonder; "it was as if the good Lord had confounded our tongues and we could no longer understand one another. . . . I couldn't stay when there was disagreement in all our thoughts, so I asked to be allowed to come back here. I don't want to be in service any more; here I live according to my own illiterate nature."

There was, one felt, true *dignity* in this "nature", which could not put up with "ignorance".

The Princess was right when she had called her "a flaming patriot".

THE CLOTHES-MENDER

ISN'T IT A SILLY SORT OF CUSTOM TO WISH
everyone new happiness every New Year's Eve, and yet—you
know—sometimes something like that does happen. May I tell
you, in this connection, about a little occurrence which really
has quite a Yuletide flavour?

During one of my trips to Moscow—many years ago
now that would be—I was kept there longer than I had expected, and I grew heartily tired of my hotel. The psalmodist
of one of the Palace churches, hearing me complain to a friend
of mine—a priest of the same church—about all the incon-
veniences I had to put up with, suddenly chimed in:

"Now, wouldn't he be just the person, Father, for my
relative? He's got a room to let straight away—facing the
street."

"What relative of yours would that be?" asked the
priest.

"Vasilii Konych."

"Ha—that's 'Maître Tailleur Lepoutan'!"

"The same, sir."

"Well, that's not at all a bad idea."

And the priest went on to explain both that he knew the
people and that the room was an excellent one, while the
psalmodist added yet another advantage.

"If," said he, "you should tear your clothes or if the bottoms
of your trousers get frayed, you'll find everything put right in
no time—so well that you won't see a thing."

I decided that all further investigations were superfluous, and
I did not even go to see the place first. I gave the psalmodist
the key to my hotel room with a message scribbled on my
card and asked him to settle my bill, collect my things and take
them round to his relative. Then I asked him to call back for
me and lead me to my new abode.

CHAPTER THE SECOND

THE psalmodist managed everything very quickly, and in a little over an hour he came round for me at the priest's.

"Come along," he said. "Everything has been unpacked already and arranged in your room, and they've got your window open—they have—and the door onto the verandah and the garden, and we've even had tea on the verandah. It's very nice there," he told me. "There are all kinds of flowers, and the dicky-birds making their nests in the gooseberries, and a nightingale trilling in a cage under the window. It's better than the country, because it's all green all round you and yet everything about the house is ship-shape, and if a button or what not gets loose, or the bottoms of your trousers get frayed —it'll be put right in no time."

The psalmodist was a very tidy person and a great dandy, and so he repeatedly emphasized this aspect of the advantage of my new quarters.

And the priest too backed him up.

"Yes," he said, "tailleur Lepoutan is such a craftsman in this particular line—you won't find another like him in Moscow or St. Petersburg."

"A specialist, that's what he is," the psalmodist said impressively, as he helped me into my coat.

Who this Lepoutan was I did not quite make out—besides, it was none of my business.

CHAPTER THE THIRD

WE set out on foot.

The psalmodist assured me that it was not worth taking a cab, because, according to him, it was only "a stone's throw away by way of *promenage*."

As a matter of fact, it turned out to be a good half-hour's walk, but the psalmodist wanted to take a *promenage*, perhaps because he also wanted to show off his cane, which was decorated with a mauve silk tassel.

The district in which the house of Lepoutan was situated lay beyond the Moskva River, towards the Yausa, somewhere near its bank. I've now forgotten even what parish it was in and what the lane was called. As a matter of fact, it wasn't even a lane, but rather a sort of little cul-de-sac, like an old-fashioned churchyard. There was a little church there, and a kind of drive which ran at an angle to it, and in this drive stood six or seven houses, all of very modest proportions, of a grey colour, built of wood, while one had a stone semi-basement. This one looked more showy and larger than the others, and right across its façade was nailed a large iron sign upon which, on a black background, in letters of gold, was prominently painted in large characters : "Maître Tailleur Lepoutan".

Obviously, this was my new abode, but I thought it strange that my host, who enjoyed the Christian name of Vasilii Konych, should call himself "Maître Tailleur Lepoutan". When the priest had called him that, I thought it was only a joke, and I did not take much notice of it, but now, on beholding this sign, I had to alter my view. Apparently—and quite seriously— it *was* his name, and I even asked my guide :

"Vasilii Konych—is he Russian or French ?"

The psalmodist looked surprised and did not seem to grasp my question.

"Why—what d'you mean ? Why should he be French ?— A pure-bred Russian, that's what he is. Why, even the clothes he makes for the market are all pure Russian—sleeveless top-coats, and all that kind of stuff—but he is better known all over Moscow for his mending : any amount of old clothes have passed through his hands and are being sold as new in the markets."

"Still," I said, feeling puzzled, "he must be of French descent ?"

Again the psalmodist expressed surprise.

"No," he retorted—"why should he be ? He's a regular local man—a Russian—and acts as godfather at christenings, and of course we Churchmen are all pure Orthodox. And why should you imagine that he has anything to do with the French nation?"

"That signboard—it has a French name on it."

"Oh, that," explained my companion. "That's nothing. That's just all splash. And, also, the main sign is in French, it's true, but there, next to the gate—see—there's another, a Russian sign. That's the more correct one."

I looked to where he pointed, and indeed beheld another signboard, which depicted a sleeveless topcoat, a coat as worn by Russian peasants, and two black waistcoats with silver buttons that sparkled like stars, with the following legend below:

"Clothing of Russian and Clerical Fashion Made. Specialist in Nap, Turning, and Mending."

Beneath this second sign the name of the man who made clothing, and turned and mended was not stated, but was merely indicated by two initials: "V. L."

CHAPTER THE FOURTH

THE room and the owner proved indeed above all praise and description, so that I at once felt perfectly at home, and soon grew quite fond of my kindly host, Vasilii Konych. Presently he and I began to meet over tea and to have long conversations and debates on various subjects. Thus, one day, as we sat sipping our tea on the verandah, we debated upon the absorbing theme of the vanity of everything under the sun and of our undying propensity to labour in the service of vanity. That is how we got onto the subject of Lepoutan.

I don't remember now by what stages we reached a point in our conversation when Vasilii Konych expressed a wish to tell me the strange story of how, and why, he appeared "under a French title".

The tale has some relation to social morals and to literature, even though it is displayed on a signboard.

Konych began simply, but in a most intriguing manner.

"My name, sir," he said, "is not Lepoutan at all, but quite a different one—and under this French title I was placed by Destiny itself.

CHAPTER THE FIFTH

"I AM Moscow-born and Moscow-bred, and of the poorest parentage. My grandad used to sell soles by the Rogozhinsky Barrier; some of the more ancient type of Old Believers used to wear these soles inside their boots. He was a fine old man, was my grandad—like a saint—all white, like a hare in moult, and he used to feed himself by the toil of his hands till his very death. He would buy some felt, cut it up into little pieces shaped like soles, string a pair on a thread, and would do the round of 'The Christians'. And you should have heard him sing out, as sweet as sweet could be: 'Soles, soles, who wants soles?' And so he would wander all over Moscow, with just about a copper's-worth of goods, and yet he earned his keep. My father was a tailor, making clothes according to the old rules. He made coats for all the most righteous Old Believers, with three pleats, as they should be, and taught me the craft as well. But ever since I was a child I possessed a special gift, and that was mending. I am not very bright at cutting, but when it comes to patching—that's my line. And I got so good at it—I'd mend a tear in the most prominent spot and you wouldn't know it had been there.

The old men used to say to my father:

'That youngster's got his talent from God, and where a man's talent is, there his happiness lies also.'

And that's how it all turned out, but before you get to your luck, you know, you need humble patience, and I was sent two serious trials: firstly, my parents died and left me when I was still very young; and secondly, the room where I lived was burnt out one Christmas Eve while I was at Mass—and I lost all my equipment: my iron and my tailor's dummy, and clothes belonging to various people, which I had there for mending. So I found myself right up against it; and yet, that's when my first step towards my new luck occurred.

CHAPTER THE SIXTH

"ONE customer, who lost his overcoat in my fire, came to me and said:

'My loss is pretty hard, and it is not pleasant to be left without a greatcoat over Christmas, but I see you can't make good the loss, and you need help yourself. If you're a reliable lad, I'll put you on the right road, but on one condition: by and by you must make up the cost of the coat.'

I answered him:

'God willing, I shall be glad to do what I can. I'll see that you get repaid before anything else.'

He told me to get dressed, and brought me to a hotel that was opposite the house of the Commander-in-Chief, and introduced me to the assistant barman and said to him in my presence:

'Here is the apprentice I told you of, who can be very useful in our line of business.'

And their business was to press all the clothes which were in the visitors' luggage and got crumpled, and also to do all kinds of necessary mending.

The assistant barman gave me a thing to do to try me out, saw that I did it well, and told me to stay.

'Now,' he said to me, 'it's Christmas, and the place is full of gentry, and they're all drinking and having high jinks, and there's still New Year to come and Twelfth-night—there will be some goings-on worse than ever—so you stay put— see?'

I said to him:

'I agree.'

And the chap who brought me there said to me:

'Well, there you are—you can make money here. Only you just do what he (that is, the assistant barman) tells you, always. If God is with you, He sends His prophet too.'

I was given a little corner with a small window in a back passage, and I got busy. There were lots and lots—I couldn't tell you how many lots of gentlemen I patched up, and it would be a sin to complain—I patched myself up pretty well too, because there was any amount of work and the pay was good. The ordinary kind of people did not put up there—only 'Trumps' used to stay there, who used to like feeling they were on the same level with the Commander-in-Chief—from window to window, that is.

The pay was particularly good for patching and mending when the damage was suddenly discovered in something that had to be worn straight away. I felt pretty uncomfortable at times: the hole would be the size of a ten-kopeck piece, and if I managed to mend it so that you couldn't tell, I'd get a gold piece.

They would never pay less than ten roubles, however small the tear. Well, naturally, there was real art in the work: just as one drop of water might run into another and you can't say there's two drops, so the clothes had to be done so that you couldn't tell they had ever been mended.

Of the money that was paid, I got a third, while another third went to the assistant barman, and the other to the servants who unpacked the gentlemen's bags in the rooms when they arrived, and brushed and cleaned the clothes. They, of course, were at the bottom of it all, because they would crumple and rub the things and sometimes jab a little hole in them; so they got two-thirds and I got one-third. Even then, there was more than enough for me in what I got, so that I even shifted my quarters from the corner in the passage, and rented a quiet little room all to myself across the yard; and a year later, the sister of the assistant barman came up on a visit from the country, and I married her—my present wife, as you see her—that's her: she's reached old age with honour, and maybe it was to her lot that God sent everything. And as for marrying her, it was like this. The assistant barman said: 'She's an orphan and you must make her happy, and then, through it all, you'll meet with great happiness too.' And she also would say: 'I—I am a lucky one,' she would say; 'God will reward you on my account.' And suddenly, as though indeed all this was the cause, there came a most unexpected surprise.

CHAPTER THE SEVENTH

"IT was Christmas-time again, and New Year's Eve. I was in my little room in the evening, mending something or other, and was about to knock off work and go to bed, when in dashed a waiter from the rooms and said :

'Come on—get a move on; there's a terrible Trump in Number One—he's walloped just about everyone, and whoever he swipes he gives a gold piece to; now he wants you—quick.'

'What's he want me for ?' I asked.

'He was dressing for a ball, and just about the last moment he finds someone's burnt a hole in his dress-clothes—right in the middle; he's walloped the lad who cleaned them, and he's given him three gold pieces. You stir your stumps—he's cross —looks like all the beasts in the world at once.'

I just shook my head, because I knew how they spoilt the clothes of the visitors on purpose—just for their own profit from the work; but I dressed and went to have a look at the Trump who looked like all the beasts in the world put together.

The payment, I knew, would be pretty good, because Number One is reckoned a Trump number in every hotel, and it was only luxury people who stopped there; while in our hotel the price of Number One was fifteen roubles a day—that's at to-day's rate, and in those days it was fifty-two roubles fifty kopecks, in paper money—and whoever had it was known as 'The Trump'.

The one I was brought to now looked as terrifying as anything —he was so big and dark-faced and wild, and in truth he did look like all the beasts put together.

'You,' he said with a snarl: 'can you mend a hole so well that it can't be noticed ?'

I replied :

'Depends what it's in. If the material's got a nap, it can be done very well, but if it's shiny satin or silk moiré stuff—I wouldn't undertake it.'

'Moiré yourself,' said he. 'Some swine, I suppose it was yesterday, sat behind me—went and burnt a hole in my dress-coat. There—have a look at it and see for yourself.'

I had a look at it and said:

'That can be done well.'

'And how long will it take?'

'I'll have it done in about an hour.'

'Go on, then,' he said, 'and if you do it well you'll get a mint of money, and if you don't, I'll give you such a hiding. You go and ask the lads here what I did to them, and you can be sure you'll get it a hundred times worse.'

CHAPTER THE EIGHTH

"OFF I went to mend the coat, and I can't say I was feeling at all happy about it, because you can't always be sure how it will turn out; if the cloth is soft it will work together better, and if it's stiffer it is hard to work in the nap so that you don't notice it.

However, I did the job well; but I didn't take it to him myself, because I didn't like his manner at all. The work is tricky—however well you do it, anyone who wants to find fault can easily make things unpleasant for you.

I sent my wife with the coat to her brother and told her to give it to him and get home herself as quick as she could; and as soon as she was back we put the door on a hook from inside and went to bed.

In the morning I got up and started on my day's jobs as usual; I busied myself with my work and waited to see what I should get from the Trump gent—whether it would be a mint of money or a crack over the head.

And suddenly, soon after one, a waiter came and said:

'The gent from Number One wants to see you.'

I said:

'I'm not going—he can do what he pleases.'

'Why?'

'Just because—I'm not going, that's all; I'd rather my work went for nothing—I don't want to see him.'

But the waiter said:

'You've nothing to be in a funk about: he's very pleased

with you and he was seeing the New Year in in your dress-suit and no one noticed any hole in it. And now he's got guests with him, they're wishing him a Happy New Year and have had a few and have got talking about your work and betting they'd find the mend, but no one's done so. And they're as pleased as can be; they're drinking toasts to your Russian artistry and want to see you. Hurry up—it'll bring you new luck in the New Year.'

And my wife also got on to me.

'Go on, go on,' says she. 'My heart feels that our new luck is about to begin.'

Well, I listened to them, and went.

CHAPTER THE NINTH

"I SAW about ten gentlemen in Number One, and they'd all had a lot to drink, and no sooner did I come in than they gave me a glass of wine and said:

'Drink with us for your Russian craftsmanship through which you can make our country famous.'

That was the sort of thing they said—they were drunk. The job, of course, wasn't all that good.

I naturally bowed and thanked them and had two glasses— one for Russia and one for their good health—'and more,' said I, 'I won't take, because I'm not used to sweet wine and also don't deserve such company.'

Then the terriblē gent from Number One said:

'You're an ass and a fool and an animal, brother—you don't realize your own worth and all you deserve through your gift. You helped me this New Year's Eve more than you know, because yesterday at the ball I changed the whole run of my life and proposed to my beloved fiancée, of a very important family, and she's said yes, and so I'll be married after Lent.'

'I wish you and your future wife,' I said, 'every happiness.'

'Well, you drink to it.'

I couldn't refuse, and had a drink, but asked to be excused any more.

'All right,' he said, 'only you tell me where you live and what your Christian name is, patronymic and surname: I want to be your benefactor.'

I said:

'I'm called Vasilii, son of Konon, and my surname is Laputin, and my workshop is just here, next door, you'll see a little signboard, it says: "Laputin".'

And as I was speaking I never noticed how all the guests suddenly seemed to kind of explode at my words and double up with suppressed laughter, while the gent I mended the coat for all of a sudden swiped me across one ear and then across the other, so that I fairly tumbled off my feet. Then he pushed me towards the door with his knee and bundled me out.

I couldn't understand a thing and ran for dear life.

Back I came, and my wife asked me:

'Quick, Vasenka, tell me how my luck has served you?'

I said:

'Now, Mashenka, don't you start questioning me about details, but if it goes on as it has begun, I'd rather not live by your luck. The gent gave me a hiding, my angel.'

My wife got very agitated—what, why and what for, and all that kind of thing; and of course I could tell her nothing because I knew nothing myself.

But while we were talking about it all, suddenly there was a noise in our lobby, a banging and a crash, and in walked my benefactor from Number One.

We both jumped to our feet and looked at him, while he, all red and worked up—with wine too, I suppose—held in one hand the *dvornik's* axe, with a long shaft, and in the other the splintered board which displayed my cheap little sign stating my poor trade and my name: 'Old Clothes Mended and Turned. Laputin.'

CHAPTER THE TENTH

"IN came the gent with the splintered signboard and straight-way flung the bits into the stove, while he said to me: 'Get dressed—hurry—you're coming for a drive with me—I want to

make your life's happiness. Otherwise I'll smash you and your
wife and all you've got here—like those boards of yours.'

Well, I figured, it was no use arguing with the brute, better
have him out of the house as quickly as possible before he did
some hurt to my wife.

I dressed hastily, and said to the wife: 'Bless me, Mashenka!'
—and away we drove.

We went to the Bronnaya, where there was a famous estate
agent, Prohor Ivanovich, and the gent straightway asked him:

'What houses have you for sale, and in what part of the town
—price about twenty-five to thirty thousand roubles, or a little
more?' It was in paper currency, of course, in those days.

'Only, I want a house,' he explained, 'that I could have
straight away, and could go into at once.'

The agent took out a copybook from a chest of drawers, put
on his spectacles, looked at one page, then at another, and said:

'There's a house that will suit you in every way, but you'll
have to add a little.'

'I can go a little higher.'

'Well, it will cost you up to thirty-five thousand.'

'That'll do me.'

'Very well, then,' he said, 'we'll get the matter through in
about an hour, and you'll be able to occupy it to-morrow,
because a deacon choked with a chicken-bone at a christening
in that house, and died, and because of that no one is living
there now.'

And this is the very house we are sitting in—you and I. They
said that the dead deacon walks about here at night and makes
choking noises, but that's all nonsense and no one's ever seen
him while we have been here. My wife and I moved in the very
next day, because the gent transferred it to us as a gift; and two
days later he came along with some half a dozen workmen and a
ladder and that signboard which talks as if I were a French tailor.

They came and nailed it up and went away, and the gent
said to me:

'There's one thing,' he said, 'that I command you: never
you dare to alter this signboard, and you're to answer to that
name.' And all of a sudden he bellowed:

174

'Lepoutan!'

I answered:

'Yes, sir!'

'Good lad,' said he. 'Here's another thousand roubles for you for household junk and what not; now, mark well, Lepoutan—you do as I order you, and all will be well with you; otherwise . . . if you start calling yourself by your old name or what—God help you if I get to hear of it. . . . As a preliminary I'll beat you to pulp, and then I'll have the law on you and take back the gift. And if you do as I want, you've only to tell me what else you need, and I'll let you have it.'

I thanked him, of course, and told him I'd got no more wishes and couldn't think of any, except one—if he would be pleased to tell me what all this meant and why I was given the house.

But this he would not tell me.

'That,' said he, 'is something you don't want to know; only remember this: henceforth you are called "Lepoutan" and that's how you stand in my Deed of Gift. Keep that name: you'll find it will pay you.'

CHAPTER THE ELEVENTH

"SO we were left to set up home in our own house, and everything went very well with us, and we reckoned that it was all through my wife's luck, because we could not get a real explanation of it from anybody for a long time, but one day two gentlemen happened to be running past here, and suddenly they stopped and came in.

My wife said:

'What can I do for you?'

And they replied:

'We want to see Monsieur Lepoutan himself.'

I came out and they looked at one another and both burst out laughing at the same time and began speaking to me in French.

I excused myself for not being able to speak the lingo.

'And how long,' said they, 'have you been under that sign-board?'

I told them how many years that would be.

'That's it. You know,' they said, 'we remember you and we've seen you before; there was a certain gent you mended a dress-suit for on New Year's Eve for a ball, and then, because of it, you had to suffer a bit of unpleasantness at the hotel.'

'You are quite right,' I said; 'there was an incident like that, but I'm only most grateful to the gentleman and through him I became a man, only I don't know his name or surname, because he wouldn't tell me.'

They told me his name—and his surname, they added, was Laputin.

'How do you mean—Laputin?'

'Of course,' they said: 'Laputin. Don't you know why he's done all this for you? He didn't want to see his name on the signboard.'

'Now fancy that,' I said. 'You know, to this day we had no idea what it was all about. We've been making full use of his benefaction and yet felt as though we were all in the dark.'

'Nevertheless,' said my guests, 'it hasn't helped him much. Yesterday,' they said, 'he struck another bad patch.'

And they told me a bit of news that made me feel very sorry for my former namesake.

CHAPTER THE TWELFTH

"LAPUTIN'S wife, to whom he proposed in the patched-up dress-suit, was even more touchy than her husband, and she adored show. Neither of them was particularly highly born —their fathers just made a pile of money on contracts—but they sought acquaintances only among the nobility. In those days we had as Commander-in-Chief in Moscow Count Zakrevsky, who himself, it was said, was only of the Polish gentry, and the real gentry, like Prince Sergei Mihailovich Golitsyn, didn't rate him highly; but the rest were flattered to be received in his house. The wife of my former namesake also pined for his honour. Only, God knows why, nothing came of it for a long time, but at last Mr. Laputin found a way to make himself agreeable to the Count, and the latter said to him :

'Come and see me, brother; I'll tell them to admit you, you just tell me what your name is, so that I don't forget.'

The other said his name was Laputin.

'Laputin?' said the Count. 'Laputin. . . . Wait, wait now— Laputin . . . I seem to remember, Laputin. That's someone's surname.'

'Quite so,' the other said. 'Your Excellency—that's *my* name.'

'Of course, of course, that is your name, brother, only I seem to remember something . . . there seemed to be some other Laputin. Perhaps it was your father, Laputin?'

The gentleman replied that his father had been a Laputin.

'That's why I seem to remember it. . . . Laputin. It may have been your father. I have a very good memory; come along then, Laputin—come to-morrow if you like; I'll tell them to admit you, Laputin.'

The other was overjoyed, and the very next day went off to see the Count.

CHAPTER THE THIRTEENTH

"BUT Count Zakrevsky, though he did say he had a good memory, on this occasion slipped up a trifle and said nothing about receiving Mr. Laputin.

The latter came dashing up.

'I'm So-and-so,' he said, 'and I wish to see the Count.'

But the doorman would not admit him.

'Orders,' said he, 'to admit no one.'

The gentleman tried arguing this way and that. 'I haven't come of my own accord,' he said, 'I've come at the Count's invitation.' But the doorman was not to be moved.

'I've orders,' said he, 'to admit no one, and if you're on business, you go to the office.'

'I'm not on business,' the gentleman protested, 'but a personal friend; the Count must have told you my name—Laputin; you must have got muddled.'

'The Count mentioned no name to me yesterday.'

'That's impossible; you must have just forgotten the name—Laputin.'

'I never forget anything, and this name I could not forget if I tried, because my own name is Laputin.'

The gentleman fairly flared up.

'What do you mean—you're a Laputin yourself! Who taught you to call yourself by that name?'

But the doorman said:

'No one's taught me anything—that's our name, and there are any number of Laputins in Moscow, only the rest are all of no importance: I'm the only one who's got on in the world.'

And while they were arguing, the Count himself came walking down the steps and said:

'Of course, that's the one I was thinking of, he's also a Laputin, and another scoundrel. And you come another day, I'm busy just now. Good day.'

Well, naturally, there was no question of any visit after that!"

CHAPTER THE FOURTEENTH

MAÎTRE Tailleur Lepoutan related this with an air of quiet sympathy, and added as a finale that the very next day he came across the great Laputin himself, whom Vasilii Konych had reason to regard as his benefactor. Konych was passing along the Boulevard with some work at the time.

"There he sat," he said, "on a seat, as sad as sad. I wanted to slip past, but the moment he saw me he said:

'Hullo, Monsieur Lepoutan! How goes it?'

'By the grace of God, and with your help, very well. And how would you be feeling, sir?'

'Couldn't be worse; I found myself in such a mess-up.'

'I've heard of it, sir, and was glad you at least abstained from touching him.'

'I couldn't touch him,' he said, 'because he is not a free-lance artisan, but only the Count's flunkey; but what I want to know is this: who bribed him to offer me this insult?'"

Konych, in his simplicity, proceeded to console the gentleman:

"'I should not look for bribery in it, sir. There are indeed lots of Laputins in Moscow, and there are some very honest ones among them—like my late grandad, for instance: he used to peddle felt soles all over Moscow.'

And no sooner had I said it than he ups and swipes me with his stick right across my back. . . . I streaked away, and haven't seen him since. I only heard that he and his wife went abroad to France, and there he lost all his money and died, and she put up a monument over him; only I heard say, she picked one up second-hand, with the same name as on my signboard: 'Lepoutan'. So we found ourselves namesakes again, after all."

CHAPTER THE FIFTEENTH

VASILII KONYCH ended his recital, and I asked him why he did not want now to change his signboard and write on it his own, legal, Russian name?

"Well, why should I, sir? Why should I stir up all that business which started my luck? It would only do harm to the district."

"How could it do harm to the district?"

"Why, of course: my French signboard, everyone knows it to be just so much splash, but it's given all our district quite a different atmosphere, and the neighbouring houses are now in quite a different class."

So Konych remained a Frenchman for the good of the inhabitants of his back alley, while his proud namesake rotted away uselessly under an assumed name at Père Lachaise.

THE DEVILCHASE

THIS IS A RITUAL THAT MAY BE SEEN ONLY IN Moscow, and even then you need to be especially lucky and to have the necessary influential connections.

I witnessed a Devilchase from beginning to end, thanks to a lucky combination of circumstances, and I wish to record it for the benefit of true connoisseurs and lovers of all that is solemn and grand in the national vein.

Although I belong to the gentry, I also stand close to "the people", since my mother was of the merchant class. Her family was a very wealthy one, but she married against their wish, because of her love for my father. My father—of sainted memory—was a great ladies' man and invariably achieved whatever he set his heart on. In the same way he was successful with my mother, but, as a result of this success of his, my mother's people gave her nothing at all, except, of course, dresses and bedding and the mercy of God, which were received together with their forgiveness and paternal blessing that was to stand for all times. My parents lived in Orel, and lived frugally but proudly, and never asked anything of my mother's wealthy relations, and had no dealings with them at all. Nevertheless, when the time came for me to leave for the University, my mother said to me:

"Please go and see uncle Ilya Fedoseich and give him my love. There's no loss of face in that, because you must respect your elder relations. After all, he is my brother, and he's a very pious man and carries great weight in Moscow; he always presents the bread and salt at all the receptions, and stands in front of all the others with the salver or ikon. . . . And the Governor-General and the Metropolitan are friends of his. . . . He can teach you a lot of useful things."

And although at that period of my life I had made a careful study of "Filaret's Catechism" and did not believe in God, I loved my mother, and so one day I said to myself: "Here I've been nearly a year in Moscow, and still haven't done anything about mother's request. What if I go at once to uncle Ilya Fedoseich and pay him a visit? I'll give him mother's message and see for myself what it is he's supposed to be able to teach me."

It was a habit of my childhood days to respect my elders, especially those who kept company with Metropolitans and Governors.

And so I got up, and brushed my clothes carefully, and went off to uncle Ilya Fedoseich.

CHAPTER THE SECOND

THAT was about six in the evening. The weather had been mild and warm, with overcast skies—in other words, it was all right. My uncle's house was well known; it was one of the most striking houses in Moscow, and everyone was familiar with it. Only I had never been inside it and had never set eyes on uncle Ilya, even from a distance.

Nevertheless I advanced boldly, thinking to myself: "If he sees me—all well and good; if not—why worry!"

I arrived inside the gates. Before the porch stood a pair of lion-like steeds, black as ebony, with flowing manes and sleek coats as lustrous as the richest sateen. They were harnessed to a brougham.

I mounted the steps of the porch and said: "I am a nephew—a student. Will you please tell Ilya Fedoseich?" And the men who stood about said:

"They'll be down in person in a moment. They are going for a drive."

At that moment there appeared the form of a man—a figure of the utmost simplicity, and very Russian, and yet most dignified and imposing. There was something in the eyes that reminded me of my mother, only their expression was different. One could see at a glance that here was a personage of some consequence.

I introduced myself. He heard me in silence, proffered his hand—very gently—and said:

"Jump in—we'll go for a drive."

I was on the point of refusing, but somehow lost my head and got in.

"To the park!" he commanded.

The leonine steeds leapt to life and bounded forward, with the back of the brougham swaying and skipping over the bumps. Once clear of the town, they raced with increasing speed.

We sat without exchanging a word, and I noticed only that uncle had jammed down the rim of his silk hat till the edge cut into his forehead over the eyebrows, and his face bore that expression of blank indifference which signifies supreme boredom.

His eyes travelled over the various objects that presented themselves to our view, and once he darted a quick glance in my direction and, for no apparent reason, let fall:

"There's no life, none at all!"

I did not know what to answer, and said nothing.

Again we were bowling along, farther and farther, and I was now wondering where he was taking me to. And then suddenly I began to feel more and more that I was in for something I had not reckoned on.

Uncle just as suddenly appeared to make up his mind about something, and he gave our coachman a series of rapid directions:

"Right. Left. Over by 'The Yard'—stop!"

I beheld a crowd of waiters hurrying towards us from the restaurant. They were all scraping and bowing profoundly before my uncle, while he sat in the brougham without moving a muscle and ordered the proprietor to be called. Off they dashed, and presently a Frenchman appeared, also full of respect. But uncle did not stir. He was tapping his teeth with the ivory knob of his cane and said:

"How many outsiders are there?"

"About thirty in the main rooms," was the Frenchman's reply, "and three private rooms are booked."

"Out with them all."

"Very well."

"It is now seven," said my uncle, glancing at his watch. "I shall be back at eight. Will everything be ready?"

"No," was the reply, "I doubt if I could manage by eight.
. . . Many have only just ordered . . . but if you'll be good
enough to come at nine, there won't be an outsider in the
place."

"All right."

"And what shall we have ready?"

"The Ethiopians, naturally."

"And what else?"

"An orchestra."

"One?"

"No—better have two."

"And shall I send for Riabyka?"

"Naturally."

"French ladies?"

"Don't want them."

"The cellar?"

"Complete."

"And the cuisine?"

"Card."

He was given the menu for the day.

Uncle examined it, and seemingly could make nothing of it,
or, perhaps, he just refused to be bothered. He tapped the
paper with his cane and said:

"All this now—for a hundred persons."

And with that rolled up the card and slipped it in his coat.

The Frenchman was radiant with joy, and at the same time
hesitated.

"I can't," he said, "serve everything for a hundred persons.
There are some very expensive things here of which there are
only five or six portions in the restaurant."

"And how do you expect me to sort out my guests? Whatever anyone wants, it must be there. Understand?"

"Yes, sir."

"Otherwise, my lad, Riabyka himself won't be on your side.
Get on with it."

We left the restaurateur and his waiters standing outside the
doors and whirled away.

By now I had become fully convinced that I was completely

out of place and tried to take my leave, but my uncle did not hear me. He was very preoccupied. We were spinning along, and every now and again stopping various people.

"Nine o'clock, at 'The Yard'!" my uncle would say tersely to each one of them.

And the individuals he said this to were for the most part important-looking old men, and they all doffed their hats and replied as briefly to my uncle:

"Your guests—your humble guest, Fedoseich."

In this manner I cannot say how many people we stopped, but I reckon there must have been a good twenty of them, and as nine o'clock was now approaching, we drove back to "The Yard". A crowd of servants tumbled out at our approach, and uncle, gently supported on both sides, was carefully conveyed from the brougham, while at the door the Frenchman himself whisked the dust off his trousers with a napkin.

"All clear?" asked my uncle.

"One general," said he, "is all behind. He very much asked to be allowed to finish in the private room."

"Pitch him out at once."

"He'll be through very soon now."

"I don't care. I've given him time enough—let him get out on the grass to finish."

I don't know what the upshot of all this would have been, but just then the general and two ladies came out, climbed into a brougham and drove away, and at the entrance, in quick succession, the guests who had been invited by my uncle in the park at once began to arrive.

CHAPTER THE THIRD

THE restaurant had been tidied up and cleaned, and was free of visitors. Only in one of the halls sat a solitary giant of a man who met my uncle in silence and, without so much as a word, took uncle's cane out of his hands and hid it away somewhere.

Uncle gave up his cane without a murmur of protest and straightway handed the giant his wallet and purse.

The uncouth and massive giant was that same Riabyka about whom the mysterious order had been given to the restaurateur in my presence. He was "a children's teacher" of some sort, but here, it appeared, he also had some specific duties to perform. He seemed as indispensable as the Gypsies, the orchestra, and all the appurtenances of a carousal that instantly appeared in full array. What I could not make out just then was what precisely the teacher was supposed to do, and it was something that, owing to my inexperience, I could never have guessed.

The brilliantly illuminated restaurant bustled with activity: music crashed, the Gypsies strolled about and helped themselves to refreshments at the buffet, while my uncle was making a tour of the rooms, the garden, the grotto and the galleries. He was looking everywhere for "unauthorized persons", and at his elbow continually walked the teacher; but when they returned to the main room, where everyone had now gathered, one could see a striking difference in their behaviour: the teacher was as sober as when he had started, while my uncle was completely drunk.

How this could have happened in so short a time I do not know, only he was in the most excellent spirits; he climbed into his chairman's seat, and the fun began. . . .

The doors were locked, and it was said of the world outside that "there is no crossing from them to us, neither can we cross to them". We were separated by an abyss—an abyss of food and drink, and above all, an abysmal orgy. I would not go so far as to call it an abominable orgy, but it was savage, elemental, of a kind that I have not the power to describe.

And indeed this should not be demanded of me, because, finding myself trapped here and cut off from the normal world, I lost heart, and for my own part hastened to become as drunk as David's sow. So I will not undertake to record how the night proceeded, because to describe it *all* is beyond the powers of my pen, and I remember only two outstanding "battle scenes" and the *finale*, but these were the scenes that were pre-eminently terrifying.

CHAPTER THE FOURTH

THE arrival was announced of someone called Ivan Stepanych —as it turned out, one of the most important industrialists and princes of commerce in Moscow.

This created a pause.

"Didn't I say, 'No one is to be admitted'?" answered uncle.

"They beg very much."

"Wherever he was before, he'd better get back there now."

The waiter left, but presently returned timidly.

"Ivan Stepanych," he said, "ordered me to tell you that they very humbly beg for admittance."

"Don't want him. I don't want him."

Others joined in: "Let him pay a fine."

"Noa, shoo him out. Don't want his fine."

But the man appeared again and reported still more apologetically.

"They are prepared," he said, "to agree to any fine—only at their time of life, they say, not to be one of the company, they say, is very mortifying to them."

My uncle rose, and his eyes blazed, but the same instant, between him and the waiter, Riabyka reared himself to his full height: with his left arm—with what seemed just a flick—he flung back the waiter as though he were a chicken, and with his right arm pushed uncle back into his chair.

From among the guests voices began to be raised in favour of Ivan Stepanych—a clamour rose to let him in: "Fine him a hundred roubles for the benefit of the musicians and let him come in."

"He's one of us—an old man—steady—God-fearing—where'll he go now? He'll probably get out of hand and make a scene before all the small fry. You must take pity on him."

Uncle hearkened to the pleadings and said:

"If it's not to be as I want, it won't be as you want it either, but as God wills: I permit Ivan Stepanych to enter, only he must beat the Turkish drum."

The ambassador left and returned.

"They ask," he said, "if they can't be fined instead."

"To hell! If he doesn't want to drum, he needn't—let him go where he likes."

After a short while Ivan Stepanych could hold out no longer and sent word to say that *he agreed* to beat the Turkish drum.

"Let him come in."

Enter an uncommonly tall, venerable-looking man of ascetic, dignified mien, with lustreless eyes, stooping shoulders, and a long beard, greeny-white and mottled. He made as if to joke and greet the company, but was checked.

"Later, later—you'll do all that later," roared my uncle. "Now beat the Turkish drum."

"Beat the drum!" joined in the others.

"Hoi, orchestra! Drum music."

The orchestra struck up a noisy piece; the venerable patriarch picked up the wooden drumsticks and began to pound the Turkish drum, in time and out of time.

The crash and roar became deafening: everyone was in ecstasies and hollering:

"Louder!"

Ivan Stepanych smote harder—harder still.

"Louder, louder—still louder!"

The patriarch beat with all his might, like the Black King of Freiligrath, and, finally, the object was achieved, the drum gave out a fearful crash, the skin burst, everyone rocked with laughter, the noise became unimaginable, and Ivan Stepanych was relieved of five hundred roubles for the broken drum by way of a fine payable to the orchestra.

He paid, wiped the sweat off his brow, and took his seat at table, and while everyone drank his health, to his intense horror he recognized his son-in-law among the guests.

More laughter, more noise, and so on, till I became insensible again. In the occasional intervals of consciousness I remember the Gypsy girls dancing, I remember how my uncle was jerking his feet as he sat in his seat; then how he got up to face someone, but instantly Riabyka appeared between them, and someone spun backwards, and uncle sat down again, and before him two quivering forks were embedded in the table. I now understood Riabyka's role.

But presently the freshness of a Moscow dawn was wafted through the windows. Again I became aware of my surroundings, but only to doubt my sanity. A battle was raging, forests were being hewn down, there was a splintering noise, thunder, swaying trees—virginal, exotic trees—behind which were crowded in a corner dusky faces, while here, by the roots, fearful axes were flashing, and my uncle was hewing, the ancient Ivan Stepanych was hewing . . . a regular scene from the Middle Ages.

This was "making prisoners"—capturing the Gypsy girls, who had taken refuge in the grotto behind the trees. Their menfolk did not defend them, but left them to their own resources. What was in jest and what in real earnest it was impossible to say: through the air hurtled plates, chairs, stones from the grotto, while the others were smashing their way into the forest, and in the foreground, more fearless than the rest, were Ivan Stepanych and my uncle.

At last the stronghold fell: the Gypsy girls were seized, embraced, covered with kisses, and each captor pushed down the bodice of each captive a hundred-rouble note—and all was over. . . .

Yes; quite suddenly, all was peace—finished! No one had intervened, but it was just—enough! One felt that, just as before there had been "no life", so now it was "enough".

Everyone had had enough, and all were pleased. Perhaps there was something in the fact that the school-teacher declared that it was time for him to be off to his "classes", but, still, that made no difference: the Walpurgis Night was over, and "life" had begun afresh.

The guests did not take leave, did not part, but simply vanished; the next instant there was no orchestra, no Gypsies. The restaurant presented a picture of complete ruin: not a drapery, not a mirror was intact . . . even the ceiling chandelier— even that lay in pieces on the floor, and its crystal prisms crackled beneath the feet of the tottering, exhausted servants. Uncle was seated alone in the middle of a sofa and was drinking *kvas*; every now and again he appeared to recall something and jerked his legs in time to imaginary music. At his elbow stood Riabyka, who was impatient to get to his classes.

We were presented with a bill—a short bill, in round figures. Riabyka carefully scrutinized the bill and demanded a reduction of fifteen hundred. After nothing but a perfunctory argument, the bill was totted up. It came to seventeen thousand roubles, and Riabyka, who studied it again, declared that this was fair enough. Uncle uttered a monosyllabic "Pay", and then put on his hat and nodded to me to follow him.

To my horror I noticed that he had forgotten nothing, and that escape for me was impossible. He filled me with extreme terror, and I could not conceive how I could remain with him alone in his present state. He had picked me up to accompany him without so much as by your leave, and now he had me firmly in tow, and I had no means of shaking him off. What was to become of me? All the wine evaporated from my brain. I was quite simply afraid of this terrible wild beast with his incredible imagination and fearful swing. But meanwhile we were already heading for the open: in the vestibule a crowd of waiters surrounded us. Uncle dictated "Five each", and Riabyka was paying out. Below we paid the *dvorniks*, watchmen, policemen, gendarmes, who had all apparently rendered us some service or other. All their demands were satisfied. But it all mounted up, and to add to it, here as far as the eye could reach across the park were the drozhkis. Their name was legion, and they were all waiting for us, waiting for "father Ilya Fedoseich, whether it would not be his pleasure to send them somewhere".

We found out how many of them there were, and each was presented with three roubles, and uncle and I climbed into the brougham, while Riabyka handed him his wallet.

Ilya Fedoseich took a hundred-rouble note out of the wallet and gave it to Riabyka.

The latter turned the note over in his hand and said roughly: "Not enough."

Uncle added two more notes of twenty-five roubles.

"Well, that's not enough either: there wasn't a single fight."

Uncle gave him a third note of twenty-five roubles, after which the teacher handed him back his cane and bowed himself out of our presence.

CHAPTER THE FIFTH

WE were left alone, uncle and I, and we were tearing back to Moscow, and behind us, with shrill whistles, yells and cries, raced at full gallop all the motley, ragtag crowd of drozhkis. I could not think what they wanted, but uncle understood. It was disgusting. They were out to extort more blackmail, and so, under pretence of rendering special honours to Ilya Fedoseich, were holding up "his worshipful honour" to public contempt.

By now we were on the fringe of Moscow, and the town lay spread before our eyes—all bathed in the gentle light of morning and wreathed in the mists of wood-smoke and the peaceful jangling of the bells that called to prayer.

To right and left of us, stretching to the city boundary, stood row upon row of warehouses. Uncle stopped by the nearest of them, walked up to a limewood vat that stood by the door, and asked:

"Honey?"

"Honey."

"How much the tub?"

"We sell it retail, by the pound."

"You sell the lot; work out what it costs."

I don't remember now, but I believe it was seventy or eighty roubles, the man worked it out.

Uncle threw down the money.

And meanwhile our cortège had descended upon us.

"Do you love me, my good city drivers?"

"Of course; we're always ready for your honour. . . ."

"Are you at my service?"

"We're very much at your service."

"Off with your wheels, then."

The drivers blinked.

"Hurry up—get a move on!" ordered my uncle.

The more quick-witted ones—about a score of them—dived under their drivers' seats, produced spanners, and proceeded to loosen the bolts.

"Good!" grunted my uncle. "Now daub them with honey."

"But, little father . . ."

"Go on!"

"All that good stuff. . . . Wouldn't it've been better . . . ?"

"Go on!"

And without insisting further, uncle got into the brougham and we sped away, while the others, the lot of them, were left with their wheelless cabs over the honey, which no doubt they did not daub onto their wheels, but probably divided among themselves or resold to the store-keeper. At any rate we were rid of them, and presently found ourselves in the Public Baths. Here I thought my end had come, and, more dead than alive, I sat in the marble bath while uncle sprawled on the floor,— not in a usual attitude, but in an almost Apocalyptic posture. All the enormous mass of his heavy bulk was supported on the floor only by the extreme tips of his fingers and toes, and between these tiny points of support his crimson body quaked beneath the jets of cold rain that lashed it, and he roared with the muffled roar of a bear that is tearing out a sore from his body. This went on for about half an hour, and all this time he continued to quiver with the same even rhythm, like a jelly on a shaky table, till suddenly he leapt to his feet, called for *kvas*, and we dressed and drove to the Kouznetzky—"to the Frenchman".

Here we both had our hair trimmed, slightly curled, and set, and then we walked to town on foot—to uncle's shop.

To me he still addressed not a word, nor would he dismiss me. Only once he said:

"Wait; not all at once. What you don't understand now, you'll tumble to by and by."

In the shop he said a prayer before the ikon, cast a proprietorial eye over everyone and everything, and took up his stand behind the cash-desk. The outside of the vessel was now .cleansed, but inside profound blackness still fermented, and it was yearning to be purified.

I tumbled to that, and now ceased to fear him. He interested me greatly; I wanted to see how he would deal with himself, whether by self-restraint or some act of fervent devotion.

About ten he began to grow very fretful, watching and waiting for the shopkeeper next door, so that the three of us could go out to tea—there was a reduction of five kopecks on a pot for three. The neighbour never came: he had died suddenly in the night.

My uncle crossed himself and said:

"We shall all die."

This death did not affect him, although for forty years they had been going together to the Novotroitzky to drink tea.

We called the neighbour from the other side and went several times to take a bite of this and that, but all teetotal. All day I stuck to the shop or chased up and down to the tavern, and just before nightfall he sent me to hire a cab to go to the All-Hallowed Virgin.

There he was well known and was received with the same deference as at "The Yard".

"I wish to fall before the All-Hallowed and weep over my sins. And this, I present to you, is my nephew—my sister's lad."

"Come in," said the nuns, "come in; from whom should the All-Hallowed receive repentance but from you, the generous benefactor of her abode. Now is the most propitious moment—it is Mass."

"Let it be finished; I like it when there is nobody about and to have a blessed twilight all round me."

He was provided with "blessed twilight": all the cressets were extinguished, except one or two, and a large lampad in a green glass before the ikon of the All-Hallowed herself.

Uncle did not fall, but crashed to his knees. Then he smote his forehead against the floor, gave a gasp, and appeared as though struck lifeless.

Two nuns and I sat down in a dark corner behind the doors. A long pause followed. Uncle was still lying on the floor without appearing to see or hear anything. It occurred to me that he had fallen asleep, and I even said so to one of the nuns. The experienced sister pondered for a moment, shook her head, and lighting a thin taper, shielded it closely with her hand and ever so quietly made her way to the penitent. Having tiptoed round him, she returned and announced in a whisper :

"It's acting all right . . . and with a twist."

"How can you tell that ?"

She bent down, motioning to me to do the same, and said :

"Look straight ahead, through the flame—where his feet are."

"I see."

"Can you see the conflict that is going on ?"

I peered into the gloom, and by and by I could indeed make it out. There was my uncle, lying in the attitude of a worshipper, but at his feet it seemed as though two cats were fighting—now one and now the other got the better of his adversary, and all this so rapidly, bobbing up and down. . . .

"Mother," I said, "where have the cats come from ?"

She replied : "It only looks to you as if they were cats ; they are not cats but temptation. See—his soul is burning Heavenwards, but his feet are still in hell."

Now I saw indeed that it was uncle's feet that were dancing the *trepak* of the previous night ; but was it possible, I wondered, that his spirit was straining towards Heaven ?

And as though in answer to my thoughts, all at once he heaved a terrific sigh and bellowed suddenly :

"I shall not rise until Thou hast forgiven me ! Thou alone art holy, while we are all fiends and devils !"—and he burst into loud tears.

And such were his tears that we too—the three of us—fell to weeping and sobbing : "O Lord, grant his prayer !"

And we never noticed how he had moved over to us, and now he was with us and he said to me in a calm, serene voice :

"Come on—let's eat."

The nuns asked him :

"Father, were you deemed worthy to behold the Reflection ?"

"No," he replied, "there was no Reflection, but this . . . I did get this."

He clenched his fist and raised it as though he were lifting a boy by the top-knot.

"You were raised to your feet ?"

"Yes."

The nuns proceeded to cross themselves—so did I—while uncle explained:

"Now," said he, "I am forgiven! Right from above—from under the dome itself—an open palm caught hold of all my hair and put me straight on my feet. . . ."

And now he was no longer an outcast, and he was happy. He made rich donations to the convent where his prayer had worked this miracle, and he experienced the joy of "life" once more, and sent my mother all her dowry, while I was guided by him into the right faith of my people.

From that day on I gradually came to know the soul of the people, in all its boundless sinning and sublime repentance. . . . This is what is known as "*The Devilchase*, that casteth out the devil of sinful thought". Only—I repeat—it can be witnessed nowhere but in Moscow, if you are deemed deserving of it, and even then only if you are lucky and possess a very influential friend among the most worthy and pious of the City Fathers.

THE ALEXANDRITE

I MUST BE PERMITTED TO MAKE A BRIEF STATE-
ment concerning a curious crystal, the discovery of which in
the depth of the mountains of Russia is linked with the memory
of the deceased Tsar Alexander Nikolaevich. I refer to the lovely
dark-green gem which was named "Alexandrite" in honour of
the late Emperor.

The name was given to the said crystal because it was first
found on April 17th, 1834, on the day Alexander II came of
age. The place where the Alexandrite was discovered was an
emerald mine in the Urals, fifty-six miles from Ekaterinburg
along the river Tokovaya, which flows into the Bolshaya
Revt. The name of "Alexandrite" was given to the stone by
the well-known Finnish mineralogist Nordenschild, for precisely
the reason that the stone was found by him—Mr. Nordenschild
—on the coming-of-age day of the late Tsar. The reasons I
have stated are, I think, sufficient to stop people from wanting
to look for others.

"Alexandrite" (Alexandrit, Chrysoberyl Cymaphone) is a
variety of the Ural Chrysoberyl. It is a precious mineral. The
colour of an Alexandrite is *dark green*, closely resembling the
colour of an emerald. By artificial light the stone sheds its green
colour and turns to *crimson*.

"The finest crystals of the Alexandrite were found at a depth
of twenty feet at the Krasnobolotsky Fields. Gems of the
Alexandrite are of the greatest rarity and are not above one
carat in weight. In consequence, Alexandrites are not only
rarely to be seen in the market, but some jewellers even know
of them only from hearsay.

"It is regarded as the stone of Alexander II."—This in-
formation I have copied from the book by M. I. Pylyaev,
published in 1877 by the Mineralogical Society of St. Petersburg
under the title: "Precious Stones, their Properties, Location
and Use".

I may add to these extracts from the work of Mr. Pylyaev concerning the Alexandrite that the rarity of the stone has been increased by two circumstances: (1) Prospectors are absolutely convinced that where Alexandrites are known to exist, it is useless to look for emeralds, and (2) the mines that provided the best specimens of the stones of Alexander II were flooded by water from a river that had burst into the workings.

Thus, I would have you note that Alexandrites are rarely to be seen at Russian jewellers', while foreign lapidaries, as M. I. Pylyaev points out, know of them only from hearsay.

CHAPTER THE SECOND

AFTER the tragic and deeply mourned death of the late Tsar,[1] under whom our contemporaries had passed their spring, their warm early days filled with hope, many of us, in conformity with a widespread human custom, desired to provide our-selves with various mementoes of the beloved Monarch. His numerous admirers therefore acquired various articles, mostly of a kind that could always be carried about the person.

Some bought miniature portraits of the dead Emperor and fixed them to their wallets or watch medallions, others engraved on their most treasured possessions the dates of his birth and death, while a few—who had the money and the chance—bought gems of the stone of Alexander II. They were mounted in rings and never taken off the finger.

Rings with Alexandrites were most eagerly sought, and formed the rarest and perhaps the most characteristic mementoes, and when anyone succeeded in obtaining one he never parted with it.

However, there were not many rings with Alexandrites to be seen, because, as Mr. Pylyaev rightly states, good specimens of the stone are both rare and costly. As a result, at one time there was a tremendous demand for Alexandrites, which, it was said, even brought about attempts at imitating the stones, but they

---

[1] Alexander II, the liberator and reformer of Russia, assassinated in 1881.

defied all attempts at imitation. The stone possesses a dichromatic peculiarity. I would have you remember that an Alexandrite is *green* in daylight, while by artificial light it is *red*.

This cannot be achieved by any artificial means.

CHAPTER THE THIRD

I OBTAINED a ring with an Alexandrite, which had come off the hand of one of the great men of the reign of Alexander II. I bought the ring quite simply—at a sale following the death of the owner. A dealer bid for it, and I got it from him. It fitted me, and after I had slipped it on my finger I never removed it.

The ring was fashioned rather curiously and symbolically; the stone of Alexander II was not alone, but had on each side of it a diamond of the purest water. They were meant to represent two of the most illustrious deeds of the past reign : the liberation of the serfs and the setting up of a grand new system of legal procedure which superseded the old "black lawlessness".

The fine, deeply coloured Alexandrite was just under one carat, while the diamonds were only half a carat each. The purpose of this again was obviously to prevent the diamonds— which represented the deeds—overshadowing the main, more modest stone, which was a reminder of the face of the noble reformer himself. The stones were set in a smooth ring of gold —without any frills—in the English fashion, so that the ring was a cherished memory and did not "reek of cash".

CHAPTER THE FOURTH

IN the summer of 1884 I made a journey to Bohemia. Having a restive propensity for getting excited over various branches of art, I became rather interested there in the local jewellery and gem-cutting craft.

Quite a number of coloured stones are to be found in Bohemia, but they are not of a high quality and are generally inferior to those of Ceylon and to our Siberian stones. The only exception is the Czech pyrope, or "fiery garnet", found in the "dry fields" of Meronitz. No better garnets exist anywhere.

Pyropes were highly esteemed in Russia in the olden days and valued greatly, but now it is almost impossible to find good, large Czech pyropes at Russian lapidaries'. In Russia you find among the cheaper jewellery either a muddy, dark Tyrolese garnet, or "water garnets"; but there are no fiery pyropes from the "dry fields" of Meronitz. All the best old specimens of this attractive, deeply coloured stone, cut as a rule in rose form, have been bought up for a song by foreigners and sent abroad, while the finest pyropes found in Bohemia go nowadays to England and America direct. Tastes there are more stable, and the English are very fond of this exquisite stone with the mysterious fire confined in it ("Fire in the Blood"), and they prize it highly. Also, the British and Americans generally like characteristic stones, such stones as pyropes, or the "moonstone", which reflects always only its own "lunar" light. In a small yet very useful little book entitled "Rules of Politeness and Good Manners", these stones are even mentioned as deserving of the taste of a real gentleman. Of diamonds it is stated that they "can be worn by anyone who has money". In Russia a different view is held on these matters: with us neither symbolism, nor beauty, nor the mystery of surprising colour is respected any more, and there is no wish to hide "the reek of cash".

In Russia we respect only "what is accepted at the pawn-broker's". That is why so-called amateurs' stones are no longer imported and are no longer known to our collectors of gems. Our people would probably think it astounding and incredible that an exquisite specimen of the flaming garnet is regarded as one of the finest ornaments of the Austrian Crown and costs a vast amount of money.

CHAPTER THE FIFTH

WHEN I went abroad, I had, among other requests, one from a friend of mine in St. Petersburg, to bring him from Bohemia two of the best garnets I could find there.

I did come across two stones of a fair size and good colour; but, to my annoyance, one of them, which was more pleasant in tone, was spoilt by very inexpert cutting. It had the shape of a diamond, but its top facet had somehow been clumsily cut straight across, and as a result, the stone had neither depth nor lustre.

However, the Czech who guided my choice advised me to buy this particular garnet and then give it to be re-cut to a well-known local cutter called Wentzel, who, my friend said, was the greatest master of his craft, as well as a very eccentric old boy.

"He's an artist—not an artisan," the Czech told me, and added that old Wentzel was a cabbalist and mystic and also, in his own way, an ecstatic poet and full of superstitions, in fact a very interesting person.

"You'll learn a lot when you meet him," my friend said. "A stone to grandpa Wentzel is not an inanimate object, but a living being. He feels in it the reflection of the mysterious life of the mountain spirits and—don't laugh—he enters into obscure contact with them through the stone. Now and again he will tell you something of the revelations he has had, and his utterances make many people think the poor old boy is not quite right in the head. He's very old, and full of whimsicalities. Nowadays he doesn't often do the work himself—his two sons are working for him—but if you ask him, and if he likes the stone, he'll do it himself. And if he does it himself, it'll be first-class, because, as I said, Wentzel himself is a great and inspired artist in his line. I've known him for years, and we drink beer together at Edlička; I'll ask him and hope he'll put the stone right for you. You will have made an excellent purchase then, and your friend in Russia will be delighted."

CHAPTER THE SIXTH

THE old man lived in one of the dark, narrow, tightly-built-up streets of the Jewish suburb, within a stone's-throw of the historic synagogue.

The cutter was a tall, gaunt old man with a slight stoop,

snow-white long hair and quick brown eyes, whose gaze expressed great concentration and a trace of something one notices in people possessed of megalomania. Although his spine was bent, he held his head high and surveyed you like a king. An actor, after seeing Wentzel, could very well make up as King Lear.

Wentzel examined the pyrope I had purchased, and nodded. Judging by this movement and by the expression of the old man's face, I was led to conclude that he approved of the stone, but apart from that, old Wentzel straightway showed himself in such a weird light, that, though our business relations still concerned the pyrope, my main interest was now centred on the old cutter himself. He stared at the stone for a very long time, munched with his toothless gums and nodded at me approvingly; then he rolled the pyrope about between his fingers, while he himself stared sharply and straight into my eyes and puckered and screwed up his face as though he had eaten a green nutshell; and suddenly he declared:

"Yes—that's *him*."

"A good pyrope?"

Instead of replying directly, Wentzel muttered that he had "known the stone for a long time".

It was easy to fancy myself before King Lear, and I replied:

"I am indeed happy to hear it, Mr. Wentzel."

My respectful manner pleased the old man, and he pointed to a seat on the bench and then himself came up to me so closely that his knees pressed against mine, and began to speak:

"He and I are old friends. . . . I've seen him when he was still at home in the dry fields of Meronitz. He was then in his pristine beauty, but I felt he was already there. . . . And who could have foretold that he would meet with so terrible a fate? Oh, you can see by examining him how far-seeing and deep are the spirits of the mountains! He was bought by a robber of a Swabian, and he gave him to a Swabian to cut. A Swabian can sell a stone well, because he has a heart of stone; but a Swabian cannot cut. A Swabian is a bully—he wants everything done his own way; he does not consult a stone—he does not see what a Czech pyrope can be made into, and a Czech pyrope is too proud to answer a Swabian. No, he and a Czech are of one spirit. A Swabian cannot make of him what he wants. Look—they wanted to make him rose-shaped—you can see that" (I saw nothing)—"but he did not submit to them. Oh yes—he, a pyrope, outwitted them; he preferred rather that the Swabians should cut off his head, and they cut off his head."

"Is that so?" I interrupted. "So he's dead."

"Dead? Why?"

"You said yourself they cut off his head."

Old Wentzel smiled pityingly.

"His head. . . . Yes, a head is an important thing, mister; but the spirit . . . the spirit is more important than the head. How many Czech heads have they cut off, and still the Czechs live. He did all he should have done when he fell into the hands of the barbarians. Had a Swabian dealt so despicably with some animal—with a pearl, or some "cat's eye" that's so fashionable to-day—nothing would have remained of them. They would have become just some silly button, fit only to be thrown away. But a Czech's different; you can't grind him up as easily as all that in a Swabian mortar! A pyrope's blood is hardened. . . . He knew what to do. He lay low—like a Czech under the Swabian—he gave his head, but hid his life in his heart. . . . Yes, mister, yes! You don't see the fire? No! And I see it—there it is, rich and eternal—the fire of the Czech mountain. . . . He lives, and—you must forgive him, mister—he's laughing at you."

Old Wentzel himself broke into a laugh and wagged his head.

CHAPTER THE SEVENTH

I STOOD before this old man, who held my stone in his hand, and was at a complete loss what to say in reply to his incomprehensible tirade. And he seemed to divine my perplexity, because he took hold of my hand, and at the same time picked up the pyrope with a pair of tweezers, raised it between two fingers to his face, and continued, his voice rising in a crescendo:

"He is a Czech prince himself—he is the primordial knight

of Meronitz ! He knew how to get away from the ignoramuses : under their very noses he disguised himself as a chimney-sweep. Yes, yes, I saw him; I saw how a Jewish dealer carried him in his pocket—the dealer matched other stones by him. But it is not for this that he had burned in the primordial fires—to rattle like a clown in the leather satchel of a profiteer. He grew tired of going about like a chimney-sweep and he has come to me for his raiment of light. Oh, we understand one another, and the Prince of the Mountains of Meronitz will now appear as a prince. You leave him with me, mister. He'll stay with me for a time—we'll put our heads together and the Prince will be a prince again."

With this Wentzel nodded to me rather brusquely and still more unceremoniously tossed the primordial knight into a very dirty, fly-spotted plate, in which lay what looked like identical garnets.

I didn't like that—I feared that my pyrope would get mixed up with the other, inferior stones.

Wentzel noticed this and wrinkled his brow.

"Wait!" he said, and stirring round the garnets on the plate with his hand, he suddenly tipped them all into my hat, then shook the hat, and without looking, plunged his hand into it and produced my "chimney-sweep".

"Do you want me to do it a hundred times, or is once enough ?"

He identified and felt the stones by their density.

"Enough," said I.

Wentzel threw the stones onto the plate once more, and nodded his head more proudly than ever.

With this we parted.

CHAPTER THE EIGHTH

IN all he said and did, in the very figure of the old cutter, there was so much eccentricity and oddness that it was difficult to view him as a normal person, and at any rate there was an atmosphere of a fairy-tale about him.

"Now," I speculated, "if such an eccentric expert on stones had lived in the days of Ivan the Terrible and had met that great connoisseur of rubies, what hours Ivan would have spent talking to him, and perhaps he would himself have sent his best bear on him! Nowadays Wentzel is an anachronism. At any pawnbroker's there are experts who must no doubt regard him with the same contempt with which he, doubtless, regards them. What a lot he has told me about a stone that only cost 25 guldens! A Czech prince, a primordial knight, and then to be tossed into a dirty plate. . . ."

No—he was obviously mad.

Yet Wentzel, as though to spite me, seemed wedged in my mind, and I could not get rid of him. I even saw him in my sleep. He and I were crawling over the Meronitz Mountains and for some reason hid from a lot of Swabians. The fields were not only dry, but hot, and Wentzel every now and again put his face to the ground, placed the palms of his hands upon the dusty rubble and whispered to me: "Try it! Try how hot it is. . . . How they burn there! No, you won't find such stones just anywhere!"

And under the influence of it all, the garnet I had purchased began indeed to appear to me as something animated "of primordial fires". The moment I found myself alone, I would remember an account I had read in my childhood days about the travels of Marco Polo, and our own Novgorodian legends about "rich stones, suited for many works". I would remember how I used to read and feel amazed that "garnets gladden the heart of man and keep away sorrow, and whoever carries them about him finds speech and understanding improved and he endears himself to people". Later, all this lost its meaning—all these legends came to be regarded by us as empty superstitions, and we began to doubt that "it is possible to soften diamonds by soaking them in the blood of goats", that "diamonds drive away bad dreams", and that if poison is brought near a person who has one on him, "he will begin to sweat"; "a sapphire strengthens the heart, a ruby increases happiness, lazulite abates sickness, emeralds heal eyes; turquoises preserve horses from falling, garnets burn away bad thoughts, a topaz stops water from boiling, agates preserve the chastity of virgins, while a bezoar-stone extinguishes all poison". And yet, after spending only a few hours with an old man and his heavy dreams, here I was prepared myself to dream with him.

CHAPTER THE NINTH

I WOULD be asleep, and yet I saw it all . . . and it seemed so pleasant, so pungent, so full of life, though I knew it was all nonsense. What a pawnbroker knew was not nonsense. He knew the value of gems . . . that was a fact. . . .

Yes, but this too had once been a fact . . . it was a fact that the Patriarch Nikon wrote to Tsar Alexis when complaining of his enemies, that they wanted to kill him and fed him with cruel poison till he would have died; but the Patriarch was clever—he had with him a "bezui-stone" and "sucked the poison out of himself". He licked and licked for a long time the bezui-stone set in his ring, but it helped him, and it was his enemies who suffered in the end. True, all this happened many years ago, when the stones in the womb of the earth, and the planets high up in the skies—all were concerned with the Fate of Man, and not as now, when in the skies and underfoot everything had grown indifferent towards Man, and there came not to him voices from above or below. None of the newly discovered planets have been assigned any duties in horoscopes; there are also many new stones, and they have all been measured and weighed and sorted out according to their specific gravity and mass, after which they convey nothing, nor do they preserve one from any ills. The time has passed when they spoke to man, and they are now as the ancient Bards, who have become "as voiceless fishes". And old Wentzel, of course, is merely playing the fool, repeating some old fairy-stories, which have become all muddled in his weakening brain.

Yet how he tormented me—this eccentric old man! Time and time again I called at his shop, and my pyrope was not only still unfinished, but Wentzel hadn't even touched it. My "primordial prince" still lay as a "chimney-sweep" on a plate among a crowd of degrading and unworthy companions.

To anyone who believed ever so little, but sincerely, that in this stone there dwelt some proud mountain spirit who could think and feel, such treatment would have appeared not only disrespectful, but barbaric.

CHAPTER THE TENTH

WENTZEL no longer interested me, but irritated me considerably. He never gave a rational answer, and sometimes I detected in his manner an uncalled-for insolence. To my most polite remarks that I had been waiting too long for the small turn of his polishing-wheel, he would pick his decayed teeth with a melancholy air and launch forth in speculations about wheels, and how many different wheels there are in the world : the wheel of a mill, the wheel of a peasant's cart, the wheel of a railway coach, the wheel of a light Viennese carriage, the wheel of a clock and the wheel of a watch, of every type and in every age. In other words, he would go on and on and would finally opine that it is easier to forge the axle of a carriage than to cut a stone, and therefore—"wait a little longer, Slav".

I lost all patience and asked Wentzel to give me back my stone as it was, but in reply the old man began to speak very softly :

"Oh, how can you do such a thing ? Why do you make it so difficult ?"

I told him I was getting very tired of it all.

"Aha," answered Wentzel. "I thought for a moment you had become a Swabian and purposely wanted to leave the Czech prince as a chimney-sweep.

And Wentzel broke into a loud laugh, opening his mouth so wide that the room became filled with the effluvia of stale hops and malt.

I fancied the old man that day had had a mug of Pilsen too much.

Wentzel even began to tell me some nonsense about having taken *him* for *walks* to Vinohrady, beyond the Nussel Steps. There—it would appear—they sat together on the Dry Mountain opposite Charles's Wall and *he* revealed to him, Wentzel, his entire history, "from the primordial days", before not only Socrates, Plato and Aristotle were born, but before the days of the Sin of Sodom and the Sodom conflagration—right up to the day when he appeared as a bug on the wall and played a trick on a peasant woman.

Wentzel seemed to recall something very amusing and fell into another fit of laughter, filling the room with the reek of malt and hops.

"That will do, grandpa Wentzel—I don't understand a thing."

"That's very strange!" he remarked incredulously, and told me that cases had been known of lovely pyropes being discovered simply in the plaster of cottage walls. There was such an abundance of the stones, that they lay above-ground and found their way into the plaster with the clay.

Wentzel, no doubt, had it all on his mind when he was sitting in the little beer-garden by the Nussel Steps, and carried it all with him to the dry mountain, where he fell into a profound and peaceful sleep and had a curious dream: He saw a poor Czech cottage in the Meronitz Mountains; in the cottage sat a young peasant woman who was spinning goat's hair with her hands, while with her foot she rocked a cradle, which with every movement tapped gently against the wall. The plaster flaked off lightly and fell to the floor in a white dust and . . . "*He awoke!*" That is to say, it was not Wentzel or the child in the cradle that awoke, but *he*—the primordial knight, sunk in the plaster. . . . He awoke and peeped out to behold the grandest sight in the world—a young mother rocking a cradle and spinning wool. . . . The Czech mother saw the garnet in the wall and thought: "That's a bug", and to prevent her child being bitten by the nasty insect, she hit it as hard as she could with her old shoe. *He* dropped out of the clay and rolled across the floor; and she saw it was a stone, and sold it to a Swabian for a handful of peas. All this happened in the days when a pyrope cost a handful of peas. It happened before the incident which has been described in the miracles of St. Nicholas, when a pyrope was swallowed by a fish, which was given to a poor woman, who was enriched by the find. . . .

"Grandpa Wentzel," said I, "you must excuse me—you're telling me a lot of very curious things, but I have no time to listen to them. I am leaving after to-morrow, early in the morning, and so to-morrow I will call on you for the last time, to take my stone."

"Very good, very good!" Wentzel replied. "Come to-morrow at dusk when they begin putting the lights on: the sweep will meet you as a prince."

CHAPTER THE ELEVENTH

I WAS there punctually at the appointed hour, when the candles began to be lit, and this time my pyrope was indeed done. "The Chimney-sweep" in him had disappeared, and the stone was absorbing and throwing out sheaves of deep, dark fire. Wentzel had somehow removed an infinitesimal fraction of the top facet of the pyrope, and its centre had risen in a clump. The garnet lapped up the light and began to play: in it there burned indeed a magic drop in a fire of incombustible blood.

"Well? What do you think of the knight?" cried Wentzel.

I was lost in admiration before the pyrope and was on the point of saying so to Wentzel. But before I could utter a word, the weird old creature suddenly did a most unexpected thing: he clutched at my ring with the Alexandrite, which now, by artificial light, was red, and shrieked:

"My sons! Czechs! Quick! Look, here is the magic Russian stone I told you of! Treacherous Siberian! All the time he was green with hope and towards evening he has become dyed in blood. He has been like that since the dawn of Creation; all these long years he hid in the earth, and allowed himself to be found only on the twenty-first birthday of Tsar Alexander, when a great wizard—magician—a warlock went to Siberia in search of him. . . ."

"You are talking rubbish," I interrupted. "This stone was discovered not by a wizard but by a scientist—Nordenschild."

"A sorcerer! I tell you—a sorcerer," screamed Wentzel. "Look what a stone it is! It has a green morning and a gory evening. . . . It is the fate—it is the fate of the noble Tsar Alexander!"

And old Wentzel turned away to the wall, dropped his head on his elbow and burst into tears.

His sons stood by in silence. Not only for them, but also for me, who had for so long beheld on my hand "the stone of Alexander the Second", this stone seemed suddenly to become charged with a profound prophetic mystery, and my heart felt heavy within me.

Say what you like—the old boy had seen and read in the stone something that was there and yet had never struck anyone before.

That is what sometimes comes of looking at a thing in an unusual frame of mind.